The Great God Gold

by

William Le Queux

The Great God Gold
by William Le Queux

Copyright © 2024

All Rights reserved.

ISBN: 978-93-61428-41-8

Published by

DOUBLE 9 BOOKS
2/13-B, Ansari Road
Daryaganj, New Delhi – 110002
info@double9books.com
www.double9books.com
Tel. 011-40042856

ABOUT THE AUTHOR

Anglo-French journalist and author William Tufnell Le Queux was born on July 2, 1864, and died on October 13, 1927. He was also a diplomat (honorary consul for San Marino), a traveler (in Europe, the Balkans, and North Africa), a fan of flying (he presided over the first British air meeting at Doncaster in 1909), and a wireless pioneer who played music on his own station long before radio was widely available. However, he often exaggerated his own skills and accomplishments. The Great War in England in 1897 (1894), a fantasy about an invasion by France and Russia, and The Invasion of 1910 (1906), a fantasy about an invasion by Germany, are his best-known works. Le Queux was born in the city. The man who raised him was English, and his father was French. He went to school in Europe and learned art in Paris from Ignazio (or Ignace) Spiridon. As a young man, he walked across Europe and then made a living by writing for French newspapers. He moved back to London in the late 1880s and managed the magazines Gossip and Piccadilly. In 1891, he became a parliamentary reporter for The Globe. He stopped working as a reporter in 1893 to focus on writing and traveling.

CONTENTS

Preface
An Explanation

The remarkable secret revealed in the following pages is not purely fiction.

The discovery, much in the form that I have here presented it, has actually been made, and its discoverer, a well-known professor at one of the Universities in the North of Europe, recently placed the extraordinary statement in my hands.

In consequence, I consulted a number of the first living authorities on the subject, who most courteously gave me their opinions and to whom I owe much assistance, while several other Hebrew scholars, less noted, evinced the greatest curiosity.

Therefore I trust that the reader himself may find this hitherto unheard-of statement of facts of equal importance and interest.

William Le Queux.

Devonshire Club, London, 1910.

Chapter One
Introduces the Stranger

"My name? Why—what does that matter, Doctor? In an hour—perhaps before—I won't trouble anybody further."

"But surely it is your duty, my friend, to let me know your name?" argued the other. "Even if it be in confidence."

The dying man slowly shook his head in the negative, moved uneasily, and stretching forth his thin trembling hand, answered in indifferent French.

"I regret that I cannot satisfy your curiosity. I have a reason—a—a strong private reason. Here is my key," he went on, speaking very slowly and with great difficulty in a weak voice scarce above a whisper. "Open my bag, doctor, and;—and you'll find there a—a big envelope. Will you give it to me?"

The Doctor, a queer, deformed little man shabbily dressed, with grey hair and short grey beard, rose from the bedside and with the key crossed to where a well-worn leather bag lay upon the floor.

As he turned his back upon his nameless patient and knelt beside the bag, a curious look of craft and cunning overspread his hard, furrowed countenance. But it was only for a second. Next instant it had vanished, and given place to that serious expression of sympathy which his face had previously worn.

He found a large blue, linen-lined envelope which he gave into the white trembling hands of the stranger.

The prostrate man looked about fifty, his unkempt hair and moustache just tinged with grey, unshaved, and with white drawn face betraying long and intense suffering.

Why was he so determined to conceal his name? What secret of his life had he to hide?

Upon his blanched features was written the history of a curious and adventurous past. Perhaps he held some strange and amazing secret. He was eccentric in only one particular—that though he knew himself to be dying, he would leave no message for any relative; refusing absolutely and stubbornly to give his name, even to the man who, now at his side, had befriended him.

The room was a small and not over cleanly one, high up in a fourth-rate hotel close to the Gare du Nord, in Paris, a room with a single bed, a threadbare carpet, and a cheap wooden washstand with the grey December light filtering through lace curtains that hung limp and yellow. The wallpaper was greasy and faded, and the bed itself the reverse of inviting.

To Doctor Raymond Diamond the dying man had been an entire stranger until three days before—a chance acquaintance which adversity had brought him. Both men were, as a matter of fact, stranded in Paris. They had, in ascending the narrow stairs of their little hotel, wished each other "Good-day." Men who are hard up always form easy acquaintanceships. The stranger had told him that he was a Dane, from Copenhagen, but the name, Jules Blanc, which he had given to the proprietor was certainly not Danish. Indeed, he had admitted to Diamond that he had not given his real name. He had reasons for withholding it.

He was a mystery, and the Doctor strongly suspected him of having absconded from his native land, and coming to the end of his resources, was now in fear of the police.

That he was well educated had been quickly apparent. Though he spoke French badly it was evident that he had nevertheless travelled extensively, and had, in his better days, been possessed of considerable means. He had been in the Near East, Asia Minor, Syria, Palestine and Egypt, and appeared to possess an intimate knowledge of those countries.

Yet his luggage had been reduced to that one small bag containing a big blue envelope and a chancre of linen.

For two days they had idled about Paris together, both practically without a *sou*.

The Doctor, when he had discovered the true state of his friend's finances, had explained that he too was "temporarily embarrassed owing to his many recent investments;" whereat they had both laughed in chorus and with light hearts spent half the day lazily lolling upon the seats in the Tuileries Gardens watching the children at play.

It was during those idle hungry hours that the stranger's remarks aroused within the Doctor the greatest curiosity. Diamond himself, an Englishman, had in his student days taken his M.D. at Edinburgh, and was also a scholar of no mean attainments, yet this Dane's knowledge of many occult matters appeared amazingly profound.

Why did he so resolutely refuse to give his name?

On the day the Doctor had met the Dane, his financial resources consisted of one solitary franc and a twenty-five centime nickel piece. His newly found friend had less. Hence the food they had had was not very abundant. The two men, however, brothers in adversity, faced the hunger problem gaily. It was not the first time that either of them had been face to face with the streets and starvation, therefore it was no new experience.

Yet the stranger ever and anon seemed deeply depressed. He knit his brows, set his teeth hard, and drew deep sighs—sighs over the might-have-beens of his past. His business in Paris was an important, an entirely secret one, he had declared. In a few days—in a week at most—it must be completed.

"And then," he added with a laugh of confidence, "I shall probably move on to the Grand."

That same evening, however, as they were walking up the Rue Lafayette towards the obscure hotel, the stranger had been suddenly seized with sharp pains in the region of his heart. Neither man had tasted food for twenty-four hours, and both were cold and faint.

Diamond, however, took the man's arm and managed to get him back to his room. There he examined him carefully, and having diagnosed the case, recognised the extreme danger, but told the patient nothing decisive.

He saw the proprietor, and from him borrowed three francs. Then he wrote a prescription which he took round to the big Pharmacie du Nord, at the corner.

The mixture revived the invalid, but in the night he collapsed again. At mid-day Diamond obtained a cup of bouillon from a cheap restaurant near, and brought it to the man who had refused his name. And he had now sat by the bedside with his fingers upon the patient's pulse all through that short gloomy afternoon.

"I'm sorry things are so bad as they are," the Doctor was saying, as he handed the invalid the big blue envelope, for he had, an hour before, told him the truth. "You ought to have had advice long ago."

The dying man smiled faintly and shook his head.

"I was warned in Stockholm," he answered in a low tone. "But I didn't heed. I—I was a fool."

The Doctor sighed. What could he say? He had recognised that the poor fellow was already beyond human aid. He had probably been suffering from the affection of the heart for the past six or seven years—perhaps more.

"And you are certain?" asked the ugly little man at last, again taking the thin, bony hand in his. "Are you quite certain that you wish to send no message to anybody?"

For a few seconds the prostrate man struggled hard to speak.

"No," he succeeded in gasping at last. "No message—to—anybody."

The Doctor pursed his lips at the rebuff. The eccentricity of the stranger had become more marked in those moments of finality.

His thin, nerveless fingers were fumbling with the bulky envelope, which seemed to contain a quantity of folded papers.

"Doctor," he whispered at last, "I—I want to burn—all these—all—every one of them. Burn them entirely."

"As you wish, my dear friend," responded the hunchback, eyeing the envelope eagerly, and wondering what it might contain. "I'll put a match to them in the stove yonder."

The invalid, by dint of great effort, managed to move himself so that his eyes could fall upon the little door in the round iron stove, in which, however, no fire was burning, even though the day was bitterly cold.

Yet he hesitated, hesitated as though he dared not trust the hungry little man who had befriended him.

"Do you wish them destroyed?" the Doctor again inquired.

The dying man nodded, at the same moment raising his finger and motioning that he could not speak.

Diamond waited. He saw that the patient was vainly endeavouring to articulate some words.

For several moments there was a dead silence.

At last the nameless man spoke again, very softly and indistinctly. Indeed, the Doctor was compelled to bend low to catch the words:

"Take them," he said. "Take them—and burn them in the stove. Mind—destroy every one."

"Certainly I will," answered the other. "Give them to me, and you shall see me burn them. I'll do so there—before your eyes."

The man held the envelope in his dying grip. He still hesitated. His eyes were fixed upon the papers wistfully, as though filled with poignant regret at a mission unaccomplished.

"Ah!" he gasped with difficulty. "To think that this is the end—the end of a lifetime's study and struggle! Death defeats me, vanquishes me—as it has vanquished every other man who has striven to learn the secret."

Diamond stood listening in wonder and curiosity. He noticed the dying man's reluctance to destroy the papers.

Perhaps he would succumb, and leave them undestroyed! What secret could they contain?

There was a long silence. The grey light over the thousands of chimney-pots was fast fading into gloom. The room was darkening.

The patient lay motionless as one dead, yet his dull eyes were still open. In his hand he still held his treasured envelope.

Again Diamond spoke, but the man with a secret made no reply. He only raised his wan hand, and shook his head sadly, indicating inability to speak.

The queer little Doctor bent once more closer to the stranger and saw that the end was near. He was hoping against hope that the man would expire before he had strength to order the destruction of those documents, whatever they were. The mysterious statements of the dying man had indicated that the papers in question contained some remarkable secret, and naturally his curiosity had been aroused.

During those three brief days of their acquaintance he had, in vain, tried to form some conclusion as to who the stranger might be. At first he had believed him to be a broken-down medical man like himself. But that surmise had been quickly negatived. He was a professional man without a doubt, but he had carefully concealed even his profession as well as his name.

The doctor had re-seated himself in the rickety rush-bottomed chair at the bedside, and sat in patience for the end, as he had sat beside hundreds of other dying men and women in the course of his career.

The patient breathed heavily, and again stirring uneasily, cast a longing look at the glass of lemonade upon the little table near by. Diamond recognised his wish, and held the tumbler to the man's parched lips.

The dying stranger motioned, and the Doctor bent his head until his ear was near the other's mouth.

"Doctor," he managed to whisper after great difficulty, "it's no use. There's no hope! Therefore will you take them to the stove—and—and burn them—*burn them all!*"

"Certainly I will," was the Doctor's reply, rising and slowly taking the envelope from the prostrate man's reluctant fingers.

He felt crisp papers within as he turned his back upon the dying man and bent down to the stove, placing himself between the invalid's line of vision and the stove itself.

A moment later, however, he opened the stove-door, placed the envelope within, and applied a match to it.

Next moment a blood-red light fell across the darkening room upon the pallid face lying on the pillow.

A pair of dull, anxious, deep-set eyes watched the flames leap up and quickly die down again, watched the crinkling tinder as the sparks died out one by one—watched until Diamond stirred up the charred folios in order that every one should be consumed.

Then he turned slightly in his bed and, stretching forth his hand as though wishing to speak, drew a long, hard breath.

"And—and so—vanishes all my hope—my life," the stranger managed to sob bitterly in a voice almost inaudible.

Again he sighed—a long-drawn sigh. And then—in the room, now almost dark, reigned a complete silence.

Death had entered there. The man with the secret had passed to that land which lies beyond human ken.

Chapter Two
Describes the Doctor's Doings

Raymond Diamond's unfortunate deformity had always been against his advancement in his profession.

The only son of old Doctor Diamond, a country practitioner of the old school, in Norfolk, he had had a brilliant career at Edinburgh, and after some years of changeful life as a *locum tenens* had bought a partnership in a practice on the outskirts of Birmingham.

His partner turned out to be a rogue who had misrepresented facts, and six months afterwards absconded to America. Diamond, however, betrayed a sharp resourcefulness. He advertised the practice in the *Lancet*, and when a prospective purchaser came to view it, he hired fourteen or fifteen men to come into the surgery, one after the other, and pay fees. Such an impression did this ruse cause upon the newly married medico, who came from London to investigate, that he bought it at once, and Diamond netted nearly twice the sum he originally gave for his partnership.

Finding that his deformity precluded him from forming anything like a lucrative practice, he accepted a berth as ship's doctor in the P&O service, and for some years sailed the Indian and China seas.

Back in London again, he drifted from one suburban practice to another, doing *locum* work, and at last built up a semblance of a practice in a cheap new suburban district down at Catford.

Even there, however, his ugliness proved much against him, and at last he was forced to retire into a Northamptonshire village, where he and his wife eked out a modest living by adopting children upon yearly payments.

It was not a very creditable means of livelihood, yet the several children beneath their cottage roof were all well treated and well cared for. And after all, Raymond Diamond, a brilliant man in many ways, was only a failure because of his physical shortcomings.

He knew his Paris well. In his younger days he had often been there. Indeed, he once resided at St. Cloud with an invalid gentleman for close upon two years. Long years of travel had rendered him a thorough-going cosmopolitan, even though his lot was now cast in a sleepy country village.

The reason of his present visit to Paris was in order to interview the father of one of his adopted daughters, but the man had not kept the appointment, and by waiting from day to day in hope of finding him, he had exhausted his slender finances, and he knew that his patient wife was in a similar condition of penury at home.

He was certainly a strikingly ugly man. His forehead was broad and bulgy, and his face narrowed to the point of the beard. His head seemed too large, his arms too long and ungainly, while his face was deeply furrowed by long years at sea. His mouth, too, was wide and ugly and when he laughed he displayed an uneven row of teeth much discoloured by tobacco.

With folded arms, he was standing by the dead stranger, silently contemplating the white upturned face which showed distinctly in the fading twilight.

"I wonder who he was?" he exclaimed aloud. "Why did he refuse his name, and why was he so particular to burn those papers? He was a queer stick—poor fellow! I suppose they have inquests in France, and I'll get something as a witness."

And he pulled the sheet tenderly across to hide the lifeless visage.

"But," he added, "perhaps I've rendered myself liable because I didn't call in a French doctor!"

Then, suddenly arousing himself, he walked softly across to the stove and, spreading his handkerchief on the floor, raked out all the tinder into it. To his satisfaction he saw, as he had anticipated, that some of the papers, closely folded as they were, had only been burned at the edges.

One of them he opened, and found it covered with typewriting.

"These will, no doubt, prove interesting," he remarked to himself as he gathered every particle up into the handkerchief, and very carefully folded it over to protect it.

The lid of an old cardboard box which he found under the bed he broke up, and placing one piece above the handkerchief and the other below, he put the whole into the breast-pocket of his shabby frock-coat.

The stranger's bag he next examined. It was old, and covered with labels of first-class hotels—many of them in cities in the Near East and the Levant. The contents were disappointing, only a couple of shirts marked with the initials "P.H.", several dirty collars, a cravat or two, and a safety razor, together with a few unimportant odds and ends.

"The proprietor must have these, in lieu of his bill, I suppose," Diamond said. "I wonder what 'P.H.' stands for? He was a well-read man without a doubt. By Jove! he took his blow as bravely as any fellow I've seen go under. With a heart like that, it's a marvel that he lived so long. If I knew who his relatives were, I'd 'wire' to them—providing I had the money," he added with a bitter smile.

Then he shrugged his shoulders, and after striking a match to reassure himself that nothing had been left inside the stove to betray the fact that papers had been burned there, he turned upon his heel and left the room.

Below, in his dingy little back room on the first floor, he saw the proprietor, and told him what had occurred.

The old man grunted in his armchair and ordered the greasy-looking *valet-de-chambre* to inform the police, but to first go and search the dead man's effects and ascertain if he had left any money.

"Monsieur Blanc was penniless, like myself," Diamond said. "Neither of us had eaten all day yesterday."

"No money to pay his bill!" croaked the old Frenchman, who looked more like a *concierge* than a hotel proprietor. "And you are also without money?" he asked glaring.

"I regret that such is the truth," was Diamond's answer with much politeness. "Has not m'sieur noticed in life that honest men are mostly poor? Thieves and rogues are usually in funds."

"Then I must ask you to leave my hotel at once," said the old man testily.

The Doctor grinned, and bowed.

"If that is m'sieur's decision, I can do nothing else but obey," was his polite answer.

"You will leave your luggage, of course."

"M'sieur is quite welcome to all he finds," was the Doctor's response, and with another bow he turned and strode out.

His plan had worked admirably. He had no desire to remain there in the present circumstances. To be ordered out was certainly better than to flee.

So he walked gaily down the stairs, and a few minutes later was strolling airily down the Rue Lafayette, in the direction of the Opera.

The hotel proprietor and the *valet-de-chambre* quickly searched the dead man's room, but beyond the bag and its contents found nothing. Afterwards they informed the police.

Meanwhile Raymond Diamond walked on, undecided how to act. He had already reached the Place de l'Opera, now bright beneath its many electric lamps, before he had made up his mind. He would go once again in search of little Aggie's father, the man who owed him money.

Therefore he turned into the narrow Rue des Petit-Champs, and halfway down entered a house, passed the *concierge*, and ascended to a flat on the second floor.

Fully twenty times he had called there before, but the place was shut, as its owner, an Englishman, was absent somewhere in the Midi. When, however, he rang, he heard movement within.

His heart leapt for joy, for when the door opened there stood Mr Mullet, a tall, thin, red-haired man with a long pale face and a reddish, bristly moustache, who, the moment he recognised his visitor, stretched forth his hand in welcome.

"Come in, Doctor," he cried cheerily. "I got back only this morning, and the *concierge* gave me your card. I expected, however, you'd grown tired of waiting, and returned to England. How's my little Aggie?"

"She grows a bonnie girl, Mr Mullet—quite a bonnie girl," answered the ugly little man. "Gets on wonderfully well at school. And Lady Gavin, at the Manor, takes quite an interest in her."

"That's right. I'm glad to hear it—very glad. Though I'm a bit of a rover, Doctor, I'm always thinking of the child you know. Why—she must be nearly thirteen now."

"Nearly. It's fully six years since I took her off your hands."

"Fully."

And the two men sat down in the rather comfortable room of the tall, cadaverous-looking man, a mining engineer, whose adventures would have filled a volume.

David Mullet, or "Red Mullet" as his friends called him on account of the colour of his hair, offered the Doctor a good cigar from his case, poured out two glasses of brandy and soda, and after a chat took out two notes of a thousand francs from the pocket-book he carried and handed them to his visitor, receiving a receipt in return.

"I've been a long time paying, I'm afraid, Doctor," laughed the man airily. "But you know what kind of fellow I am! Sometimes I'm flush of money, and at others devilish hard up."

"I'm hard up, or I wouldn't press for this."

"My dear Doctor, it's been owing for two years. And I'm very glad to get out of your debt."

"Well, Mr Mullet," Diamond said, "eighty pounds is a lot to me just now. I haven't had a square meal for days, and to tell the truth I've just been ordered out of my hotel."

"My dear fellow, that's happened to me dozens of times," laughed the other. "I never feel sorry for the proprietor. I only regret that I can't give tips to the servants. I suppose you'll go back home—eh?"

"To-night, or by the first service in the morning."

"By Jove, I'd like to see my little Aggie. I wonder," exclaimed the man, "I wonder if I could manage to get across?"

"It isn't far," urged the Doctor.

But "Red Mullet" hesitated. He had a cause to hesitate. There was a hidden reason why for the past three years he had not put foot on English soil.

He shook his head sadly as he recognised that discretion was the better part of valour. He was too wary a man to run his neck into a noose.

"No," he said, "I think that in a few weeks I'll ask you to bring little Aggie over here to see me. You won't mind the trip—eh?"

"Not at all," was the reply. "Aggie will hardly know her father, I expect. She looks upon me as her parent."

"That was what we arranged, Doctor. She was to take your name, and you were to bring her up as your own daughter. I have a reason for that."

"So you told me six years ago."

"Red Mullet" nodded, and stretched out his long legs lazily as he contemplated the smoke of his cigar ascending to the ceiling. Recollections of his child had struck a sympathetic chord in his memory. There were incidents in his life that he would fain have forgotten. One of them was now recalled.

Quickly, however, the shadow passed, and his brow cleared. He became the same easy-going, humorous man he always had been, possessing a merry *bonhomie* and a fund of stories regarding his own amusing experiences in various out-of-the-way corners of the world.

At last the Doctor, with eighty pounds in his pocket, rose and wished his friend adieu.

Then he walked to a *brasserie* in the Avenue de l'Opera, where he dined well, concluding his meal with coffee and a liqueur, and at nine o'clock he left the Gare du Nord for Calais and London.

The reason of his sudden flight from Paris was the fear of having contravened the law by not calling in a French medical man when he knew that the case of the mysterious Blanc was hopeless. Detention would mean trouble and much expense. Therefore he deemed it best to get across to England at the earliest possible moment.

At six o'clock next morning he found himself in a small hotel called the Norfolk in Surrey Street, Strand, where he had on one or two occasions stayed. The waiter having brought up his breakfast, he locked the door and, going to the table, he took from his pocket the packet of charred paper and broken tinder which he had abstracted from the stove in Paris.

With infinite care he opened the handkerchief and spread it out. The tinder had broken into tiny fragments and some had been reduced to black powder, while the half-charred paper split as he attempted to open it.

He had switched on the light, for the London dawn had not yet spread. Then, seating himself at the table, he proceeded to examine and decipher the remains of the papers which the dying man believed he had entirely destroyed.

For some time he could make nothing of the lines of written words, which had neither beginning nor end.

Suddenly, however, he held his breath. He sat erect, statuesque, his dark eyes staring at the paper.

Then he re-read the written lines eagerly.

"Great Heavens! How strange!" he cried. "How utterly astounding! That man who refused his name had learned the greatest and most important secret this modern world of ours contains! And it is in my hands—*mine*! My God! Is it true—is it really true what this man alleges?"

He paused and again re-read the smoke-blackened, half-burned pages. For some moments he sat with his mouth open in utter astonishment. He could scarcely believe his own eyes.

"His secret—his amazing secret, one unheard of—is mine!" he gasped, glancing around the room, as though half-fearful lest he had been overheard. "I shall be a rich man—one of the richest in all Europe! Before six months is out the whole world will be at the feet of Raymond Diamond!"

Chapter Three
Shows One of the Fragments

"Well," declared the Doctor, speaking to himself, "even my success in intra-laryngeal operations was not half so interesting as this!"

And again he bent to examine the half-charred fragments before him. Some were in typewriting, one was in a small fine script. One hardly legible was in German, others were in English, interspersed here and there with words which he recognised were in Hebrew character.

In that small bedroom, beneath the rather dim electric light, the deformed little man sat pouring over the folios so dry that they cracked and crumbled when touched.

Much was undecipherable; the greater part had indeed been utterly consumed, but here and there he was enabled to read consecutive sentences, and those he made out utterly staggered him.

Indeed, so full of interest, so curious, and so amazing they would have staggered anybody.

He held in his hands the dead man's secret—a secret that on the face of it, seemed to be the strangest and at the same time the most unsuspected in all the world.

Suddenly he sat back, and, staring straight across the narrow room, exclaimed aloud:

"Why, there are men in the city this very day who'd give me ten thousand pounds for the remains of these papers! But would I sell them? No—not for ten times that amount! Who knows what this discovery may not be worth?"

He chuckled to himself. Already he felt himself a wealthy man, a man who could dictate his own terms in financial circles—a man who would be welcomed in audience by crowned heads themselves!

He sighed, and the heavy exhalation blew a quantity of fragments of tinder away upon the carpet.

"I wish I hadn't burned them quite so much," he said regretfully. "Had I had a newspaper handy I could have lit that instead. Or—or I might easily have delayed their destruction until—until after the end. Yet he seemed quite conscious, up to the very last moment. No wonder he regretted death before the fulfilment of the great work he had commenced—no wonder he contemplated moving to the Grand Hotel at an early date! And yet," he added, after a pause, "it's all very intricate, very indistinct, and requires a greater scholar than myself to properly understand and unravel it."

The chief document, consisting of about ten typewritten pages in English, had been badly burned. It was this which he was now engaged in trying to decipher. At the top left-hand corner the sheets had originally been held together by a paper-fastener, but that corner had been consumed as well as all round the edges. The centre alone of three folios remained readable, even though it had been yellowed by smoke.

"There seem very many references to Israel, to Nebuchadnezzar, King of Babylon, and to the Book of the Prophet Ezekiel. Yet they seem to convey nothing. Ah!" he sighed, "if only I could reconstruct the context. There are Biblical references, too. I must obtain a Bible."

So he rose, rang for a waiter, and asked him whether there was such a thing in the hotel as a copy of Holy Writ.

The man, a young German, naturally regarded the visitor as an eccentric person or a religious crank, but he went at once and borrowed a small Bible from the chambermaid—a volume which afterwards proved to contain, between its leaves, small texts of her Sunday-school days, several pressed flowers, and a lock of hair.

A reference given upon one of the crinkled folios was "Ezekiel xxviii, 24."

Reseating himself after the young German had left, Raymond Diamond hastily turned over the pages of the little well-thumbed Bible and found what proved to be the prophecy of the restoration of Israel.

Another reference in the next line of the half-burnt screed was Ezekiel xl, xli and xlii, no verses being designated.

On turning to these chapters, the doctor found that they contained a description of Ezekiel's vision of the measuring of the temple.

Continuing, he read the further dimensions of the temple, the size of the chambers for the priests, and the measures of the outer court "to make a separation between the sanctuary and the profane place."

All this conveyed to the deformed man but little.

That it had some connection with the strange secret was apparent, but in what manner he failed to distinguish.

He had gathered broadly that the dead man's discovery was an amazing one, and that a strange secret was revealed by those documents when they were intact, but it was all so mystifying, so astounding, that he could scarce give it shape within his own bewildered brain.

The enormous possibilities of the discovery had utterly dumbfounded him—it was a discovery that was unheard of.

In order to present to the reader some idea of the fragments of the dead man's papers lying upon the table before him, it may be of interest if the present writer gives a photographic representation of one of the badly burned folios.

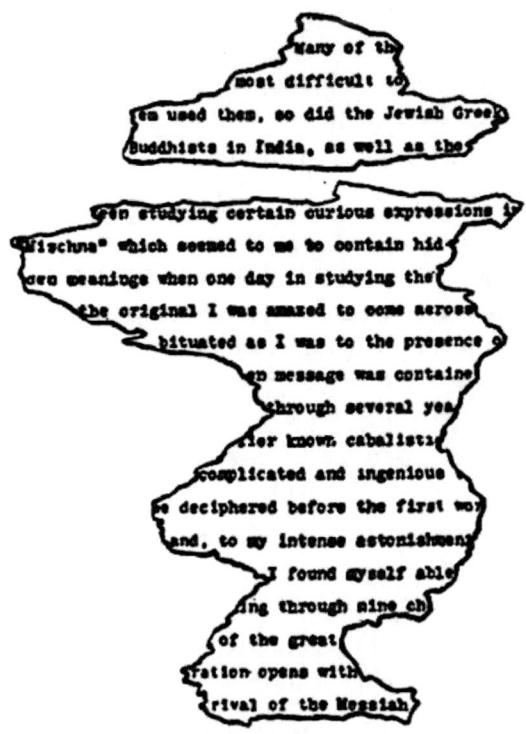

As will easily be seen, the undestroyed fragment of the document showed but little that was tangible. Of interest, it was true, but the interest was, alas! a well-concealed one. The dead man was a scholar. Of that there was no doubt whatsoever. The doctor had recognised from the first that he was no ordinary person.

The document seemed to be a portion of some statement made by a person as to the curious and unexpected result of certain studies.

He who made the declaration had apparently been a student of the Talmud, and especially the school of the Amoraim, or debaters, who about A.D. 250 expounded the "Mishna."

Raymond Diamond had long ago read Wunsche, Bacher and Strack, and from them had learned how the Amoraim had expounded the "Mishna," and how their labours had formed the Gemara, while the united Mishna and Gemara formed the books of the Talmud. By that time, and even earlier, the teachers of Judaism were also working in the schools of Babylonis. Hence the Talmud now exists in two forms—the Palestinian Talmud, or Talmud of Jerusalem, and the Babylonian Talmud. Rabbi Jehuda compiled the "Mishna" which, in general, sums up the outcome of the activity of the Sopherim, Zugoth and Tannaim, and thus became the canonical book of the oral law.

He was recalling these facts as he sat staring at the half-charred fragments on the table before him.

"The person making the declaration," he said aloud to himself, "appears to have discovered certain hidden meanings in the 'Mishna.' Well—one can read hidden meanings in most writings, I believe, if one wishes. Yet he seems to have come across something which amazed him—some cabalistic message very complicated and ingenious. It caused him great astonishment when he found himself able to—able to what? Ah! that's the point," he sighed.

Then, after another long pause, he decided that "nine ch—" meant "nine chapters," and that the final lines of the page dealt with some declaration opening with the arrival of the Messiah.

"Yes," he said in a hard decisive tone, straightening his crooked back as well as he was able. "There is a mystery explained here—a great and most astounding mystery."

Chapter Four
Concerns a Consultation

Late that same afternoon Raymond Diamond walked up the long muddy by-road which led from Horsford station to the village, about a mile distant.

Horsford was an obscure little place, still quite out-of-the-world, even in these days of trains and motor-cars.

About four miles west of Peterborough on the edge of the fox-hunting country, it was a pleasant little spot consisting of a beautiful old Norman church, with one of the finest towers in England and one long, straggling street mostly of thatched houses.

There were only two large houses—Horsford House, at the top of the hill on the Peterborough side, and the Manor, an old seventeenth-century mansion, half-way down the village.

It was not yet dark when the Doctor, the only arrival by train, turned the corner by the Wheel Inn and entered the village. As he did so, Warr, who combined the business of publican and village butcher, wished him a cheery "Good evenin', Doctor."

And as the little man trudged up the long street he was greeted with many such salutes, to all of which he answered mechanically, for he was thinking—thinking deeply.

The fragrant smell of burning wood from the cottages greeted his nostrils—the smell of that quiet little village which for some years had been his home.

He breathed again in that rural peace, as a dozen cows slowly plodded past him.

At last he turned from the main street, up a short, steep hill where, at the end of a small *cul-de-sac*, stood a long, old-fashioned, two-storied cottage with its dormer-windows peeping forth from the brown thatch. In summer, over the whole front of it spread a wealth of climbing roses, but now, in winter, only the brown leafless branches remained.

In the small, well-kept front garden were a number of well-trimmed evergreens, while an old box-hedge ran around the tiny domain.

As he lifted the latch of the gate, Mrs Diamond, a neat, well-preserved woman in black, threw open the door with a cheery welcome, and a moment later he was in his own old-fashioned little dining-room, warming himself at the fire, which, sending forth a ruddy glow, illuminated the room.

For such a humble home, it was quite a cosy apartment. Upon the old-fashioned oak-dresser at the end were one or two pieces of blue china, and on the oak overmantel were a few odd pieces of Worcester and Delft. On the walls were one or two engravings, while the furniture was of antique pattern and well in keeping with the place.

The doctor possessed artistic tastes, and was also a connoisseur to no small degree. In the days when he had possessed means, he had been fond of hunting for curios or making purchases of old furniture and china, but, alas! in these latter days of his adversity he had experienced even a difficulty in making both ends meet.

"I received your telegram, Raymond dear," exclaimed Mrs Diamond. "I'm so glad you were successful in finding Aggie's father. It's taken a great weight from my mind."

"And from mine also," he said with a sigh seated before the fire with his hands outstretched to the flames. "Mullet wants me to take the child over to Paris to see him in a week or so."

"Why does he not come over here?"

The Doctor pulled a wry face, and shrugged his shoulders ominously.

His wife, by her speech, showed herself to be a woman of refinement. She had been the widow of a medical man in Manchester before Diamond had married her. Though it was much against her grain to submit to registration as a foster-mother of children, yet it had been their only course. Raymond Diamond was too ugly to succeed in his profession. The public dislike a deformed doctor.

He told his wife how he had been at the end of his resources in Paris, and how, just at the moment when things had looked blackest, "Red Mullet" had returned. But he made no mention of meeting the stranger, or of the record of the curious secret which, between two pieces of cardboard, now reposed carefully in his breast-pocket.

Its possession held him in a kind of stupor. From what he had been able to gather—or rather from what he imagined the truth to be—he already felt himself an immensely wealthy man. He was, in fact, already planning out his own future.

The dead stranger had said he intended to remove to the Grand Hotel. Diamond's intention was to go further—to purchase a fine estate somewhere in the grass-country, and in future live the life of a gentleman.

Mrs Diamond noticed her husband's preoccupied manner, and naturally attributed it to financial embarrassment.

A few moments later the door opened, and a pretty, fair-haired girl, about thirteen, entered, and finding the doctor had returned, rushed towards him and, throwing her arms about his neck, kissed him, saying:

"I had no idea you were back again, dad. I went down the station-path half-way, expecting to meet you."

"I came by the road, my child," was the Doctor's reply as he stroked her long fair hair. "I've been to Paris—to see your dad, Aggie," he added.

"My other dad," repeated the child reflectively. "I—I hardly remember him. You are my own dear old dad!" And she stroked his cheek with her soft hand.

Aggie was the doctor's favourite. He was devoted to the daughter of that tall, thin man who was such a cosmopolitan adventurer, the child who was now the eldest of his family, and who had, ever since she had arrived, a wee weakly little thing, always charmed him by her bright intelligence and merry chatter.

She was a distinctly pretty child, neat in her dark-blue frock and white pinafore. In the village school she was head of her class, and Mr Holmes, the popular, good-humoured schoolmaster, had already suggested to the Doctor, and also to Lady Gavin at the Manor, that she should be sent to the Secondary School at Peterborough now that he could teach her no more.

The Doctor drew Aggie upon his knee, and told her of her father's inquiries and of his suggestion that she should go to Paris to see him.

Paris seemed to the child such a long way off. She had seen it marked upon the wall-maps in school, but to her youthful mind it was only a legendary city.

"I don't want to leave Horsford, dad," replied the girl with a slight pout. "I want to remain with you."

"Not in order to see and know your father?"

"You are my dad—my only dad," she declared quickly. "I don't want to see my other dad at all," she added decisively. "If he wants to see me, why doesn't he come here?"

"He can't my dear," replied the doctor. "But tell me. Have you seen Lady Gavin since I've been away?"

"No, dad. Mr Farquhar and his sister have come to stay at the Manor, so she's always engaged."

"Frank Farquhar is down here again, eh?" asked Diamond quickly. Then he reflected deeply for a few moments.

He was wondering if Farquhar could help him—if he dare take the young man into his confidence.

Nowadays he was "out of it." He knew nobody, buried there as he was in that rural solitude.

"Is Sir George at home?" he asked the child, who, like all other children, knew the whole gossip of the village.

"No, dad. He started for Egypt yesterday. Will Chapman told me so."

The Doctor ate his tea, with his wife and five "daughters" of varying ages, all bright, bonnie children, who looked the picture of good health.

Then, after a wash and putting on another suit, he went out, strolling down the village to where the big old Manor House, with its quaint gables and wide porch, stood far back behind its sloping lawn.

Generations of squires of Horsford had lived and died there, as their tombs in the splendid Norman church almost adjoining testified. It was a house where many of the rooms were panelled, where the entrance-hall was of stone, with a well staircase and a real "priests' hole" on the first floor.

He ascended the steps, and his ring was answered by a smart Italian man-servant. Yes. Mr Farquhar was at home. Would the doctor kindly step into the library?

Diamond entered that well-known room on the right of the hall—a room lined from floor to ceiling with books in real Chippendale bookcases, and in the centre a big old-fashioned writing-table. Over the fireplace were several ancient manuscripts in neat frames, while beside the blazing fire stood a couple of big saddle-bag chairs.

Sir George Gavin, Baronet, posed to the world as a literary man, though he had risen from the humble trade of a compositor to become owner of a number of popular newspapers. He knew nothing about literature and cared less. He left all such matters to the editors and writers whom he paid—clever men who earned for him the magnificent income which he now enjoyed. Upon the cover of one of his periodicals it was stated that he was editor. But as a matter of fact he hardly ever saw the magazine in question, except perhaps upon the railway bookstalls. His sole thought was the handsome return its publication produced. And, like so many other men in our England to-day, he had simply "paid up" and received his baronetcy among the Birthday honours, just as he had received his membership of the Carlton.

Diamond had not long to wait, for in a few moments the door opened, and there entered a smart-looking, dark-haired young man in a blue serge suit.

"Hulloa, Doc! How are you?" he exclaimed. "I'm back again, you see— just down for a day or two to see my sister. And how has Horsford been progressing during my absence—eh?" he laughed.

Frank Farquhar, Lady Gavin's younger brother, occupied an important position in the journalistic concern of which Sir George was the head. He was recognised by journalistic London as one of its smartest young men. His career at Oxford had been exceptionally brilliant, and he had already distinguished himself as special correspondent in the Boer and Russo-Japanese campaigns before Sir George Gavin had invited him to join his staff.

Tall, lithe, well set-up, with a dark, rather acquiline face, a small dark moustache, and a pair of sharp, intelligent eyes, he was alert, quick of movement, and altogether a "live" journalist.

The two men seated themselves on either side of the fireplace, and Farquhar, having offered his visitor a cigar, settled himself to listen to Diamond's story.

"I've come to you," the Doctor explained, "because I believe that you, and perhaps Sir George also, can help me. Don't think that I want any financial assistance," he laughed. "Not at all. I want to put before you a matter which is unheard of, and which I am certain will astound even you—a journalist."

"Well, Doc," remarked the young man with a smile, "it takes a lot to surprise us in Fleet Street, you know."

"This will. Listen." And then, having extracted a promise of silence, Diamond related to the young man the whole story of the dead stranger, and the curious document that had been only half-consumed.

When the Doctor explained that the papers had not been wholly burned, Frank Farquhar rose quickly in pretence of obtaining an ash-tray, but in reality in order to conceal the strange expression which at that, moment overspread his countenance.

Then, a few seconds later, he returned to his chair apparently quite unmoved and unconcerned. Truth to tell, however, the statement made by the dwarfed and deformed man before him had caused him to tighten his lips and hold his breath.

Was it possible that he held certain secret knowledge of which the Doctor was ignorant, and which he could turn to advantage?

He remained silent, with a smile of incredulity playing about his mouth.

The truth was this. Within his heart he had already formed a fixed intention that the dead man's secret—the most remarkable secret of the age—should be his, and his alone!

Chapter Five
Spreads the Net

The deformed man existed in a whirl of excitement. He already felt himself rich beyond his wildest dreams. He built castles in the air like a child, and smiled contentedly when rich people—some of the hunting crowd—passed him by unrecognised.

During the three days that followed, Frank Farquhar held several consultations with him—long earnest talks sometimes at the Manor or else while walking across that heath-land around the district known to the followers to hounds as the Horsford Hanglands.

The villagers who saw them together made no comment. As was well known, the little Doctor and Lady Gavin's clever young brother were friends.

Diamond had enjoined the strictest secrecy, but Farquhar, as a keen man of business and determined to put his knowledge to the best advantage, had already exchanged several telegrams with some person in London, and was now delaying matters with Diamond until he obtained a decided reply.

On the fourth day, just after breakfast, Burton, the grave old butler, handed the young man a telegram which caused him to smile with satisfaction. He crushed it into his pocket and, seizing his hat, walked along to the Doctor's cottage. Then the pair took a slow stroll up the short, steep hill on to the Peterborough road, through the damp mists of the winter's morning. Away across the meadows on the left, hounds were in full cry, a pretty sight, but neither noticed the incident.

"Do you know, Doctor," exclaimed the young man as soon as they got beyond the village, "I've been thinking very seriously over the affair, and I've come to the conclusion that unless we put it before some great Hebrew scholar we shall never get down to the truth. The whole basis of the secret is the Hebrew language, without a doubt. What can we do alone—you and I?"

The little Doctor shook his head dubiously.

"I admit that neither of us is sufficiently well versed in Jewish history properly to understand the references which are given in the fragments which remain to us," he said. "Yet if we go to a scholar, explain our views, and show him the documents, should we not be giving away what is evidently a most valuable secret?"

"No. I hardly think that," answered the shrewd young man. "Before putting it to any scholar we should first make terms with him, so that he may not go behind our backs and profit upon the information."

"You can't do that!" declared Diamond.

"Among scholars there are a good many honourable men," replied Frank Farquhar, with a glance of cunning. "If we proposed to deal with City sharks, it would be quite a different matter."

"Then to whom do you propose we should submit the documents for expert opinion?" inquired the deformed man, as he trudged along at his side.

"I know a man up in London whom I implicitly trust, and who will treat the whole matter in strictest confidence," was the other's reply. "We can do nothing further down here. I'm going up to town this afternoon, and if you like I'll call and see him."

The Doctor hesitated. He recognised in the young man's suggestion a desire to obtain his precious fragments and submit them to an expert. Most deformed men are gifted with unusually shrewd intelligence, and Raymond Diamond was certainly no exception. He smiled within himself at Frank Farquhar's artless proposal.

"Who is the man?" he asked, as though half-inclined to adopt the suggestion.

"I know two men. One is named Segal—a professor who writes for our papers; an exceedingly clever chap, who'd be certain to make out something more from the puzzle than we ever can hope to do. I also know Professor Griffin."

"I shall not allow the papers out of my possession."

"Or all that remains of them, you mean," laughed the young man uneasily. "Why, of course not. That would be foolish."

"Foolish in our mutual interests," Diamond went on. "You are interested with myself, Mr Farquhar, in whatever profits may accrue from the affair."

"Then if our interests are to be mutual, Doctor, why not entrust the further investigation to me?" suggested the wily young man. "I hope you know me sufficiently well to have confidence in my honesty."

The Doctor cast a sharp look at the little young fellow at his side.

"Why, of course, Mr Farquhar," he laughed. "As I've already said, you possess facilities for investigating the affair which I do not. If what I suspect be true, we have, in our hands, the solution of a problem which will startle the world. I have sought your assistance, and I'm prepared to give you—well, shall we say fifteen per cent, interest on whatever the secret may realise?"

"It may, after all, be only historical knowledge," laughed young Farquhar. "How can you reduce that into 'the best and brightest?' Still, I accept. Fifteen per cent is to be my share of whatever profit may accrue. Good! I only wish Sir George were home from Egypt. He would, no doubt, give us assistance."

The Doctor purposely disregarded this last remark. He held more than a suspicion that young Farquhar intended to "freeze him out."

"When are you going up to town?" he asked.

"This afternoon. I shall see my man in the morning, and I feel sure that if I put the problem before him he'll be able, before long, to give us some tangible solution," was Frank's reply. "When I act, I act promptly, you know."

The Doctor was undecided. He knew quite well that young Farquhar was acquainted with all sorts of writers and scholars, and that possibly among them were men who were experts in Hebrew, and in the history of the House of Israel.

He reflected. If the young man were content with fifteen per cent, what had he further to fear?

Therefore, after some further persuasion on Frank's part, he promised to write out an agreement upon a fifteen per cent, basis, and submit the fragments to the young man's friend.

They returned to the village, and the Doctor promised to call upon him at noon with an agreement written out.

This he did, and in the library at the Manor Frank appended his signature, receiving in return the precious fragments carefully preserved between the two pieces of cardboard.

When the deformed man had left, Frank Farquhar lit a cigarette, and stretching his legs as he sat in the armchair, laughed aloud in triumph.

"Now if I tie down old Griffin the secret will be mine," he remarked aloud. "I've already 'wired' to Gwen, so she'll expect me at eight, and no doubt tell her father."

At five o'clock Sir George's red "Mercedes" came round to the front of the house to take Frank into Peterborough, and half an hour later he was in the "up-Scotsman" speeding towards King's Cross, bearing with him the secret which he felt confident was to set the whole world by the ears.

He dropped his bag at his rooms in Half Moon Street, had a wash and a snack to eat at his club, the New Universities, round in St. James's Street, and then drove in a taxi-cab to a large, rather comfortable house in Pembridge Gardens, that turning exactly opposite Notting Hill Gate Station.

Standing behind the neat maid-servant who opened the door was a tall, dark-haired, handsome girl not yet twenty, slim, narrow-waisted, and essentially dainty and refined.

"Why, Frank!" she cried, rushing towards him. "What's all this excitement. I'm so interested. Dad has been most impatient to see you. After your letter the day before yesterday, he's been expecting you almost every hour."

"Well, the fact is, Gwen, I couldn't get the business through," he said with a laugh. "We had terms to arrange—and all that."

"Terms of what?" asked the girl, as he linked his arm in hers and they walked together into the long, well-furnished dining-room.

"I'll tell you all about it presently, dear," he replied.

"About the secret?" she asked anxiously. "Dad showed me your letter. It is really intensely interesting—if what you suspect be actually the truth."

"Interesting!" he echoed. "I should rather think it is. It's a thing that will startle the whole civilised world in a few days. And the curious and most romantic point is that we can't find out who was the original holder of the information. He died in Paris, refusing to give his real name, or any account of himself. But there," he added, "I'll tell you all about it later on. How is my darling?"

And he bent until their lips met in a long, fervent caress.

Her arms were entwined about his neck, for she loved him with the whole strength of her being, and her choice was looked upon with entire favour by her father. Frank Farquhar was a rising man, the adopted candidate for a Yorkshire borough, while from his interest in Sir George Gavin's successful publications he derived a very handsome income for a man of his years.

"I've been longing for your return, dearest," she murmured in his ear as he kissed her. "It seems ages ago since you left town."

"Only a month. I went first to Perthshire, where I had to speak at some Primrose League meetings. Then I had business in both Newcastle and Manchester, and afterwards I went to Horsford to see my sister. I was due to stay there another fortnight, but this strange discovery brings me up to consult your father."

"He's upstairs in the study. We'd better go up at once. He's dying to see you," declared the bright-eyed girl, who wore a big black silk bow in her hair. She possessed a sweet innocent face, a pale soft countenance indicative of purity of soul. The pair were, indeed, well matched, each devoted to the other; he full of admiration of her beauty and her talents, and she proud of his brilliant success in journalism and literature.

At the throat of her white silk blouse she wore a curious antique brooch, an old engraved sapphire which Sir Charles Gaylor, a friend of Dr Griffin, had some years ago brought from the excavation he had made in the mound of Nebi-Yunus, near Layard's researches in the vicinity of Nineveh. The rich blue gleamed in the gaslight, catching Frank's eye as he ascended the stair, and he remarked that she was wearing what she termed her "lucky brooch," a gem which had no doubt adorned some maiden's breast in the days of Sennacherib or Esarhaddon.

The first-floor front room, which in all other houses in Pembridge Gardens was the drawing-room, had in the house of Professor Griffin been converted into the study—a big apartment lined with books which, for the most part, were of "a dry-as-dust" character.

As they entered, the Professor, a short, stout, grey-haired man in round steel-framed spectacles, raised himself from his armchair, where he had been engrossed in an article in a German review.

"Ah! my dear Farquhar!" he cried excitedly. "Gwen told me that you were on your way—but there, you are such a very erratic fellow that I never know when to expect you."

"I generally turn up when least expected," laughed the young man, with a side-glance at the girl.

"Well, well," exclaimed the man in spectacles; "now what is all this you've written to me about? What 'cock-and-bull' story have you got hold of now—eh?"

"I briefly explained in my letter," he answered. "Isn't it very remarkable? What's your opinion?"

"Ah! you journalists!" exclaimed the old professor reprovingly. "You've a lot to answer for to the unsuspecting public."

"I admit that," laughed Frank. "But do you really dismiss the matter as a 'cock-and-bull' story?"

"That is how I regard it at the moment—without having been shown anything."

"Then I can show you everything," was Farquhar's prompt reply. "I have it all with me—at least all that remains of it."

The old man smiled satirically. As Regius Professor of Hebrew at Cambridge, Dr Arminger Griffin was not a man to accept lightly any theory placed before him by an irresponsible writer such as he knew Frank Farquhar to be.

He suspected a journalistic "boom" to be at the bottom of the affair, and of all things he hated most in the world was the halfpenny press.

Frank had first met Gwen while he had been at college, and had often been a visitor at the professor's house out on Grange Road, prior to his retirement and return to London. He knew well in what contempt the old man held the popular portion of the daily press, and especially the London evening journals. Therefore he never sought to obtrude his profession when in his presence.

"Well?" said the old gentleman at last, peering above his glasses. "I certainly am interested in the story, and I would like to examine what you've brought. Burnt papers—aren't they?"

"Yes."

"H'm. Savours of romance," sniffed the professor. "That's why I don't like it. The alleged secret itself is attractive enough, without an additional and probably wholly fictitious interest."

Frank explained how the fragments had fallen into his hands, and the suggestion which Doctor Diamond had made as to the possibility of a financial value of the secret.

"My dear Frank," replied the professor, "if it were a secret invention, a new pill, or some scented soap attractive to women, it might be worth something in the City. But a secret such as you allege,"—and he shrugged his shoulders ominously without concluding his sentence.

"Ah!" laughed the young man. "I see you're sceptical. Well, I don't wonder at that. Some men of undoubted ability and great knowledge declare that the Bible was not inspired."

"I am not one of those," the professor hastened to declare.

"No, Frank," exclaimed the girl. "Dad is not an agnostic. He only doubts the genuineness of this secret of yours."

"He condemns the whole thing as a 'cock-and-bull' story, without first investigating it!" said Farquhar with a grin. "Good! I wonder whether your father will be of the same opinion after he has examined the fragments of the dead man's manuscript which remain to us?"

"Don't talk of the dead man's manuscript!" exclaimed the old professor impatiently, "even though the man is dead, it's in typewriting, you say—therefore there must exist somebody who typed it. He, or she, must still be alive!"

"By Jove!" gasped the young man quickly, "I never thought of that! The typing is probably only a copy of a written manuscript. The original may still exist. And in any case the typist would be able to supply to a great degree the missing portions of the document."

"Yes," said the other. "It would be far more advantageous to you to find the typist than to consult me. I fear I can only give you a negative opinion."

Chapter Six
Gives Expert Opinion

Frank Farquhar was cleverly working his own game. The Professor had scoffed at the theory put forward by Diamond, therefore he was easily induced to give a written undertaking to regard the knowledge derived from the half-burnt manuscript as strictly confidential, and to make no use of it to his own personal advantage.

"I have to obtain this," the young man explained, "in the interests of Diamond, who, after all, is possessor of the papers. He allowed me to have them only on that understanding."

"My dear Frank," laughed the great Hebrew scholar, "really all this is very absurd. But of course I'll sign any document you wish."

So amid some laughter a brief undertaking was signed, "in order that I may show to Diamond," as Frank put it.

"It's really a most businesslike affair," declared Gwen, who witnessed her father's signature. "The secret must be a most wonderful one."

"It is, dear," declared her lover. "Wait and hear your father's opinion. He is one of the very few men in the whole kingdom competent to judge whether the declaration is one worthy of investigation."

The Professor was seated at his writing-table placed near the left-hand window, and had just signed the document airily, with a feeling that the whole matter was a myth. Upon the table was his green-shaded electric reading-lamp, and with his head within the zone of its mellow light he sat, his bearded chin resting upon his palm, looking at the man to whom he had promised his daughter's hand.

A scholar of his stamp is always very slow to commit himself to any opinion. The Hebrew professor, whoever he may be, follows recognised lines, and has neither desire nor inclination to depart from them. It was so with Griffin. Truth to tell, he was much interested in the problem which young Farquhar had placed before him, but at the same time the suggestion made by Doctor Diamond was so startling and unheard of that, within himself, he laughed at the idea, regarding it as a mere newspaper sensation, invented in the brain of some clever Continental swindler.

From his pocket the young man drew forth the precious envelope, and out of it took the cards between which reposed three pieces of crinkled and smoke-blackened typewriting, the edges of which had all been badly burned.

The first which he placed with infinite care, touching it as lightly as possible, upon the Professor's blotting-pad was the page already reproduced — the folio which referred to the studying of the "Mishna" and the cabalistic signs which the writer had apparently discovered therein.

The old man, blinking through his heavy round glasses, examined the disjointed words and unfinished lines, grunted once or twice in undisguised dissatisfaction, and placed the fragment aside.

"Well?" inquired Farquhar, eagerly, "does that convey anything to you?"

The Professor pursed his lips in quiet disbelief.

"The prologue of a very elegant piece of fiction," he sneered. "The man who makes this statement ought certainly to have been a novelist."

"Why?"

"Because of the clever manner in which he introduces his subject. But let us continue."

With delicate fingers Frank Farquhar handled the next scrap of typewriting and placed it before the great expert.

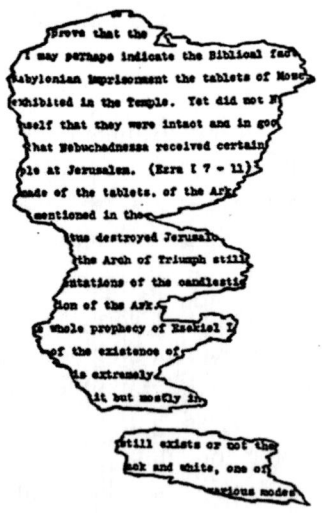

The folio in question apparently attracted Professor Griffin much more than the first one presented to him. He read and re-read it, his grey face the whole time heavy and thoughtful. He was reconstructing the context in his own mind, and its reconstruction evidently caused him deep and very serious reflection.

A dozen times he re-read it, while Frank and Gwen stood by exchanging glances in silence.

"The first portion of the statement on this folio is quite plain," remarked the Professor at last, looking up and blinking at the young man. "The writer indicates the Biblical fact that, after the Babylonian imprisonment the tablets of Moses were never again exhibited in the Temple. Surely this is not any amazing discovery! Every reader of the Old Testament is aware of that fact. The prophet Ezekiel himself was one of the temple priests deported to Babylon by Nebuchadnezzar in 597 B.C. You'll find mention of it in Ezekiel, i, 2-8. His message consisted at first of denunciations of his countrymen, both in Babylon and in Palestine, but after the fall of Jerusalem in 586 B.C. he became a prophet of consolation, promising the eventual deliverance and restoration of the chosen people. Give me down the Bible, Gwen, dear, and also Skinner—the 'Expositor's Bible.' You'll see it in the second case—third shelf to the left."

The girl crossed the room, and after a moment's search returned with the two volumes, which she placed before her father.

"Nebuchadnezzar received certain vessels from the temple at Jerusalem. Well, we know that," remarked the old man, as he opened the copy of Holy Writ and slowly turned its pages.

"The reference in the book of Ezra," he said, referring to the open book before him, "concerns the proclamation of Cyrus, King of Persia, for the building of the temple in Jerusalem, how the people provided for the return, and how Cyrus restored the vessels of the temple to Sheshbazzar, the Prince of Judah." Then, turning to Gwen, he said: "Read the verses referred to, dear—seventh to the eleventh in the first chapter."

The girl bent over the Bible, and read the verses aloud as follows:

"Also Cyrus the King brought forth the vessels of the house of the Lord, which Nebuchadnezzar had brought forth out of Jerusalem, and had put them in the house of his gods;

"Even those did Cyrus King of Persia bring forth by the hand of Mithredath the treasurer, and numbered them unto Sheshbazzar, the Prince of Judah.

"And this is the number of them: thirty chargers of gold, a thousand chargers of silver, nine and twenty knives,

"Thirty basons of gold, silver basons of a second *sort* four hundred and ten, *and* other vessels a thousand.

"All the vessels of gold and silver *were* five thousand and four hundred. All *these* did Sheshbazzar bring up with *them* of the captivity that were brought up from Babylon unto Jerusalem."

"Surely that is sufficient historical fact!" the old Professor said in his hard, "dry-as-dust" voice. "Again, farther on, there is, you see, a statement that Titus destroyed Jerusalem and that he built the Arch of Triumph in Rome and placed a representation of the candlesticks upon it. Does not every schoolboy know that! Bosh! my dear Frank!"

"True," exclaimed Frank, "but see! in the next line but one is a reference to the existence of something in 'the whole prophecy of Ezekiel' — something in 'black and white.'"

Professor Griffin shrugged his shoulders.

"Ezekiel develops the doctrine of individual responsibility and of the Messianic kingdom as no prophet before him," was the Professor's reply. "It may refer to that. The prophet's style is not of the highest order, but is extraordinarily rich and striking in its imagery. The authenticity of the book is now admitted, all but universally, but the corrupt state of the Hebrew text has, for ages, been the despair of students. Cornhill, in 1886, made a brilliant attempt to reconstruct the Hebrew text with the aid of the Septuagint."

Griffin noticed that his young friend did not quite follow that last remark, so he added:

"The Septuagint is, as you may perhaps know, the earliest Greek translation of the Old Testament scriptures made directly from the Hebrew original during the third century before Christ for the use of the Hellenistic Jews. In the literary forgery produced about the Christian era, known as the 'Letter of Aristeas,' and accepted as genuine by Josephus and others, it is alleged that the translation was made by seventy-two men at the command of Ptolemy II. You will find portions of it in the British Museum, and from it we find that the translation is not of uniform value or of the same style throughout. The Pentateuch and later historical books, as well as the Psalms, exhibit a very fair rendering of the original. The prophetical books, and more especially Ezekiel, show greater divergence from the Hebrew, while Proverbs frequently display loose paraphrase."

"But is there anything in those typed lines which strikes you as unusually curious?" demanded young Farquhar, pointing to the smoked and charred fragment upon the blotting-pad.

The Professor was silent for a moment, his eyes fixed upon the disjointed and unfinished sentences.

"Well—yes. There is something," was his answer. "That statement that something exists in 'the whole prophecy of Ezekiel.' What is that something?"

"Is it what Doctor Diamond suspects it to be, do you think?"

"I can form no definite conclusion until I have investigated the whole," was the great scholar's response. "But I would, at this point, withdraw my own light remarks of half an hour ago. There may be something of interest in it, but what the picturesque story is all leading up to I cannot quite imagine."

"To a secret—to the solution of a great and undreamed-of mystery!" declared Frank excitedly.

"The last few lines of this scrap before me certainly leads towards that supposition," was the answer of Gwen Griffin's father.

"Then you do not altogether negative Diamond's theory that there is here, if we can only supply the context, the key to the greatest secret this world has ever known!"

"Ah! that is saying a good deal," was the reply. "Let me continue the investigation of this wonderful document which the dying man was so anxious to destroy."

And by the sphinx-like expression upon the old man's face it was apparent that he had already gathered more information than he was willing to admit.

The truth was that the theory he had already formed within his own mind held him bewildered. His thin fingers trembled as he touched the dried, crinkled folio.

There was a secret there—without a doubt, colossal and astounding—one of which even the greatest scholars in Europe through all the ages had never dreamed!

The old man sat staring through his spectacles in abject wonder.

Was Doctor Diamond's theory really the correct one? If so, what right had these most precious papers to be in the hands of an irresponsible journalist?

If there was really a secret, together with its solution—then the latter must be his, and his alone, he decided. How it would enhance his great reputation if he were the person to launch it forth upon the world!

Therefore the old man's attitude suddenly changed and he pretended to regard the affair humorously, in the hope of putting Frank off his guard.

If the world was ever to be startled by the discovery it should, he intended, be by Professor Arminger Griffin, and not through any one of those irresponsible halfpenny sheets controlled by Sir George Gavin and his smart and ingenious young brother-in-law.

Both Frank Farquhar and Gwen noticed the old man's sudden change of manner, and stood puzzled and wondering, little dreaming what was passing with his mind.

Few men are—alas!—honest where their own reputations are at stake.

Chapter Seven
In which the Professor Exhibits Cunning

Frank was fully aware that Professor Griffin was an eccentric man, full of strange moods and strong prejudices. Most scholars and writers are.

"But, dad," exclaimed his daughter, placing her soft hand upon his shoulder, "what do you really think of it? Is there anything in this Doctor Diamond's theory?"

"My dear child, I never jump to conclusions, as you know. It is against my habit. It's probably one of the many hoaxes which have been practised for the last thousand years."

The girl exchanged a quick glance with her lover. She could see that Frank was annoyed by the light manner with which her father treated the alleged secret.

"Well, Professor," said the young man at last, "this, apparently, is the next folio, though the numbering of each has been destroyed," and he placed before the man in spectacles another scrap which presented the appearance as shown.

In an instant the old man became intensely interested though he endeavoured very cleverly to conceal the fact. He bent, and taking up a large magnifying-glass mounted in silver—a gift from Frank on the previous Christmas—he carefully examined each word in its order.

"Ah!" he exclaimed, "the first three lines, underlined as you see, are apparently a portion of some prophecy regarding the captivity of the Jews in Babylon, 'the period of the Blood-debts,' after which comes the period when the oppression will lose its power, which means their release by Cyras. Come now, this is of some interest!"

"Read on, dad," urged the dainty girl, excitedly. "Tell us what you gather from it."

The pair were standing hand-in-hand, at the back of the old man's writing-chair.

"Not so quickly, dear—not so quickly. That's the worst of women. They are always so erratic, always in such an uncommon hurry," he added with a laugh.

Then, after a pause during which he carefully examined the lines which followed, he pointed out: "You see that somebody—not the writer of the document, remember—has stated that Moses' tablets 'The Cha—', which must mean the Chair of Grace, between two cherubims of fine gold, a number of other things, including the Ark of the Covenant itself and the archives of the Temple down to B.C. 600 are—what?"

And he raised his head staring at the pair through his round and greatly magnifying-glasses.

"Doctor Diamond's theory is that the treasures of Solomon's Temple are still concealed at the spot where they were hidden by the priests before the taking of Jerusalem by Nebuchadnezzar."

The Professor laughed aloud.

"My dear Farquhar," he exclaimed, "on the face of this folio it would, of course, appear so. One may read it as a statement of fact that all the relics of the Temple and all the great treasures of the ages bygone—the Treasure of Israel—are concealed 'beneath', somewhere—'which is a series' of something. To this, there are three entrances, one only being accessible. Then in the final lines, we have another prophecy that the tablets shall 'remain in their hiding-place—that is with the Ark of the Covenant—till the coming of the Messiah who alone may open the treasure-house, or place of concealment, in order that he may show proof of—', and the rest is lost." he added with a sigh of disappointment.

"I admit," said Frank, "that is one reading of it. But what is your reading—that of an expert?"

The old man merely shrugged his shoulders and said:

"I don't think that the Doctor's theory is the correct one. The belief that the Treasure of Solomon's Temple still exists is far too wild and unsubstantiated. Of course, it is not quite clear in history what became of the contents of the Temple, but I think we may safely at once dismiss any possibility of the relics of Moses as being intact after a couple of thousand years or so. Stories of hidden treasure have appealed to the avarice of man throughout all the ages, from the days of the Roman Emperors, down to the day before yesterday, when a ship went forth to search for the lost gold of President Kruger. There have been hundreds, nay thousands of expeditions to search for treasure, but in nearly every case the searchers have returned sadder and poorer men. No, Frank," he exclaimed, decisively, "I don't think any one would be such an utter fool as to attempt to suggest that the Treasure of Israel still exists. At least no scholar would. Whoever would do such a thing would be a clumsy bungler, ignorant of both the Hebrew language and the history of the Hebrew nation. Doctor Diamond, from what you tell me, is, I gather, one of such."

"But they are not the Doctor's documents," Frank hastened to point out. "As I've told you, a man dying in Paris ordered him to burn them. He did so, but they were not all consumed."

"The Doctor worked a trick upon a dying man," sniffed the Professor. "Hardly played the game—eh?"

"I quite agree with you there," answered young Farquhar. "Yet, according to the Doctor's version, he was in no way responsible for the fact that only half the folios were consumed."

"Well, whatever it is," declared the Professor, very decisively, "it seems to be some rather clumsy 'cock-and-bull' story. In what I've read. I, as a scholar, could pick many holes. Indeed, such a screed as this could never have been concocted by any one with any pretence of knowledge of old Testament history. There are certain statements which are utterly absurd on the face of them."

"Which are they?" inquired Frank eagerly.

"Oh—several," was the rather light reply. "As you are not a scholar, my dear boy, it would be useless me going into long and technical explanations. The disjointed bits of prophecy are, I admit, really most artistic," he added with a laugh.

If the truth be told, Arminger Griffin was concealing the intense excitement that had been aroused within him. He was making a discovery—a wonderful, an amazing discovery. But to this young journalist, who would merely regard it as a good "boom" for one of his irresponsible halfpenny journals, he intended to pooh-pooh it as a mere clumsy fairy tale.

"Well," he asked, a moment later, in an incredulous tone. "What else have you to show me?"

"No more typewriting," was Frank's reply. "The only other folio is one of manuscript, and it will probably interest you, for it contains two Hebrew words," and he placed before the great expert a half-consumed fragment of lined manuscript paper which bore some close writing in English of which the present writer gives a facsimile here.

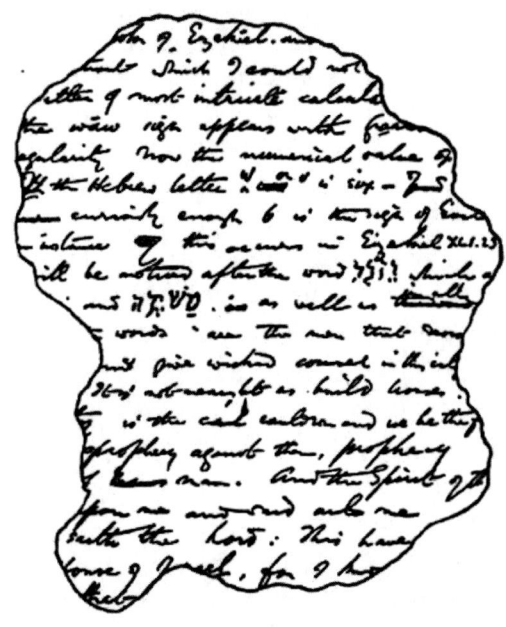

"H'm," grunted the old man, after a swift glance at it. "A copy, evidently. The Hebrew words are too clumsily written. No scholar wrote them. Probably it's a translation from German or Danish—I think you said that the man who called himself Blanc, was really a Dane—eh?"

"Yes. He told Diamond that he came from Copenhagen," Farquhar replied.

But the old man was too deeply engrossed in the study of the neat manuscript. How he wished that the context had been preserved, for here, he recognised, was the key, or rather the commencement of the key to the whole secret. He was now anxious to get rid of Frank Farquhar, and be allowed to pursue his investigations alone. There was certainly much more in it than he had at first suspected.

With such a sensation as that contained in the half-burnt documents to launch upon the world, he would be acclaimed the most prominent scholar of the day. The whole of academic Europe would shower honours upon him.

"What does it mean about the 'wâw' sign?" inquired the young man. "Does that convey anything?"

"Nothing," laughed the Professor with affected indifference. "What can one make out of such silly nonsense? It says, apparently, that in Ezekiel the 'wâw' sign appears with great regularity. Well, so it does in all Hebrew texts. The letter 'a' appears often in English doesn't it? Well, so does the Hebrew 'w' or 'v'. Therefore it's all bunkum—that was my first impression—and I still retain it!"

Gwen looked genuinely disappointed. She had hoped that this wonderful manuscript which had fallen into her lover's hands would turn out, as he had declared it would, to be of utmost value, both to history and also of financial value to its possessors.

But her father, recognised as one of the first authorities of the day, had decisively condemned it as a clumsy fraud.

"The reference given in the manuscript is, I see, Ezekiel xli. 23," remarked the girl, and turning over the pages of the Bible which she still held in her hand she exclaimed:

"Here it is. Let me read it: 'And the temple and the sanctuary had two doors. And the doors had two leaves *apiece*, two burning leaves; two *leaves* for the one door, and two for the other *door*. And *there were* made on them, on the doors of the temple, cherubims and palm trees, like as *were* made upon the walls; and *there were* thick planks upon the face of the porch without. And *there were* narrow windows and palm trees on the one side and on the other side, on the sides of the porch, and upon the side chambers of the house, and thick planks.'"

"Yes," remarked the old man. "The first Hebrew word in the manuscript means either 'palace' or 'temple'. That occurs as the third word of the quotation. But there is no mention of 'cupbearer'. If I recollect aright, there is a mention of the doors of the Temple in the First Book of Kings. I believe it's in the sixth chapter. Look, dear, and see if you can find it."

His daughter turned over the leaves quickly, found the chapter he had indicated, and scanned over the verses.

"Ah!" she cried, a moment later. "Yes. You are right, dad. Here it is, beginning at verse 31: 'And for the entering of the oracle he (Solomon) made doors *of* olive tree: the lintel *and* side posts *were* a fifth part *of the wall*. The two doors also *were* of olive tree: and he carved upon them carvings of cherubims and palm trees and open flowers, and overlaid *them* with gold, and spread gold upon the cherubims, and upon the palm trees. So also made he for the door of the temple posts *of* olive tree, a fourth part *of the wall* And the two doors *were of* fir tree: the two leaves of the one door *were* folding, and the two leaves of the other door *were* folding. And he carved *thereon* cherubims and palm trees and open flowers: and covered them with gold fitted upon the carved work.'"

"I looked up the reference in Ezekiel," remarked Frank, "but I could not understand it. Perhaps, you, Professor, may be able to throw some light upon it?"

The old man turned to the speaker, and held up his thin, almost waxen hands.

"How can I?" he asked with an air of bewilderment well feigned. "How can I possibly? The latter half of this fragment of scribble is a mere copy of a verse out of the Old Testament, and seems to have nothing whatever to do with the theory—whatever it may be—expounded in the upper part of the page."

"Then what is your candid opinion, dad?" asked Gwen, placing her hand softly upon her father's shoulder again as she stood behind him, and at the same time turning her eyes affectionately upon the tall, good-looking, young man at her side.

"My candid opinion, my dear," grunted the old Professor, "is that it is one of the many extraordinary theories we have had of hare-brained persons who have gained a smattering of Hebrew, and believe themselves to have discovered some very wonderful secret. To put it bluntly, Gwen— the whole thing is bunkum!"

The young man said nothing. His spirits fell. Of course, he had expected the Professor, in the habit of all scholars, to throw cold water upon Doctor Diamond's suggestion, but he was hardly prepared for such a drastic dismissal of the subject.

"Well," he exclaimed at last, "I don't wish you to come to any premature conclusion, Professor. You have really not had sufficient opportunity yet of thoroughly investigating the affair, have you?"

"No. That's quite true. I—well—I'd like to keep these scraps for a day, or say a couple of days—if I might, my dear Frank. I'll be most careful of them, I promise you, and they shall not leave my possession. As a matter of fact," he added, "Ginsberg from Berlin happens to be in London, and I'm extremely anxious to show them to him, and hear his views."

Frank Farquhar was a smart young man, and in a second realised danger in this.

"I fear, Professor, that I cannot allow you to show them to Professor Ginsberg. I made a promise to Diamond that they should be shown only to yourself."

"Very well, very well," laughed the Professor, "if you care to trust them with me till the day after to-morrow I will promise to show them to nobody. I only wish to study the extraordinary statement myself, and consult certain original Hebrew texts."

At first Frank was reluctant, remembering his promise to Doctor Diamond. But at Gwen's persuasion he was induced to leave them to be locked up in the old-fashioned oak bureau at the further end of the cosy room. The three then passed into the small drawing-room on the same floor, where Gwen, at her lover's request, sat at the piano and sang in her sweet contralto several pretty French *chansonettes* which she had learnt.

Chapter Eight
Presents another Curious Problem

In the solution of a problem such as that placed before Professor Griffin, knowledge meant power.

Though he had successfully concealed his excitement he had, truth to tell, learnt much from the perusal of those charred papers—much that held him in utter amazement. A theory had presented itself of which no one had ever before dreamed.

He had derided the manuscript as a clumsy story by some half-educated person. But, within himself, he knew quite well that the problem had been propounded and the suggestion made by some person equally well-read as himself, some Hebrew scholar of highest attainment, if not of highest standing. Alas, in these days of impudent self-advertisement, it is not the cleverest man who is the most notable, or who looms largest in the public eye. The same rule applies to Professors of Hebrew, as to men in every other walk of life.

That night, after Frank had left and Gwen had kissed him good-night and gone to her room, he sat for over an hour, smoking his long pipe in silence at his study fireside. He had resolved that he would be the first to reveal the startling secret to the world. Yes. He would write an article in the *Contemporary*, and he knew full well that words, coming from such a high authority as himself, would be quoted by almost every newspaper in the whole civilised globe.

It was astounding—never before in the whole history of the world had such a wonderful discovery been made. The Christian religion would be shaken to its very foundations—not weakened, be it said, but actually strengthened a thousandfold.

He laughed aloud as he sat with his pipe in his hand, his eyes cast down upon the bright red hearthrug.

"What would the Bishops of the Anglican Church, the Cardinals of the Romish Church, the Rabbis of the Jewish Synagogues and all the other heads of our religion give for possession of this secret which is mine—mine only!" he exclaimed, speaking to himself in a low whisper. "What would men in the city, the financiers, speculators, and the thousand-and-one varieties of money 'sharks' give me to reveal the truth to them. The truth?" he repeated thoughtfully. "The truth? No. I have not yet got at the actual truth. To discover it will be my work to-morrow. And I will not pause for a single instant until all is plain, and I have the secret open and revealed."

Again he hesitated, smoking on in silence, his brow heavy and thoughtful, for he had taken off his glasses and placed them in their big, bulky case.

"Two men, this fellow Diamond, whoever he may be, and Frank Farquhar stand between myself and the secret!" he muttered to himself with a grin. Then he rose impatiently and snapped his fingers. "They shall not stand in my way for long," he laughed. "The secret is mine—it is in *my* possession!"

The Professor rose early next day, as was his habit.

As he sat at the breakfast table, Gwen who looked bright and fresh in her neat white blouse and plain navy serge skirt, noticed that he was unusually silent and morose. They were devoted to each other, but at such times when her father, rendered irritable by his studies, betrayed impatience she always remained silent.

"I've asked Frank over to luncheon, dad," she ventured at last to remark.

Whereupon the old man replied in a snappy voice: "I fear I shall not be bade. I'm going along to the Museum, and may be there all day. I have a number of researches to make. Apologise for my absence."

Gwen promised to do this; but instead, an hour later, she sent her lover a wire, suggesting that, as the Professor would be absent, they should lunch together at Princes', which idea the young man gladly adopted.

At eleven Professor Griffin, descending from a cab, entered a small office in Oxford Street, the office of a firm of photographers whose specialty is the reproducing of ancient documents for the official publications of the British Museum, the Paleographical Society and similar institutions. To the manager, he produced the carefully preserved scraps of typewriting and manuscript, and ordered photographic reproductions to be made with as great a speed as possible.

The manager examined the charred folios closely, and declared that the work would be useless for reproduction in any journal or magazine.

"I don't want them for that purpose," was Griffin's reply.

"We'll do them as clearly as possible on whole plates, Professor," was the man's reply, "but they will not come out very satisfactorily, I fear."

"As long as I can decipher them easily is all I care," replied the older man. "I shall call for the originals at four o'clock."

"We will have finished with them by that time, sir. I will send them down to the studio at Acton."

"And take the utmost care of them please," urged the Professor.

"We are used, as you know, sir, to handling the most valuable manuscripts in the world. The Museum give us all their work, and we often have, in our safes, manuscripts worth thousands of pounds each," replied the manager.

A sudden thought occurred to Griffin, and taking from the table the scrap of writing upon the ruled paper, he held it up to the light to examine its watermark. The design was at once apparent—the head of a lady of the seventeenth century with hair dressed in the style of Charles the First, low-cut bodice, puffed sleeves, and a necklet of pearls, while above the words placed in a semi-circle was "Sevigne Paper."

"H'm," grunted the old man, "evidently one of those imitation English papers, made in France. Well, Macdonald, get as good results as you can from the scraps, won't you?"

The photographer's manager, who knew Griffin well, and who had often photographed Hebrew and Greek manuscripts for him, assured him that the very greatest care should be taken in the work.

Thereupon, the Professor rose and left, urging that the originals should be returned from Acton well before four o'clock.

In his thick and somewhat shabby overcoat and soft felt hat, he walked through the drizzling rain to the British Museum, where, as he entered, the attendants saluted him. In that national institution he was a well-known figure, for during the greater part of his lifetime he had studied there, especially in the Department of Manuscripts.

It was to that he at once made his way. The Keeper of the Department was absent, but a man of Professor Griffin's reputation has the "run of the place;" therefore after wishing good-day to one of the assistant-keepers he began searching the catalogue of manuscripts for the Hebrew ones which he wished to consult, writing their numbers upon a slip. This he handed to the assistant-keeper who, having glanced at the numbers and recognised to which they referred, regarded him with a glance of quick curiosity.

"One of the earliest originals of the Book of Ezekiel—eh, Professor?" remarked the man. "And the other is the Muratori Manuscript."

"Exactly," was Griffin's reply, and when the man had left the little room in which he was standing, he drew from his pocket a small book in which overnight he had made pencilled memoranda from the half-confused fragments which Frank had placed before him. Then he waited in undisguised anxiety.

Presently the assistant-keeper returned with two of the most important Biblical manuscripts the Museum possessed, and placed them before the man whose opinion upon Hebrew originals of Holy Writ was always decisive.

The first manuscript, one of the earliest originals of the Book of Ezekiel and one used by the revisers of the Bible a few years ago, was upon yellow and discoloured parchment of great age, bound in old calf of the early sixteenth century. The binding had practically perished, but the writing within was still plain and quite decipherable to an expert.

Originally written upon a long roll, it had in later times been cut into folios and bound, as being readier of access, and easier to consult. Of its early history from the time of being written until A.D. 1421, practically nothing was known. In the year in question it was brought to Constantinople from Palestine, and in 1627 was given by the Patriarch to Charles the First.

The Professor removed his hat and overcoat seated himself, and with reverent fingers turned the time-dimmed pages from which a portion of our Holy Bible had been translated.

To the person unacquainted with early Hebrew script the pages were covered by meaningless hieroglyphics; but to him they were as clear as any printed column in the *Times* newspaper.

He searched through until he discovered a certain passage. Then, eagerly consulting his notebook, he began translating it, word for word, writing down the English equivalent upon the paper that had been placed before him.

He did not hurry, but alone in the little room, he worked on, slowly and deliberately. For fully two hours he continued but the result was, judging from the expression upon his face, by no means gratifying.

The assistant-keeper came and went, for the Professor, being such a great authority, was always allowed to work in the keeper's private room. Indeed only a man of Griffin's rare attainments and knowledge would have been able to translate from the original Hebrew of that ancient character, so often indistinct and involved in meaning and in sense.

At times, with a rapid hand, he made an exact reproduction of the original, especially that of chapter xli, verse 23 to the end which, as will be recollected, was given in the dead man's manuscript as an illustration.

Heedless of the fact that he had had no luncheon, he continued copying the original very carefully and with a sure and expert touch until he had made a complete copy of the original of chapters xl, xli, xlii, xliv, and xlvii, a work which occupied him till nearly four o'clock.

He took no count of time, so wholly engrossed was he in his work. The assistant-keeper entered prior to his departure at four o'clock when the department closed, and began bustling about, hoping that the "dry-as-dust" old fellow, being disturbed, might abandon his work for that day.

But nothing interrupted him in making his rapid copying of those Hebrew characters that had been written before the birth of Christ.

Presently, in sheer despair, the assistant-keeper remarked:

"That's rather heavy work for you, Professor, isn't it?"

"No. Not exactly," was the old man's quick reply without looking up, "I am about to make a most interesting investigation; therefore, I dare not employ any copyist. He might so easily make mistakes."

"An investigation!" echoed the younger man. "Why, curiously enough for the past three days we've had a man here copying that same book for some mysterious purpose. He finished only yesterday afternoon. But he refused to tell me the reason he was making the copy other than that he, like yourself, was making some investigations. He used the same expression as yourself, curiously enough."

"Another searcher!" gasped the Professor, laying down his pen, and staring at the speaker. "Another investigator of the original of the Book of

Ezekiel! Who was he? What was he like?" demanded the old man quickly, his face blanched in an instant.

"I don't know who he was, for we've never seen him here before. He was an old gentleman, a foreigner evidently—and a scholar, for he wrote the Hebrew characters almost as quickly and accurately as you yourself."

Professor Arminger Griffin sat back in his chair, his mouth open, staring into space.

Was it possible that some one else besides himself had obtained knowledge of the great secret, and was actively engaged upon investigations!

And the stranger who had copied that very manuscript which he was copying, was an unknown foreigner and a scholar into the bargain!

Was it possible that the secret was already out?

Chapter Nine
Concerns "The Other Man"

"What was the stranger like?" asked the Professor eagerly, his thin hand resting upon the ancient parchment he had been so carefully copying.

"A short, stout, elderly man with white pointed beard," was the assistant-keeper's reply. "Four days ago he came here, carrying with him a number of references which he turned up in various early Hebrew manuscripts. But it was the one you have there before you which attracted him most. He worked three days upon it, and made a complete and most accurate copy."

"He didn't tell you whence he came, or for what purpose he was making the researches?"

"No, for, as you well know, Professor, students seldom do. They are not very communicative, unless they be young," laughed the official. "But he was a foreigner."

"Undoubtedly. From the north of Europe, I should say—Norwegian or perhaps Russian, not German, I think. But he spoke most excellent English."

"A scholar?"

"Without a doubt. He went about his work in that careful methodical manner that at once betrayed the specialist. He concluded his work only yesterday."

"How was he dressed?"

"Fairly well. He wore a dark-grey suit and a black bow cravat."

"His searches were confined to Ezekiel?"

"No, not exactly. He copied some references from our earliest manuscript of Deuteronomy—you examined it a few months ago, I remember. The thirty-second chapter seemed to attract him, as he copied it in its entirety."

"Ah, that's the Song of Moses," remarked the Professor. "'Give ear O ye heavens, and I will speak; and hear O earth, the words of my mouth.' I wonder what can be his object," he added thoughtfully.

"He merely told me that he was making an investigation in order to put a remarkable theory to the test."

Griffin started. A remarkable theory was being put to the test by this stranger! Was it possible that another scholar was in possession of the dead man's secret, besides himself!

He held his breath. Then, when a few moments later he had recovered himself, he began to make many inquiries concerning the unknown foreigner. But it was already past four o'clock, and the assistant-keeper had his train to catch to his home at Epping. Therefore he declared that he knew no more, and taking the precious manuscript, replaced it with the others and hastily bade the Professor "Good afternoon."

"Good afternoon," was the old man's reply. "I am sorry you are in such a hurry. I'll return to-morrow."

Then he struggled into his overcoat, and left the Museum full of vague misgivings.

Already dark outside, the street-lamps were lit, and the steady downpour was unceasing. But he trudged across to the photographer's, and there obtained the scraps of half-destroyed manuscript, which only a few moments before had been brought back from the studio at Acton.

"We shall have prints ready for you to-morrow evening," said the manager. "I'll send them to you, shall I?"

"No, don't do that," Griffin said quickly. "I would rather call for them. I'll be in about this time to-morrow."

Then placing the packet in his pocket, he walked along Oxford Street in the direction of Tottenham Court Road.

His mind was full of the alarming discovery that another person was investigating the same problem as himself. This meant that the secret was known, and if known to another, what more likely than that the stranger possessed a complete manuscript—a manuscript which gave the context, not only of the curious statement, but of the directions of how the truth could be verified.

Of the latter, he possessed only that one scrap of written manuscript. There must have been other folios, but all were, alas! missing. They had, no doubt, been consumed by the flames before the eyes of the dying man.

He was beside himself with anxiety. It could not have been Diamond himself who had been at the Museum, for the Doctor was not a Hebrew scholar and, besides, he had been told by Frank that the man was badly deformed. Therefore, his deformity would certainly have impressed itself upon the assistant-keeper.

By the "Tube" from Tottenham Court Road Station he travelled to Notting Hill Gate, and turning into Pembridge Gardens, let himself in with his latch-key.

Frank was with Gwen in the drawing-room, and they were taking their tea *tête-à-tête* when the old man entered. After luncheon he had taken her to a matinée, and the happy pair had only just returned.

"Tell me, Frank," asked the Professor, almost before he had time to greet him, "did that friend of yours, Diamond, show those papers to any one else besides you, do you think?"

"Certainly not. Why?" inquired the young man in some surprise.

"Oh, nothing," replied the Professor with slight hesitation. "I—well—I only thought that it would be a little unfair to trouble me if somebody else had already been making any researches."

"Nobody has seen it save myself, I can assure you. Diamond is a most careful and cautious man," Frank declared. "He brought them straight over from Paris, and came at once to me."

"He might possibly have shown them to somebody in Paris," the elder man suggested.

"I asked him, and he distinctly told me that nobody save myself had set eyes upon them."

The Professor sank into an armchair, and in silence took the cup of tea which Gwen handed to him.

"You're tired, dad," she said. "I see it in your face!"

"A little, dear. I've been at the Museum all day."

"I wish you wouldn't go to that horrid old place. It always gives you a headache, you know," said the girl anxiously.

"Ah, my child," replied the old man with a sigh, "the place holds, for me, much that is interesting in life—in fact all that is interesting, except your own neat little self."

The girl laughed merrily, declaring that compliments should not be paid to her in the presence of Frank.

But the old man, sighing rather wearily, said:

"Well, Gwen, it's the truth. I have nothing much to live for, except yourself and my studies. When your dear mother died, the sun of my life was extinguished. And now you have grown up to take her place."

She and Frank exchanged quick meaning glances.

"I hope always to live near you, dear old dad, even after we're married," she said. "I shall never desert you."

Her father smiled, saying:

"That is what every girl says to her parents before marriage. Few, however, fulfil their promise."

"Well, dad, don't let's talk about parting till the time really comes," exclaimed his daughter, in an endeavour to change the topic of conversation. Only a moment prior to the Professor's return she and Frank had been discussing the future, and considering that very point.

"Have you been making researches in the Museum in connection with the burnt papers, Professor?" asked young Farquhar, who, standing in his well-cut suit of blue serge, looked a splendid specimen of the lithe, athletic young Englishman.

"Yes, I have."

"And the result?"

The Professor shook his head in the negative.

"At present I have failed to discover the slightest title of corroboration of your friend Doctor Diamond's wonderful theory. The construction which may be placed upon the scrappy statements are many, but none upon which I can yet form any absolute conclusion."

He made no mention that he had caused photographic negatives of the burnt papers to be secured, or that, within his pocket, there reposed an accurate copy of the accepted original of the Book of Ezekiel.

"You are still in opposition, then, to Diamond's theory?" asked the young man.

"Of course."

"But why?"

The Professor drank his tea slowly, and replaced the cup upon the little table.

"Well," he answered with much deliberation, "because Biblical history is entirely opposed to it. The first Book of Kings relates in detail the building of the temple by Solomon in B.C. 1012, the dimensions of the Porch, the Holy Place, and the Holy of Holies. Within and without the building was conspicuous by the lavish use of gold from Ophir and Parvaim. Above the sacred Ark, which was placed as of old in the Most Holy Place, were made new cherubim, one pair of whose wings met above the Ark and another pair reached to the walls behind them. In the Holy Place, besides the Altar of Incense, which was made of cedar overlaid with gold, there were seven golden candlesticks instead of one, and the table of the shew-bread was replaced by ten golden tables bearing beside the shew-bread the innumerable golden vessels for the service of the sanctuary. Instead of the brazen laver we know that there was a 'molten sea' of brass, a masterpiece of Hiram's skill, for the ablutions of the priests. It was called a 'sea' from its great size, being five cubits in height ten in diameter and thirty in circumference, and containing, it is estimated, about sixteen thousand gallons of water. It stood upon twelve oxen, three towards each quarter of the heavens, and all looking outwards. The brim itself, or lip, was wrought 'like the brim of a cup, with flowers of lilies,' or curved outwards like a lily or lotus flower. The front of the porch was supported, after the manner of some Egyptian temples, by the two great brazen pillars Jachin and Boaz, eighteen cubits high, with capitols of five cubits more, adorned, as we are told, with lily-work and pomegranates.

"But," he added, "all this is historical fact. In the temple reposed the most valuable collection of gold and jewels ever gathered together, and the dedication of the House of Jehovah, the God of Israel, was the grandest ceremony ever performed under the Mosaic dispensation. And if you read 1 Kings, viii, and 2 Chronicles, v, you will there learn how, at the ceremony, Jehovah gave the sign of His coming to take possession of His house. Then Solomon built his own house, placing within it the wonderful 'wealth of Ormuz and Ind,' and to him came the Queen of Sheba, an event which marked the culminating-point of his glory. The very king who built the glorious temple, and to whom Jehovah had twice given solemn warning in his old age, however, and under the influence of his wives, turned his heart away from God. He served Ashtoreth, the moon-goddess of the Zidonians, and Moloch, the 'horrid king' whom the Ammonites worshipped with human sacrifice. Solomon died in B.C. 976, and very shortly after his death the prophecy of Ahijah was fulfilled: his kingdom was rent in twain, and the parts, weakened by the disruption, formed the separate kingdoms of Judah and of Israel."

"It will be interesting to trace the history of the temple from that date down to the siege of Jerusalem by Nebuchadnezzar," remarked Frank.

"That occurred about three hundred years after Solomon's death—at least according to our latest chronologers," replied the Professor, "and it is in tracing that history that we have many of the points before us negatived most decisively. Let me instance one or two of them."

"Yes, do, dad," cried Gwen, greatly interested. "I'm quite excited, over the mysterious affair."

"Then listen, child," the old man said. "But, first go and get a Bible from the study."

And the girl rose to do her father's bidding.

Chapter Ten
Fact or Fiction

"I may perhaps with advantage give you very roughly some historical facts which tend to negative Diamond's theory," the Professor said, turning to Farquhar while Gwen was absent.

"That is what I'm most desirous of hearing," replied the young man. "I can claim no special knowledge like yourself. Indeed, no man in England is more capable of expressing an opinion than you are."

The Professor passed his hand through his scanty grey hair and smiled. He saw that his wide knowledge impressed this young man whose only thought was a "sensation" in one or other of the Gavin group of publications.

Then, when Gwen had re-entered the room with a Bible in her hand, he said in that slow, deliberate habit of his, the habit of the scholar and deep thinker:

"The theory of this Doctor Diamond is that the treasures of Solomon's temple were hidden by the priests prior to the taking of Jerusalem by Nebuchadnezzar. Well, that is a bold but quite unsubstantiated assertion. As early after Solomon as the reign of Jeroboam the First, King of Judah, the golden calves, the symbols of the Heliopolitan deity, were set up in the two extremities of the kingdom, and the temple was put to sacrilegious usages. These sins were continued by his successors, until in the reign of Asa, the third King of Judah, the impure orgies of Ashtoreth were suppressed, for 'having his heart perfect with Jehovah all his days' the king repaired Shishak's plunder—the first plunder of the temple, mark you—with 'rich offerings of gold and of silver.' Asa made war against the Ethiopians, and on returning to Jerusalem the prophet Azariah, son of Oded, met him and exhorted him and his subjects to be strong heart in hand in seeking God. He gave an affecting description of the former state of Israel: 'For a long season Israel hath been (or was) without the true God, and without a teaching' priest, and without law. (2 Chronicles, xv, 3.) His words roused the hearers to a new and more thorough reformation. The idols were removed from all the cities of Judah and Benjamin, and those which had been won from Ephraim. The altar of burnt-offering, which had been polluted by Jeroboam, was renewed, and in the third month of the fifteenth year (B.C. 940) Asa called a great convocation at Jerusalem. Jehoshaphat followed his father's piety, but the darkest night of Israel's spiritual declension came with the accession of Ahab, seventh King of Israel, and husband of Jezebel. The service of Baal was established throughout Israel, a grove was made for the orgies of Ashtoreth, and by Jezebel's orders the prophets of Jehovah were put to death, all except one hundred who were hidden in a cave by Obadiah, the governor of Ahab's house."

"But was the temple already plundered?" asked Gwen, seated with her chin resting upon her hand, listening intently.

"We know that it was plundered seriously by Shishak, King of Egypt, who carried off many of its greatest treasures, including the celebrated golden shields of Solomon's house, which Rehoboam replaced by brass to keep up the display," was the Professor's prompt reply. "Recent discoveries at Karnak tell the whole story of the conquest from the Egyptian point of view. The kingdom of Judah, it seems, became for a long time tributary to Shishak, and upon the walls of the great temple at Karnak there are the sculptured representation of the siege and the hieroglyphics 'Fuda Melchi' — meaning 'The Kingdom of Judah.' That was, you will bear in mind, the first spoliation."

"Were there others?" asked Frank. "I mean others that are authenticated by recent discoveries?"

"Yes, Jehoram reigned in Jerusalem from B.C. 895-892, and after his marriage with Athaliah, daughter of Ahab, the temple was again despoiled, and the daughters of Judah were once more prostituted to the rites of Ashtoreth," replied Professor Griffin. "Joash, in B.C. 884, repaired the fabric of the temple by public subscription, for he was the inventor of the modern money-box—and there were enough funds left over, we are told, to purchase vessels for the sanctuary. (2 Kings, xii, 4-6; 2 Chronicles, xxiv, 4-14.) This, however, did not last long, for in the reign of Amaziah, ninth King of Judah, Jehoash, King of Israel, defeated him in B.C. 826, took him prisoner and, entering Jerusalem again, reached the temple and conveyed all its treasures to Samaria.

"In the reigns of Jeroboam the Second, Shallam, Menaham and Pekehiah, other vessels and treasures were provided for the temple. Jonathan built the high gate, but his successor, Ahaz, after plunging into all the idolatries of the surrounding nations, making molten images for Baal and sacrificing his children to Moloch in the valley of Hinnom, found himself, according to our best chronologer, Ussher, involved in war. He was therefore compelled to apply for help to Tiglath-pileser, the 'Tiger-Lord of Asshur,' King of

Assyria, against Syria and Israel, and declaring himself his vassal, sent him all the treasures then left in the temple. Ahaz, we learn from 2 Kings, xvi, 10-18, profaned the temple by dismounting the brazen altar and replacing it by another. Likewise the 'Great Sea of Solomon,' too large to be removed at previous despoliations, was dismounted from its supporting oxen, and the lavers from their bases, which were also sent to the King of Assyria, together with the coverings which had been built for the King's entry to the house, and for the shelter of the worshippers on the Sabbath. The golden vessels of the House of God were cut in pieces and sent with the rest, and the sanctuary itself was shut up. Hezekiah, who came after him in B.C. 726, reopened and restored the Holy Place, though it was now devoid of most of its treasures.

"To trace the history of the Temple through the days of Hoshea, son of Elah, Manasseh and Amon is perhaps unnecessary. Under Josiah, whose reign marks the last dying glory of the earthly kingdom of David, idolatry was put away, the Temple was renovated and the Ark of the Covenant which had been hidden restored to its place. (2 Chronicles, xxxiv, 3-13; xxxv, 3.) During these repairs the high priest Hilkiah found the sacred copy of the book of the law and delivered it to Shaphan, the scribe, who read it before the king. It was afterwards publicly read, and incited a new zeal among the people, and once again was the sanctuary filled with gold and silver vessels. Therefore you will see that by this period there could not have been any of the actual treasures placed by Solomon remaining in the Temple."

"The Ark of the Covenant was still there," remarked young Farquhar.

"That is not at all certain," was the old man's reply. "Many of the events chronicled in the Old Testament are corroborated by the inscriptions found by Flinders Petrie in Egypt and by Layard at Nineveh. Others are negatived, and our chronology rendered uncertain. Certain it is, however," he went on, "that in the fourth year of the reign of Jehoiakim, eighteenth King of Judah (B.C. 608-597), Nebuchadnezzar arose, and a few years later advanced to Jerusalem, which he took after a brief siege. The vessels of the sanctuary were carried off to Babylon, where they were dedicated in the temple of Belus. If you turn to 2 Kings, xxiv, 13, you will there read: 'And he carried out thence all the treasures of the house of the Lord, and the treasures of the king's house, and cut in pieces all the vessels of gold which Solomon, King of Israel had made in the temple of the Lord, as the Lord had said.'"

"Surely it was Ezekiel who went as one of the prisoners of Nebuchadnezzar to Babylon," remarked Gwen.

"Yes," replied her father, "on the second occasion when the Babylonian king attacked the city. But," he added, "in the reference I have just given you, you will note that the vessels are described as 'those that Solomon had made.' Either therefore they had been too massive for removal on the many previous occasions when the temple was plundered or they had been made to replace the ancient originals. The latter is my own theory. Now, as I dare say you will recollect, in B.C. 586, on the tenth day of the fifth month, Ab, Nebuchadnezzar again advanced against the rebellious city of Jerusalem and destroyed it. The two great pillars of the temple porch, Jachin and Boaz, and Solomon's brazen sea with the twelve bulls supporting it, were broken in pieces and their brass transported to Babylon, together with a great number of captives. And on the third day of the catastrophe, in the nineteenth year of Nebuchadnezzar, the temple and the city were committed to the flames with the palaces of the king and princes, and all the chief houses of Jerusalem, and their walls levelled to the ground."

"Then that was the actual end of Solomon's temple," remarked Frank Farquhar. "Is that authentic?"

"Without a doubt," said the Professor. "Yet did not Jeremiah comfort the Jews amid all these judgments by contrasting His destruction of the other nations of their present oppressors with His correction of themselves? 'Fear thou not, O Jacob, my servant, saith Jehovah, for I am with thee; for I will make a full end of all the nations whither I have driven thee; *but I will not make a full end of thee, but correct thee in measure*; yet will I not leave thee wholly unpunished.' Surely no words could more fully express the principle of Jehovah's dealings with the Jews, His own people, in every age."

"Belshazzar, at his feast in Babylon, put to sacrilegious uses the vessels of the temple, did he not?" asked the young man.

"Yes," answered Griffin, and addressing Gwen said: "Turn to the fifth chapter of Daniel, dear, and read out the first four verses."

The girl found the place and read as follows: "Belshazzar, the King, made a great feast to a thousand of his lords, and drank wine before the thousand. Belshazzar, whiles he tasted the wine, commanded to bring the golden and silver vessels which his father Nebuchadnezzar had taken out of the temple which was in Jerusalem; that the King and his princes, his wives and his concubines, might drink therein. Then they brought the golden vessels that were taken out of the temple of the house of God which was at Jerusalem; and the King, and his princes, his wives, and his concubines, drank in them. They drank wine and praised the gods of gold, and of silver, of brass, of iron, of wood, and of stone."

"And at that moment," remarked the Professor, "was seen the prophetic handwriting on the wall: '*Mene, mene, tekel, upharsin*,' being followed by the city's surprise by Cyrus the Great, and its fall and destruction. Then under

Cyrus, the Israelites returned from their captivity, and by his decree another temple was built by Zerubbabel, the prince of Judah, who was leader of the migration. Cyrus caused his treasurer Mithredath to deliver up the vessels which Nebuchadnezzar had carried away from Jerusalem, five thousand four hundred in number, to Zerubbabel to be re-consecrated to the service of Jehovah."

"Is it to this second temple which our manuscript relates, do you think?" queried Frank. "Or is it to Solomon's temple?"

"Of the temple of Zerubbabel we have but few particulars," answered the Professor, "and no description that would enable us to realise its appearance. But there are some dimensions given in the Bible and elsewhere which are extremely interesting as affording points of comparison between it and the temple of Solomon and Herod after it. The first and most authentic are those given in the Book of Ezra (Ezra vi, 3-4) when quoting the decree of Cyrus, wherein it is said: 'Let the house be builded, the place where they offered sacrifices, and let the foundations thereof be strongly laid; the height thereof three-score cubits, and the breadth thereof three-score cubits, with three rows of great stones and a row of new timber.' Josephus quotes this passage almost literally, but in doing so enables us with certainty to translate the word here called 'row' as storey, as indeed the sense would lead us to infer—for it could apply only to the three storeys of chambers that surrounded Solomon's, and afterwards Herod's temple, and with this again we come to the wooden talar which surmounted the temple and formed a fourth storey. It may be remarked that this dimension of sixty cubits in height accords perfectly with the words which Josephus puts into the mouth of Herod when he makes him say that the temple built after the Captivity wanted sixty cubits of the height of that of Solomon. For as he had adopted the height of a hundred and twenty cubits in the Chronicles for that temple, this one remained only sixty. This temple was still standing in Herod's time, and was repaired by him. Hecataeus mentions that the altar was twenty cubits square and ten high. But he unfortunately does not supply us with the dimensions of the temple itself. Therefore if the priests and Levites and Elders of families were disconsolate at seeing how much more sumptuous the old temple was than the one which on account of their poverty they had just been able to erect, (Ezra, iii, 12-13; Joseph Ast., xi, 4, 2) it certainly was not because it was smaller, as almost every dimension had been increased one-third; but it may have been that the carving and the gold and other ornaments of Solomon's temple far surpassed this, and the pillars of the portico and the veils may all have been far more splendid, so also probably were the vessels; and all this is what a Jew would mourn over, far more than mere architectural splendour."

"It is a pity we do not know more about this second temple," remarked Gwen, in a tone of disappointment and regret.

"For our present purpose its history, down to the taking of Jerusalem by Titus, does not concern us, my dear," remarked the old scholar, drawing his hand rather wearily over his white brow. "The problem before us evidently has to do with the days of Jehoiakim, prior to the advance of Nebuchadnezzar. Later facts and traditions do not concern us at the moment. I think, however, I have given you an outline of the varied history of the temple and its treasures based upon the very latest readings of Egyptian, Assyrian and other inscriptions, sufficient to show you quite plainly that Solomon's treasure could not possibly have existed in the reign of Jehoiakim, and that the theory of this friend of yours, Diamond, is utterly and entirely without the foundation of tradition or of ancient legend."

"Well," remarked the young man, "such an opinion coming from your mouth is, of course, final, Professor. Yet you must admit that the statement, even as it stands, is full of interest."

"Full of very cleverly conceived mystery—and mystery is always attractive," laughed the Professor, looking at him through his big, round, highly magnifying spectacles.

In the statement he had made there was one discrepancy, one that only a scholar would notice. He had purposely withheld one Biblical reference— one which, above all, had caused him to reflect and believe that the writer of the half-burnt screed was correct, that the secret and its key were actually genuine.

But it was his fixed intention to turn Frank Farquhar from further investigation, and to laugh at Doctor Diamond as a fool, ignorant of any knowledge of the history of the Hebrew race.

A silence fell. Gwen Griffin and her lover were both staring straight at the fire without uttering a word.

The old man sat watching the effect of his words upon the pair, and before Frank left, he handed back to him the charred remnants which he had received from the photographer.

But his thoughts were of that other man—the short, white-bearded foreigner, his rival—who was so busy with his researches, the stranger from across the Channel who also held the remarkable secret.

Chapter Eleven
The Great God Gold

After dining at the club Frank Farquhar strolled round to Half Moon Street, and throwing himself into an armchair before the fire, gave himself up to reflection.

He was recalling what the Professor had said. It was true that all stories of lost treasure were nowadays received with incredulity, and surely this was the most amazing and most wonderful of them all.

Arminger Griffin, Regius Professor of Hebrew, treated the whole matter as a huge joke. Historical fact was wholly against the suggestion contained in these half-burned scraps which, before his departure from Pembridge Gardens, the Professor had handed back to him. Ah! if they could only reconstruct the context of those disjoined words.

He took a cigar and lit it. But a moment later he tossed it impatiently into the fire. It tasted bitter. The Professor had dashed all his hopes to the ground, for was not his opinion on such a matter final.

As he bade good-night to Gwen in the hall and held her soft hand in his she had whispered to him words of encouragement. "Father is really devoid of any romance," she declared. "There may be something in the secret after all. Could you not endeavour to find the person who made that remarkable declaration?"

Her suggestion he was now carefully considering.

The stranger who had died in Paris was apparently not the person who made the declaration. The latter was in all probability alive. If so, could he not furnish many more facts than the scrappy information they at present possessed?

Yet what right had Doctor Diamond to the secret — and for the matter of that, what right had he himself?

That the hard-up stranger in Paris feared lest the documents should fall into other hands was shown by his last act of causing them to be burned. Such a course made it appear as though the stranger had no right to the possession of the papers. In all probability he had not!

Gwen's suggestion, however, appealed to him. Yet to find that one man in the whole world who knew the truth would, he foresaw, be a work fraught with greatest difficulty. The only manner by which he could be approached, if found, would be upon pretence of restoring to him the charred remains of his valuable statement.

The telephone-bell rang, and he rose and answered it. The editor of one of the great daily journals controlled by his brother-in-law, Sir George, spoke from the office in Fleet Street, at that hour of the evening a hive of industry. A question of policy had arisen, and the editor, one of the shining lights of modern journalism, consulted Frank as representative of the proprietor, Sir George being still in Egypt.

Frank, after a brief conversation, left the matter entirely in the editor's hands, and replacing the receiver walked back from the big roll-top writing-table to the fireplace, where he stood with both arms leaning on the mantelshelf gazing thoughtfully into the blazing coals.

A few moments later his man entered saying:

"A gentleman to see you, sir—Doctor Diamond."

Frank started. His visitor was the very man of all men he wished most to consult, therefore he gave orders for him to be shown in at once.

"Why, my dear Doctor," cried the young fellow, as the ugly little old man entered, "this is a real surprise! I thought of running down to Horsford to see you in the morning. Take off your coat and sit down. I want to have a serious chat with you."

"I got no reply to my two letters, Mr Farquhar," said the crook-backed little man in explanation of his visit. "So I thought I'd just run up and see how you are progressing with our business."

Frank helped him off with his shabby frieze coat and, having installed him comfortably by the fire and given him a cigar, replied:

"Well, Doctor, the fact is I did not reply to your letters because I had nothing definite to report. I trust you will not attribute my silence to any want of courtesy. I have been busy over the matter ever since I returned to London."

"And with what result?" asked the crafty-eyed little man.

"Nothing very satisfactory, I regret to say," was the young man's answer. "Yet I am not discouraged. Professor Griffin, before whom I have placed it, gives as his opinion that there is probably, something in the theory, but he will not quite commit himself to any absolute declaration."

"Is he really competent to judge?" Diamond queried.

"Competent! Why, my dear sir, he's one of the first Hebrew scholars in the world! He is daily engaged in making researches. History, as we are acquainted with it, may negative the theory advanced in those scraps of typewriting, yet Old Testament history is, as you know, very involved and often very contradictory."

"Well," exclaimed the Doctor, "to tell the truth, Mr Farquhar, I'm getting anxious. What I fear is that too many people will get knowledge of it. Then, with the secret out, we shall have others trying to investigate. And with such a gigantic business before us, is it any wonder that I'm becoming impatient?"

"Many a good business is spoilt by being in too great a hurry," Frank declared. "Remain patient, and leave matters entirely to me," he added reflectively. "I've been wondering whether, if we made diligent and secret inquiry, we might not discover the actual person, whoever he may be, who made the curious declaration. It certainly was not your dead friend."

The Doctor hesitated. The idea at once commended itself to him.

"No," he said. "Often when I have recalled all the romantic facts, I have been inclined to suspect that the man who died, although a scholar, had no right to possession of those papers. He intended to make money with them if death had not come so unexpectedly. His very words proved that."

"Exactly my opinion," declared Frank. "Now if we could but find out who the mysterious discoverer really is, we might approach him under pretence of handing back to him the remains of the papers."

"Ah! You still have them safely, eh?" demanded the Doctor.

"Certainly. They are locked in from prying eyes in my desk yonder."

"May I have them?"

"Of course," was Frank's unhesitating reply, though he had no desire to part with them at that juncture. Yet he had, unfortunately, no excuse for keeping them further. He could not say that the Professor held them, as he had given his visitor a solemn promise not to allow the documents out of his possession.

So he rose, unlocked a drawer with the key upon his chain, and handed to the deformed man the packet containing the half-burnt statement.

"Well," remarked Diamond, as he took the precious documents in his hand, "if you think it a wise course, let us adopt it."

"Yes, but where are we to commence our search?"

"The stranger said he was a Dane. He came from Copenhagen. Is it not probable," suggested the Doctor, "that the discoverer was some friend of his residing in that city?"

"More than likely," Farquhar agreed. "Yes. Let us try Copenhagen. We must first find out who are the professors of Hebrew resident there. I will write to our Copenhagen correspondent to-night and ask for a list. Then, if necessary, I will run over there myself. In this matter we must lay out a decisive line of inquiry and follow it up."

"Quite so," exclaimed the hunchback. "Copenhagen must be our starting-point. The initial difficulty, however, as far as I discern, is that we do not know our dead friend's name. If we did and could trace him, we might discover whether he knew anybody who was a Hebrew scholar."

"The Danish police would furnish us with names and descriptions of persons lately missing from the capital."

"So they would, that's a brilliant idea," exclaimed the Doctor. "My opinion is that the reason why he refused his name to me, even at the final moment, was because he was wanted by the police, and intended that they should remain in ignorance of his end."

"If so, it makes our inquiry far easier," declared Frank. "And suppose we find him?" he asked.

"If we find him," answered Diamond, looking straight into the eyes of the ambitious man opposite—"if we find him, we will compel him to furnish to us the context of the statement."

"Compel—eh?" repeated the other, a hard smile playing about the young man's lips. Diamond was a queer figure and strange persons had always attracted him. Through the ugly little doctor he had gained this remarkable knowledge of an uncanny secret withheld from the world for over two thousand years. He was reflecting what a "boom" the discovery would be for that great daily newspaper of which he was one of the Board of Directors.

"Then you agree that we shall at once turn our attention to Copenhagen—eh?" he asked.

"Certainly—the sooner the better."

"We have no photograph of your friend—a most unfortunate fact."

Diamond gave a detailed description of the dead man, and his friend, crossing to his writing-table, wrote it carefully at his dictation.

"I've been in Copenhagen several times," Frank remarked, "so I know that city fairly well. I wonder whether the man we seek is a professor at the University?"

"Our first object is to establish the dead man's identity."

"He may have lied, and perhaps was not a Dane after all! He may have been a Norwegian, or even a Swede."

Diamond raised his deformed shoulders and answered:

"True, as he was so bent upon concealing his identity he may well have lied to me regarding his nationality. Yet we must risk that, don't you think?"

"But you told me that you were convinced that he was a Scandinavian."

"Yes. But he might have come from Stockholm, or Gothenburg or Christiania."

"Our first inquiries must be of the Danish police," Frank said decisively. "I'll write to-night to our correspondent in Copenhagen."

"Would it not be best for you to go there and make inquiries yourself?"

"I may do that. Most probably I shall."

"Stories of treasure are always attractive," remarked the Doctor, casting a crafty glance at his young friend. "I hope, Mr Farquhar, you will make no mention in any of your papers regarding it."

"My dear Doctor, don't worry yourself about that," Frank laughed. "Of treasure stories we've of late had a perfect glut. For a long time, for instance, I've taken a deep interest in the wrecks of vessels known to have contained treasure, the exact location of which are known. As an example, we have the ship *Grosvenor* now lying off the Pondoland Coast with over a million and a half pounds of treasure in her rotting hold. Then there's the *Ariston*, in Marcus Bay, with 800,000 pounds worth; the *Birkenhead*, on Birkenhead Reef, with a similar amount; the *Atlas*, near Yarmouth, with 700,000 pounds, the *Dorothea*, on Tenedos Reef, with 460,000 pounds; the *Abercrombie*, lying under the Black Rock, with 180,000 pounds; and the *Merenstein*, on the coast of Yutton Island, with 120,000 pounds. In addition to these there are H.M.S. *Chandos* with 60,000 pounds in coin in her hold, the troopship *Addison* with 20,000 pounds in gold, and the *Harlem II*, lying half covered by sand with her hold full of silver bars. All these and many others are lying in positions perfectly well known, and only await salvage. Why, in one gale off the West African coast in 1802 seven ships were wrecked, all of them containing a vast treasure. Besides, the contents of the vessels I have mentioned have all been verified from their bills of lading still in existence. No, my dear Doctor," the young man added with a laugh, "had the story been an ordinary one of treasure it would not have interested me in the least, I assure you; and as for publishing any details, why, my dear sir, is it not to my own personal interest to keep the matter as secret as possible? Please do not have any apprehension on that score."

"I have not," declared the hunchback; "my great fear, however, is that this professor friend of yours may chatter."

"He will not. I have impressed upon Griffin the value of silence," said Frank. "Besides, he is a 'dry-as-dust,' silent man, who says nothing, so absorbed is he in his studies in his own particular sphere."

"Good. Then we will now transfer our attention to Copenhagen."

"I shall write to-night. Remain patient and wait the reply of the Danish police. I'm open to bet anything that your friend was compelled to make himself scarce from Denmark, and carried with him confidential documents which were not his property and with which he had no right to deal."

"Then if that really turns out so, it also proves another thing."

"What's that?"

"Why, if the documents were to be of any commercial value, they must have contained the actual key to the secret."

"No doubt. The key was written clearly in those manuscript folios, all of which were burned save one," was Frank's reply. "It is the context of that document which we must obtain at all costs and at all hazards. And if the dead man has not lied I'm firmly of opinion that it will be found within the city of Copenhagen."

Chapter Twelve
Describes an Important Discovery

Professor Griffin, for a scholar was a man of unusually rapid action.

He was convinced that another person was following the same course of inquiry as himself. Therefore he determined to act quickly and decisively.

Next day he returned to the British Museum, and after three hours' work completed the copy of the manuscript. Then he turned his attention to two fragments of the Hebrew manuscript of the Book of Ezekiel, one of the fourth century in the Oriental Room, and the other of the fifth century in the Harleian collection.

While studying these, he recollected that some fragment of early manuscript of Ezekiel had been recently found in the Genisa in Old Cairo by Mr Alder and his companions, and that several of them were in the Bodleian Library at Oxford. Therefore, he searched the catalogue, noted the numbers, and that evening took the train to the university centre, staying the night at the Randolph Hotel.

Next morning he was in consultation with his friend, Professor Cowley, and Number 2611 of the Hebrew manuscript was brought. It proved to be the text of Ezekiel from chapter xiv, 22 to chapter xlvii, 6.

"Ah!" exclaimed Griffin, the instant he glanced at it. "It is too modern, I fear, for it contains the vowel-points."

"Yes," answered his friend. "I fear it will be of no value to you, if you seek a very early manuscript."

Griffin had made no explanation of the reason of his inquiry.

"The oldest manuscript of Ezekiel is, as you know, in the Imperial Library in St. Petersburg," Professor Cowley remarked. "I have here some photographic reproductions," and from a portfolio he produced some facsimiles which had been published by the Paleographical Society some years ago. They were splendid reproductions, and to Griffin of most intense interest.

He sat and for a long time examined them most carefully. He made no remark to his friend, but from the expression upon his face after making a pencilled calculation upon the blotting-pad before him, it was evident that his search had not been unrewarded.

The only other actual manuscript in the Bodleian proved to be a parchment fragment of chaps, x, 9 to xiv, 11. But this containing vowel-points and accents on both Mashrahs, was, at a glance, dismissed as comparatively modern, its age being about A.D. 220.

The facsimile of the St. Petersburg manuscript was to him most interesting and from it Griffin made copious notes. Then, that same afternoon, he left for Cambridge, where next day he inspected several early manuscripts in the University Library, and at evening was back again in Pembridge Gardens, where he dined alone with Gwen.

The girl was anxious to ascertain what her father had discovered, but he was most reticent, knowing well that all would be told to Frank Farquhar on the following day.

Suddenly she said:

"Frank has gone abroad, dad."

"Abroad? Where to?"

"To Copenhagen. He left Victoria at eleven this morning and travels by Flushing, Kiel and Korsor. I saw him off."

"Copenhagen!" repeated the Professor thoughtfully, and in an instant he recollected that the dead stranger was a Dane, from Copenhagen. What clue was young Farquhar following?

That night he sat alone in his study reading and re-reading the copy of the first manuscript he had consulted in the British Museum, and comparing it most carefully with the extracts he had made from the facsimile of the St. Petersburg codex.

Then he took from a shelf a copy of the Old Testament in Hebrew and English, and compared the Hebrew with the early texts.

"After all," he remarked aloud to himself, "there is little or no difference in our modern Hebrew text, except that in the older manuscripts the name of the Deity is written larger, in order to render it prominent. Ah! if I could only reconstruct the context!"

From his table he took up a large envelope, and breaking it open, drew forth the whole-plate photographic reproductions of the precious fragments of the dead stranger's manuscript. These he placed before him beneath his reading-lamp, and studied them long and carefully, especially the scrap of handwriting.

Turning again to the extract he had made from the codex in St. Petersburg he re-examined it. The portion was Ezekiel, ii, 9-10 in Hebrew, the English of which was as follows: "And when I looked, behold an hand *was* sent unto me; and, lo, a roll of a book *was* therein. And he spread it before me; and it *was* written within and without: and *there* was written therein lamentations, and mourning, and woe."

These two verses had attracted him at Oxford, and they again riveted his attention. It almost seemed as though he read in them some riddle meaning something tangible, for he was making upon a slip of paper frequent and rapid arithmetical calculations.

At half-past ten Gwen came, and kissing him good-night, urged him to go to bed, but nevertheless he continued his work far into the night, until the fire had burned itself out and he rose cold and tired.

He sighed, for though he had alighted upon something mysterious and hitherto undiscerned in that early text, yet its meaning was altogether uncertain.

Its discovery only served to increase the mystery a hundredfold.

As he lay in bed, two facts caused him apprehension. The first was the existence of the mysterious foreigner who was following the same line of inquiry as himself, and the second was the true reason of Frank Farquhar's visit to Copenhagen.

That the mysterious foreigner was making active investigations had again been proved by Professor Cowley at Oxford, for he had remarked that only on the previous day those selfsame fragments of Ezekiel had been carefully inspected by a white-bearded man whose description answered in every detail to the man who had searched in the Oriental Room of the British Museum.

"He seemed extremely interested in the text of Ezekiel," professor Cowley had remarked. "He was a scholar, too, from the north of Europe I should say."

The mysterious searcher seemed a kind of will-o'-the-wisp, who had taken exactly the same course as himself, only he had progressed a day or so ahead. Was it possible that he held the selfsame knowledge as that contained on the half-destroyed statement?

Next day Griffin again visited the British Museum, in order to make further researches, and on entering, his friend the assistant-keeper exclaimed:

"Oh! Professor! That foreign old gentleman, who is interested in Ezekiel, was here again yesterday afternoon."

"Here again!" echoed Griffin. "Have you found out who he is?"

"No—except that he is evidently a scholar."

"What manuscripts did he consult?"

"Only one—the early fragment of Deuteronomy," was the assistant-keeper's reply.

"May I see it?"

"Certainly," and the official gave orders for the precious piece of faded parchment to be brought.

It proved to be a Hebrew manuscript of a portion of the fifth chapter of Deuteronomy beginning at the twenty-third verse, and ending at the thirty-first Griffin who read Hebrew as he did English, glanced through it, and saw that in English, the first verse could be translated as, "And it came to pass, when ye heard the voice out of the midst of the darkness, (for the mountain did burn with fire), that ye came near unto me, *even* all the heads of your tribes, and your elders; And ye said, 'Behold the Lord our God hath shewed us His glory and His greatness, and we have heard His voice out of the midst of the fire: we have seen this day that God doth talk with man, and He liveth.'"

As he read rapidly the Hebrew words his face brightened. Something was revealed to him. The stranger was evidently following an exactly similar line to himself, and had, by copying that Biblical fragment, advanced a stage nearer the truth!

"This fragment is published in facsimile, if I remember aright?" he asked the assistant-keeper of manuscripts.

"Yes, by the Paleographical Society. I have a copy if you wish the loan of it."

And the Professor gladly accepted the loan of the large thin volume of reproductions of the rarest treasures among the Biblical manuscripts.

The researches of the foreigner showed him to be in possession of some additional facts. What were they? Ah! if he could only meet the man whose footsteps he was following, if he could only watch unseen, and note what authorities he was consulting.

For a week he haunted the Museum at all hours, hoping to meet the old man who held possession of the dead man's secret.

He wrote to Professor Cowley at Oxford, and received a reply stating that the foreigner had been again to the Bodleian on the previous day inspecting the two fragments of early texts of Deuteronomy preserved there.

Griffin lost no time in again going down to Oxford, and next morning early called at the library. He remained there all day, but to his disappointment the mysterious old man did not reappear. He had no doubt left Oxford before the Professor's arrival.

From those two fragments of Deuteronomy which had so interested the stranger, Griffin could make out nothing. They did not contain anything bearing upon the theory that he had been following. Yet he was told that the stranger had spent five hours in studying them and making certain arithmetical calculations.

He was sitting in the same silent, restful, book-lined room in which the stranger had sat. He was in the same chair, indeed, and before him was the same writing-pad upon which he had written.

The precious fragment was lying upon the pad of red blotting-paper. At his side stood the official who had handed the stranger the piece of crinkled parchment which he had sought.

"Yes," he was saying, "he made a number of calculations, covering many sheets of paper, and when he left, he said that his work was unfinished, and that he intended to return. But we have not seen him since."

As Professor Griffin was gazing long and steadily upon that early fragment of Hebrew text, the official, who of course, knew the Professor well, added: "Curiously enough, after he had gone, I found lying on the table a piece of paper on which he had been making his calculations. Here it is," and he placed before the Professor a piece of crumpled paper bearing upon it what appeared to be a sum of multiplication and addition.

Griffin examined it eagerly, and, used as he was to the arithmetical values of the letters of the Hebrew alphabet—for each letter was a numerical value—he saw instantly that the stranger's secret had fallen into his hands! He held his breath as the assistant-librarian placed a second scrap of paper before him.

By those two discarded scraps astounding truths had been suddenly revealed to him!

Chapter Thirteen
Shows a Face in the Night

To the ordinary observer the sum upon the scrap of paper would have conveyed nothing.

Professor Griffin studied it carefully, however, and mentally submitted it to certain tests.

What was written upon the paper was as follows:

$$7 . 3 . 4 . 1 . 0 . 9$$
$$5$$

$$3 . 6 . 7 . 0 . 5 . 4 . 5$$
$$7 . 1 . 9 . 2 . 2 . 0$$

$$4 . 3 . 8 . 9 . 7 . 6 . 5$$
$$Y \ O \ D \ H$$
$$4 . 3 . 8 . 9 . 7 . 6 . 5 . 0$$
subtract Gi-mel

"Of the Temple that...."

The Professor begged leave to take it with him to London, whereupon the assistant-librarian replied: "It seems very much as though our friend the stranger is applying some numerical cipher to that fragment of Deuteronomy, does it not? Of course, Professor, you may have it—and welcome. I confess I cannot make head or tail of it."

"Nor I either," laughed Griffin, blinking through his spectacles. "Yet it interests me, and I thank you very much for it. Apparently this foreigner believes that he has made some discovery. Ah!" he added, "how many cranks there are among Hebrew scholars—more especially the cabalists!"

And in pretence of ignorance of the true meaning of that curious arrangement of figures, the Professor placed the scrap of paper in his breast-pocket, and returned to the Randolph Hotel, where he had tea, afterwards sitting for a long time in the writing-room with the stranger's discarded calculation spread before him.

In the left-hand corner of the piece of paper was something which puzzled him extremely. In a neat hand were written the figures, 255.19.7. And while awaiting his train, he lit his big briar pipe, and seating himself before the fire, tried to think out what they could mean.

But though he pondered for over an hour he failed to discern their object. They were evidently the stranger's signature.

He applied the Hebrew equivalents to them, and they were as follows: "Bêth. He. He, A-leph-Teth. Za-yin." But they conveyed to him absolutely nothing.

Seated alone in the corner of the first-class carriage, he again took out the scrap of paper, and held it before him. That there was a cipher deciphered into the words "of the Temple that," was apparent.

He started with the ordinary numerical values of the Hebrew alphabet. They were 7.3.4.1.0.9. which meant: Za-yin, Gi-mel, Da-leth, A-leph, the zero, and Teth. These were multiplied by He, which meant 5. Then 719220, meaning certain other letters, were added and multiplied by yodh, or ten. From each number of the total 3, or Gi-mel, was subtracted, and the English translation of the figures that remained was: "of the Temple that—"

To such a man, versed in all the cabalistic ciphers of the ancients, the truth was plain. Extremely involved and ingenious it was, without a doubt, but by careful study of this he would, he saw, be able to find the key being used by the aged man who had in such an uncanny way signed himself "255.19.7."

He replaced it carefully in his pocket, and lighting his pipe, set back in the carriage to reflect.

Ah! if he could only come across that will-o'-the-wisp who was engaged in the search after the truth. Probably he possessed the context of the burnt document, and could supply the missing portion. But if so, how had it fallen into his hands?

The affair was a problem which daily became more interesting and more extraordinary.

At Westbourne Park Station, when the collector came for his ticket, he fumbled for it in his pocket, but was unable for some time to find it. Then at Paddington he took a taxi-cab home, arriving in time for a late dinner.

Gwen bright and cheerful, sat at the head of the table as was her habit, inquisitive as to her father's movements and discoveries.

But to her carefully guarded inquiries he remained mute. He had been down to the Bodleian, he said, but that was all. The old man longed to get back to the restful silence of his own study to examine the scrap of paper left by the stranger, and from it to determine the exact key to that very ingenious numerical cipher.

The man who was in search of the same secret as himself was a weird person, to say the least. Both in London and in Oxford, he had come across the aged man's trail. That he was unknown in England as a scholar was apparent, and that he was a deeply read man and student of Hebrew was equally plain.

He was not a Jew. Both the Library assistants at the British Museum and at the Bodleian had agreed upon that point.

They had declared that he was from the north of Europe. Was he a Dane from Copenhagen, like the dead man who had preferred to be known as Jules Blanc?

Arminger Griffin ate his dinner in impatience carefully avoiding the questions his pretty daughter put to him. Then he ascended to the study, having bidden her good-night. She had received no news of Frank, it seemed. For what reason had the young man so suddenly left for Copenhagen? The question caused him constant apprehension. Could he have discovered any clue to the existence of the context of the document?

More than once during the day he had been half tempted to go himself to Denmark, but the discovery of the aged stranger's arithmetical calculations induced him to remain in London and watch.

Having switched on the light he crossed the room, and seating himself at the table felt in his pocket for the scribbled calculation. He failed to find it. He was horrified. It had gone!

He must have pulled it from his pocket at Westbourne Park while searching for his ticket. His loss was, indeed, a serious one. In frantic haste he searched all his other pockets, but in vain. The scraps of crumpled paper which contained the key to a portion of the cipher upon which the stranger was working was gone!

He sank into his armchair in despair.

Before his vision rose those mystical figures 255.19.7. written in fire. What was the hidden meaning therein contained?

One line of the sum he recollected: "7.3.4.1.0.9." multiplied by 5. Mental calculation resulted in the answer of 3670646. There was a sum to add to it. But alas! he could not remember the figures of it.

Therefore the clue, so unexpectedly obtained, was lost.

So he sat alone, his head buried in his hands in deepest despair.

Gwen crept in in silence, but seeing her father's attitude, crept out again without disturbing him, and read in the drawing-room alone, until it was time to return to her room.

"Shall I ever solve the mystery?" cried the Professor aloud to himself as he paced the room presently. "Misfortune has befallen me! With that fragment deciphered I could by careful study have learned the key and then read what that mysterious searcher has undoubtedly read. Ah! if I could only meet him. Then I would follow and watch his movements. But alas! I am always too late—too late!"

As he sank again into a chair, plunged in the wildest despair, the dark figure of a tall, thick-set, military-looking man of about forty, in a long dark overcoat, passed and repassed the house in the rainy night.

For some time, he had been waiting at Notting Hill Gate Station, almost opposite the end of Pembridge Gardens, glancing at the clock now and then, as though impatiently watching for someone. Then, at last, as if full of determination he had crossed the Bayswater Road, and strolled slowly past Professor Griffin's house, eyeing its lighted windows with considerable curiosity as he went by.

He continued his walk as far as the end of the road which led into Pembridge Square, and there halted for shelter for a full five minutes beneath the portico of a house. Then he retraced his steps, re-passing the house which had aroused so much interest within him, until he came to the station where he again stood in patience.

The watcher was an active, rather good-looking man, though the reason of his presence there was not at all apparent. To pass the time he bought an evening paper, and stood in the corner reading it, yet in such a position that he could watch everybody who entered or left the Underground Railway Station. There was a slight foreign cast in his features. His keen dark eyes were searching everywhere, while the clothes he wore were the clothes of a man of refined taste.

From time to time there played about his dark face a sinister smile—a smile of triumph. He was evidently not a man to be trifled with, and it seemed very much as though he held the owner of that comfortable house in resentment.

The words he muttered as he stood there pretending to read were, in themselves, sufficient indication of this:

"They thought to trick him—to trick me—but by Jove, they'll find themselves mistaken!" and his claw-like hand gripped the newspaper until it trembled in his grasp.

He lit a cigarette, and twice crossed the road. Standing at the corner of Pembridge Gardens, he again looked up the street, dark, misty, and deserted on that winter's night.

"They laugh at us without a doubt," he muttered to himself. "They laugh, because they think he's fool enough to give away the secret. Yes, they take him for a blind idiot. Frank Farquhar has gone upon a fool's errand to Denmark, intending to 'freeze us out' of what is justly ours. When he returns, he will find that I have checkmated both him and his friend Griffin, in a manner in which he little expects."

His countenance was full of craft and cunning; his smile was sufficient index to his character.

Soon after ten o'clock, while standing at the corner of Pembridge Gardens, he suddenly drew back into the shadow, turned upon his heel and crossed the road to the station, in order to avoid notice.

Having gained the opposite pavement, he drew back again into the shadow, and saw a female figure in a short dark skirt, and wearing a handsome white fox boa, hurrying across the road in his direction.

She passed him, and he for the first time caught sight of her pretty face. It was Gwen Griffin.

Apparently she was in a frantic hurry, for she rushed into the booking-office and in her haste to get a ticket, dropped her purse. Then, when she had run down the stairs to the platform, the silent watcher followed leisurely, obtained a ticket for Earl's Court, but was careful not to gain the platform until the girl had already left.

"I thought the story would alarm her," he laughed to himself as he stood awaiting the next "Circle" train. "Ah, my fine young fellow, you've made a great and a most fatal error!" he added with a dry laugh, as he paced the platform.

Chapter Fourteen
In which Owen Becomes Anxious

When just on the point of retiring, the maid had brought Gwen up a telegram from Frank, stating that something serious had occurred, that he had returned to London unexpectedly, and that he was unable to come to the house as he preferred not to meet her father, and urging her to meet him at Earl's Court Station at a quarter past ten that night.

In greatest alarm, and wondering what could possibly have occurred, the girl had dipped on the first things that had come to her hand and had dashed out to meet her lover.

Before going forth she had taken the maid into her confidence, saying:

"I have to go out, Laura. You need not mention anything to my father. Leave the front door unbolted. I will take the latch-key."

The dark-eyed girl, with whom Miss Gwen was a great favourite, promised to say nothing, and had let her young mistress quietly out.

Gwen was puzzled why Frank should appoint to meet her at Earl's Court. If the interview was to be a secret one, why had he not committed a breach of the *convenances* and asked her to his rooms? She had been there to tea once—in strictest secrecy, of course—but in company with a girl friend.

What untoward circumstances could have arisen to bring Frank back before he reached Copenhagen? He could not have got further than Hamburg, she reflected—if as far.

At Earl's Court she alighted, and having ascended the stairs in eager expectation, passed through the booking-office into the Earl's Court Road, expecting her lover to meet her.

But she was disappointed. He was not there. She glanced at the railway dock, and saw that it was already twenty-five minutes past ten. The receipt of the strange message had upset her. She felt that something terrible must have occurred if Frank "preferred" not to face her father. What could it be? She was half frantic with fear and apprehension.

From out the misty night the tall man standing in the shadow on the opposite side of the road was watching her every movement. At the kerb stood a taxi-cab which he had hailed, and now kept waiting. He had remarked to the driver that he expected a lady and would wait until she arrived.

For fully a quarter of an hour he allowed the girl to pace up and down the pavement outside the station, waiting with an impatience that was apparent. That message which she believed to be from Frank had filled her mind with all sorts of grave apprehensions. He would surely never appoint that spot as a meeting place if secrecy were not imperative.

She noticed that there were quiet deserted thoroughfares in the vicinity. There he no doubt intended to walk and explain the situation.

Yet why did he not come, she asked herself. Already he was half an hour late, while she, agitated and anxious, could scarcely contain herself.

Suddenly, however, a tall good-looking man in a dark overcoat stood before her and raised his silk hat. She was about to step aside and pass on when the man begged her pardon, and uttered her name, adding:

"I believe you are expecting my friend, Frank Farquhar?"

"Yes," she replied. "I—I am." And she regarded the stranger inquiringly.

"He has sent me, Miss Griffin, as he is unfortunately unable to keep the appointment himself?"

"Sent you—why?" asked the girl, looking him straight in the face.

"He has sent me to tell you that something unexpected has happened," replied the man.

"What has occurred?" she gasped. "Tell me quickly."

"Well," he said with some deliberation. "I do not know whether you are aware that Mr Farquhar was interested in a great and remarkable secret—a secret which he was occupied in investigating?"

"Yes," she answered quickly. "I know all about it. He told me everything."

"The *contretemps* which has occurred is in connection with that," the stranger said. "He was on his way to Copenhagen, but was compelled to return. He has, I believe, gained the key to some extraordinary cipher or other, and therefore he wishes to see you at once, and in secret. He told me that at present his return to London must be kept confidential, as there are other unscrupulous people most anxious to learn the truth upon which such enormous possibilities depend."

"He wants me to go to him," the girl cried. "Where is he then?"

"Not far away," the man replied. "If you will allow me to escort you, I will do so willingly, Miss Griffin."

The girl hesitated. She naturally mistrusted strange men. He saw her hesitation, and added:

"I trust you will forgive me for not being with you at the time Frank appointed, but—well, I don't wish to alarm you unduly, but he was not very well. I was sitting with him."

"Then he's ill!" she cried in alarm. "Tell me. Oh! do tell me what has occurred."

"He will tell you himself," was the ingenious reply. "But," he added, as though in afterthought, "I ought to have given you my card." And he produced one and handed it to her. The name upon it was "William Wetherton, Captain, 12th Lancers."

"Do relieve my anxiety, Captain Wetherton," the girl implored. "Tell me what has happened."

"As I have already said, Farquhar has made a great discovery, and wishes at once to consult you. His indisposition was only temporary—an attack of giddiness," he added, and he saw that she was wavering. "I'm an old friend of Frank's," he went on, "and he consulted me, as soon as the matter of the Hebrew secret came into his hands. Of course, he has very often mentioned you," he laughed.

He was a well-spoken man, and beneath his smile the girl did not detect his cunning. Her natural caution was overcome by her frantic desire to see Frank, and hear what he had discovered. An instant's reflection showed her that if he could not meet her it was only natural that he should send his friend Captain Wetherton—a man of whom he had spoken on several occasions. He was stationed at Hounslow, Frank had told her, and they often spent the evening together at the club and some "show" afterwards.

"There's a 'taxi' across the way," the Captain pointed out. "Let us take it—that is if I may be permitted to be your escort, Miss Griffin?"

"Is it far?"

"Oh, dear no," he laughed, and raising his hand he called the cab he had already in waiting. The vehicle drew across, and as he entered after her he spoke to the man. He had already given him the address before he had approached her. As he sat by her side, the man's face changed. In the semi-darkness she could not get a good look at his features, yet his chatter was gentlemanly and good-humoured. From his remarks it was apparent that he had known her lover for a long time, and held him in high esteem.

"As soon as Frank's telegram arrived, I rushed out," said the young girl. "It was a great surprise, for I believed him to be on his way to Copenhagen."

"They'll probably miss you at home, won't they?" he asked, with a glance of admiration at the girl's sweet face.

"Well," she laughed, "my father doesn't know I'm out. Laura, the maid, will leave the door unbolted and I've got the latch-key."

The man seated at her side smiled, turning away his head lest she might wonder.

Acquainted as Gwen was with the streets of the West End, she saw that the course taken by the "taxi" was through Brompton Road and Knightsbridge to Hyde Park Corner, then straight up South Audley Street and across one of the squares, Grosvenor Square she believed it to be.

"Why isn't Frank at his own rooms in Half Moon Street?" she asked with some curiosity.

"Because, having discovered the secret, he is now in fear of his rivals, so is compelled to go into hiding. I, alone, his best friend, know his whereabouts. Quite romantic, isn't it?" he laughed.

"Quite. Only—well, only—Captain Wetherton, I do wish you would tell me what has really occurred. I feel that you are keeping something from me."

"I certainly am, Miss Griffin," was his prompt reply, a reply which contained more meaning than he had intended. "Frank, in sending me to you, made the stipulation that he should have the pleasure of telling you himself. All I can say is that I believe the knowledge of the secret will be the means of bringing to him wealth undreamed of, and a notoriety world-wide."

He was purposely keeping her engrossed in conversation, in order that they might cross Oxford Street; hoping that in the maze of turnings beyond that main thoroughfare she might lose her bearings.

Suddenly the "taxi" pulled up with a jerk before a closed shop, in a dark, rather unfrequented but seemingly superior street, and the Captain opened the side door with his latch-key, disclosing a flight of red-carpeted stairs.

"Here are my rooms," Wetherton explained. "Frank has sought refuge with me here. He is upstairs."

Gwen ascended the stairs quickly to the second floor, where the Captain opened the door with his key, and a moment later she found herself in a large, well-furnished bachelor's sitting-room where the electric lamps were shaded with yellow silk.

It was evidently the room of a man comfortably off, for the furniture had been chosen with taste, and the pretty knick-knacks and quaint curios upon the table showed the owner of the place to be a man of some refinement.

"Where is he?" inquired the girl, looking around blankly, her cheeks flushed with excitement.

The man turned upon her, and laughed roughly in her face.

She drew back in horror and alarm when, in an instant, she realised how utterly helpless she now was in the stranger's hands. He had closed the door behind him and pushed back the bolt concealed beneath the heavy portiere.

"He is not here!" she gasped. "You've—you've lied to me. This is a trick!" she gasped.

"Pray calm yourself, my dear little girl," he said, coolly lighting a cigarette. "Sit down. I want to have a quiet chat with you."

"I will not, sir!" she answered, with rising anger. "Allow me, please, to go. I shall tell your friend Mr Farquhar of this disgraceful ruse."

"You can tell him, my dear girl, whatever you please," the fellow laughed insolently. "As a matter of fact, your lover does not know me from Adam. So you see it's quite immaterial."

"It is not immaterial," she declared, with a fierce look of resentment: "You shall answer to him for this!"

"Possibly it will be you who will be compelled to answer to him, when he knows that you have accompanied me here alone to my rooms, at eleven at night—eh? What will your lover say to that, I wonder?"

"I have the telegram," she cried, opening the little bag she carried.

It was not there!

"See," he laughed. "I have the telegram!" And before her eyes he tossed it into the fire.

She bent to snatch it from the flame, but he seized her white wrist roughly and threw her backward upon the hearthrug. He had extracted the message from her bag as they had sat together in the darkness of the cab.

Struggling to her feet she screamed for help, and fought frantically with the man who had decoyed her there; fought with the fierce strength of a woman defending her dearest possession, her honour.

She saw how the man's countenance had changed. There was an evil expression there which held her terrified.

She begged mercy from him, begged wildly upon her knees, but he only laughed in her face in triumph. She saw, now that the telegram was destroyed, that this man who had posed as Frank's friend could make his vile story entirely complete.

She was helpless in the hands of a man whose very face betrayed his vile unscrupulousness.

In the struggle she felt his hot foetid breath upon her cheek. Her blouse of pale blue *crêpe-de-chine* was ripped right across the breast as she endeavoured to wrench herself from his grasp.

"Ah! Have mercy on me!" she screamed. "Let me go! Let me go! I'll give you anything—I—I—I'll be silent even—if you'll only let me go! Ah! do—if you are a gentleman!"

But the fellow only laughed again, and held her more tightly.

Her bare chest heaved and fell quickly before him. Her breath came and went.

"You think," he said in a cruel hard voice, "you think your lover will not believe me. But I see upon your flesh a mark—a natural blemish that you cannot efface. Listen to me quietly. Hear me, or else I shall tell him of its existence, and urge him to discover whether or not I have spoken the truth. Perhaps he will then believe me!"

"You brute!" cried the girl in sudden and breathless horror. "You blackguard! you intend to ruin me in Frank's eyes. Let me go, I say! Let me go." Again she struggled, trying to get to the window, but with his strong arms encircling her she was helpless as a child, for with a sudden effort he flung her backwards upon the couch, inert and senseless.

Chapter Fifteen
Reveals the Rivals

Sir Felix Challas, Baronet the well-known financier and philanthropist, was seated in his cosy library in Berkeley Square, dictating letters to his secretary between the whiffs of his mild after-breakfast cigar. He was a man of middle age, with slight side whiskers, a reddish face, and opulent bearing. In his frock-coat, fancy vest, and striped trousers, and white spats over his boots, he presented the acmé of style as far as dress was concerned. The whole world knew Sir Felix to be something of a dandy, for he had never, for the past ten years or so, been seen without a flower in his buttonhole. Like many another man in London he had amassed great wealth from small beginnings, until he was now a power in the world of finance, and as a philanthropist his name was a household word.

From a small leather shop somewhere in the Mile End Road he had risen to be the controlling factor of several of the greatest financial undertakings in the country; while the house of Challas and Bowen in Austin Friars was known in the City as one of the highest possible standing.

Though he owned that fine house in Berkeley Square, a beautiful domain in Yorkshire which he had purchased from a bankrupt earl, a villa at Cannes, racehorses, motors, and a splendid steam-yacht, he was still a bachelor, and a somewhat lonely man.

The papers mentioned his doings daily, gave his portrait frequently, and recorded with a flourish of trumpets his latest donation to this charity, or to that. Though he made enormous profits in his financial deals, yet he was a staunch churchman, his hand ever in his pocket for the various institutions which approached him. Indeed, if the truth were told, he, like others, had bought his birthday Baronetcy by making a princely donation to the Hospital Fund. This showed him to be a shrewd man, fully alive to the value of judicious advertisement.

In the years gone by he had mixed with many of the shady characters of the complex world of the City, but now, in his opulence, he had apparently cut himself adrift from them all, and prided himself upon his eminent respectability.

As he sat there that winter's morning, leaning back in his big leather armchair before the fire, he was dictating a letter to the governors of a great orphanage at Bristol, promising to defray the cost of building a much needed wing of the institution.

Then, having done so, he added to his secretary, a rather smug looking man in black:

"And you might also write a paragraph to-day, Stone, and send it to the Press Association. You know what to say—'magnificent gift,' and all that sort of thing. They'll send it out to the newspapers."

"Yes, Sir Felix," answered the man, making a note in shorthand.

"Let's see, what else is there? Ah! The Malms Syndicate! Write saying that I withdraw," he remarked.

His secretary hesitated.

"But that, Sir Felix, means ruin to all three. They are all poor men."

"That's just what I intend," he answered with a smile. "We shall do that business ourselves, as soon as they are out of it."

So Mr Stone scribbled rapidly a letter in shorthand, which meant the ruin of three honest men, who, believing in the great financier's promises, had taken upon themselves liabilities which they could not meet.

Such letters are not infrequent. The great philanthropist, whom the world looked up to as a model man, who did his utmost for the benefit of suffering humanity, and who had been rewarded by his Sovereign, collected his wealth by ways that would often not bear investigation. But being a big man, he was able to do things which a little man would fear to do. For were not Challas and Bowen, with their huge operations and big bank balances, above suspicion?

While dictating another letter, the butler, an elderly and pompous person, entered announcing: "Mr Jannaway, Sir Felix."

"That will be enough for to-day, Stone," the red-faced man said to the secretary, who rose at once, and followed the servant out of the room.

Next moment the man who had posed on the previous evening as "Captain Wetherton" entered the room, looking smart and spruce in a well-cut suit of blue serge.

"Well, Jim?" exclaimed the financier anxiously, as he rose to meet his visitor. "I've been expecting you all the morning. What news—eh?"

"Oh! It's all right," answered the man cheerily, flinging himself into an armchair without invitation, apparently quite at home in Challas's house.

"Found out anything of interest?" inquired Sir Felix, pushing over the big silver cigar-box that stood upon the smoking-table.

"Well—I hardly know," he answered hesitatingly. "Where's the girl?"

"In Charlie's rooms. I've had a devil of a scene with her. She's obdurate."

"A day's confinement there will break her spirit, no doubt," remarked Sir Felix. "Especially if she believes she'll lose her lover."

"I don't know," he answered dubiously. "She's got a mind of her own, I can tell you. She's a regular little spit-fire."

The red-faced man laughed.

"Well, Jim," he said. "You ought to know how to manage women, surely. Did my scheme work well?"

"Excellently. She got your 'wire,' and went to Earl's Court at once. I followed and after a little persuasion she fell into the trap. While she was unconscious, I took the latch-key, and at half-past two let myself and old Erich into the house in Pembridge Gardens."

"Well—did he find anything?"

"Yes. Griffin has taken photographic copies of the burnt papers, before giving them back into Farquhar's hands, and from his copies of various early manuscripts of Ezekiel and Deuteronomy it's quite plain that he is making a very careful and complete study."

"It seems, then, that Griffin's intention, is to discover the cipher for himself, and leave the ugly little Doctor out in the cold," Sir Felix remarked with a snap. "But, Jim, this business is ours and nobody else's. We must crush anybody and everybody, who attempts in any way to decipher that secret record. When the Dane brought it to me at the Ritz, in Paris, I laughed at the idea. Treasure-hunting was never in my line. But," he added with a smile, "I took care to have a complete copy of his precious document made before I gave it back to him the next morning, and it is now in the safe over yonder. Like to see it?"

Jim Jannaway, the man who had on the previous night represented himself to be "Captain Wetherton," the friend of Frank Farquhar, expressed eagerness to see it. Therefore the financier rose, and with the gold master-key upon his watch-chain, opened the heavy steel door, and handed his visitor a typed document bound in a dark green cover—a complete copy of the manuscript which Doctor Diamond had partly burned in that obscure hotel at the Gare du Nord.

The context of the half intelligible sentences was there—the context which Professor Griffin was longing to obtain. And moreover, as the man turned over the pages, reading swiftly, he came across a geometrical figure—a plan marked with numbers and corresponding explanations.

"Who made the discovery?" asked Jim Jannaway, late of His Majesty's Army and now gambler, card-sharper, and swell-mobsman.

"The devil only knows," laughed Sir Felix. "He says he did himself. The fellow was hard up and I gave him a hundred francs, but I believed the whole thing to be a huge hoax, until I consulted old Erich and he began to puzzle his brains. Then I saw that there might be something in it. My only fear is that Griffin and his friends may get ahead of us. But you've done well, Jim. You always do."

"I do the dirty work of the firm," laughed the man addressed, removing his cigar from his lips, "and devilish dirty work it is at times."

"Well, you can't complain of the pay. Isn't it better to live as you are, a gentleman of means, than as I found you five years ago, a 'crook' who might be arrested at any moment?"

"I don't complain at all, my dear fellow. Only—"

"Only what?"

"Well, I really don't see your object in enticing the girl to Charlie's rooms. It might be awkward for us."

Sir Felix laughed, snapping his fingers.

"What? Are you growing afraid?" he asked.

"Not at all, only I can't see your object."

"The object is simply to compromise her," he said grimly. "She's a confounded pretty girl. I saw her at the theatre with her aunt a week ago, and she was at Lady Ena's wedding the other day, with her lover, Frank Farquhar. Of that man we must be wary. With his confounded newspapers, he has power," he added.

"That's the very reason why I fear we are treading on dangerous ground."

"Bosh! leave all to me. The girl is in Charlie's rooms, there let her stay for the present," answered the man whom the world believed to be a pillar of the church, and a devout philanthropist.

Jim Jannaway saw that this man whom he served—the man who held him in his toils—had some mysterious evil design upon the unfortunate girl. He could not, however, discern exactly what it was. He had ordered him to keep her in that upstairs room, "and break her spirit," as he put it.

The midnight search of the Professor's study had revealed that he was in active pursuit of the truth. That meant Sir Felix taking steps to checkmate his efforts. Ever since the first moment it had been known by a chance visit to the hotel while Jules Blanc was lying there dead, that the fragments of the strange document had fallen into Doctor Diamond's hands, private inquiry agents, employed by Sir Felix, had been silently watching the movements of the deformed Doctor, Frank Farquhar, and his friend, the Professor. All had been reported to the red-faced man sitting there at his ease—the man who controlled financial interests worth millions.

Sir Felix had been convinced by the foreign expert he had consulted that there really was something in the theory of the unknown discovery, and he intended that none should learn the truth except himself. He had Jim Jannaway, the unscrupulous, at his elbow, ready to do any dirty work, or make any risky move which he ordered. In a day Jim could, if he wished, summon up half a dozen of the most dangerous characters in London, pals of his, to assist him, for be it said he always paid well—with Sir Felix's money, of course.

Against such a combination as Challas and Bowen, though Mr Thomas J. Bowen lived in New York and was seldom in London, no private person could stand. The great firm, with their agents all over the world, gathered confidential information from everywhere, and could plot to crush any one who attempted to carry through a business that was against their interests.

Hence any attempt on the part of Doctor Diamond, or Professor Griffin, to solve the problem in face of the opposition of Sir Felix, was foredoomed to failure, if not to disaster. But alas! both men were in ignorance of the fact that a complete copy of the dead man's document was in the possession of the man whose hatred of the Jews, his enemies in business, was notorious; and who would therefore go to any length in order to secure, for his own satisfaction, the sacred relics and vessels of Solomon's Temple—providing they still existed.

Chapter Sixteen
Owen Learns the Truth

When the Professor seated himself at the breakfast-table and the news of Miss Gwen's absence was broken to him by Laura, the parlour-maid, he started up in surprise.

"Miss Gwen went out late last night instead of going to bed, sir, and took the latch-key," the girl was compelled to admit.

The old man pursed his thin lips. His daughter was not in the habit of going out on midnight escapades.

"Late last night Miss Gwen received a telegram, sir," the girl added. "It seemed to excite her very much; she dressed at once, and went out."

The Professor rose from the table without eating, and went to the study to think.

Upon the blotting-pad lay a sheet of ruled manuscript paper. He stared at it in horror as though he saw an apparition, for there upon the paper, scrawled boldly in blue chalk, were the mystic figures:

255.19.7

They danced before his eyes, as he stood staring at them. How came they there, in his own study? What could they mean?

He looked around bewildered. Nothing was out of place—nothing disturbed. Those puzzling figures had been written there by some unseen hand.

During his wakeful hours that long night he had applied Hebrew letters of those numerical values to the array of figures. But the result was chaotic. It was some mystic sign. But what, he could not determine.

He had found them on that scrap of paper cast aside at the Bodleian Library, and now again they appeared in the privacy of his own study, to puzzle and confound him.

Through the next hour he waited, from moment to moment, in the expectation of a telegram from Gwen explaining her absence and assuring him of her safety. But, alas! none came. Therefore, he put on his boots and overcoat and went round to the police-station, where the inspector on duty received him most courteously, and took a minute description of the missing young lady, a statement which, half an hour later, had been received over the telegraph at every police-station throughout the Metropolitan area.

He had taken the precaution to place one of Gwen's photographs in his pocket, and this he handed to the inspector.

"Well do our very best, Professor, of course," the officer assured him. "But young ladies are often very erratic, you know. We have hundreds of girls reported missing, but they usually turn up again the next day, or a couple of days later. Their absence is nearly always voluntary, and usually attributable to the one cause, love!"

"But my daughter's lover is in Denmark," the Professor protested.

"That is what you have been led to believe," remarked the inspector with an incredulous smile. "Girls are very cunning, I have two myself, sir."

"But you will help me, will you not?" urged the old gentleman earnestly.

"No effort shall be spared to discover your daughter, sir," answered the rosy, clean-shaven man seated at his desk. "I'll report the matter to our superintendent at once. Do you," he added, "happen to know what dress she was wearing? I will want a close description of it, also the laundry mark on her underlinen. Your servants will, no doubt, be able to supply the latter. Perhaps I'd better step round with you and see them."

So the inspector at once accompanied the Professor back to Pembridge Gardens, and there was shown some of the girl's clothes with the laundry mark upon them. Afterwards he left, leaving the old man in the highest state of apprehension.

He put aside all thought of the inquiry upon which he had been engaged. His sole thought was for the safety of his child.

Meanwhile Jim Jannaway and Sir Felix Challas were still in deep consultation in the privacy of that quiet, sombre study in Berkeley Square.

"Erich left for Paris by the nine o'clock service this morning," Jim was saying. "He wants to consult some early manuscript in the National Library, he says."

"He's a decidedly clever old fossil," declared the Baronet, knocking the ash off his cigar, "and I'm convinced he's on the right track. If we can only keep these other people off, mislead them, or put them on a false scent, we shall win."

"Erich has done that already," laughed the other. "He's been down to Oxford and pretended to study certain manuscripts, knowing well that Griffin's researches must lead him there. By putting Griffin on a false scent he's simply tangling him up. Oh! yes, I agree, Erich Haupt is a wary old bird."

"Then he is now making investigations in various quarters with the sole object of misleading Griffin, eh?" laughed Sir Felix. "Really, it's quite comical."

"Yes, and he lets drop just sufficient information to excite the curiosity of the officiate of the various libraries and place them on the *qui vive*. He does that, so that they shall inform Griffin."

"Excellent!" declared the Baronet. "As soon as he returns from Paris I must see him. I wonder if the secret record really does exist? If it does, then, by Jove! I'll hold the key to the whole Jewish religion. But one thing is quite evident, my dear Jim, we must crush out all this opposition with a firm, relentless hand. You understand?"

"I quite follow," remarked the great financier's unscrupulous "cat's-paw."

And they continued the discussion of the present rather insecure situation.

Sir Felix Challas wore his mask with marvellous cleverness. The world — the people who read of him in the newspapers — never suspected that the man whose name so often headed subscription lists for charitable objects, and whose handsome donation was the signal for a hundred others, was an unscrupulous schemer. His had been the hand that, by clever financial juggling in which some other person was always the principal, had brought ruin to thousands of happy homes. He had, indeed, if the truth were told, climbed to the pedestal of notoriety and esteem, over the bodies of the men, both capitalists and workmen, he had, with such innate cunning, contrived to ruin.

The strange story told by that shabby Dane as he sat in the gorgeous room of the Grand Hotel in Paris, had attracted him from the very first. Here was a chance of getting the better of his natural enemies, the Jews. Ah! how he hated them! Yes. He would search, and if he found any of those sacred relics, his intention was to laugh in the face of the whole Hebrew community and hold the discovery up to the derision of the Christians.

What mattered it to him that the Dane had died in penury in that obscure hotel near the Gare du Nord? His secret agent, who had watched the poor fellow from the moment he left the Grand Hotel, had informed Sir Felix of the man's tragic end, but he had only smiled with evident satisfaction. The agent had ascertained that the present document had not been found among the dead man's possessions, hence the Baronet believed that the man, before his death, had destroyed it. It was a blow to him when he discovered that certain fragments of it had been carefully preserved by Doctor Diamond. It meant that opposition had arisen—a very serious opposition which he must forcibly crush down.

"Charlie returns from Brussels to-day, doesn't he?" the Baronet was asking.

"Yes. He ought to be back in his rooms by now. And he'll find the girl there. I've left him definite instructions how to act."

"The girl must be sworn to silence," Sir Felix said with heavy brow. "She must assist us. We must compel her."

Jim Jannaway nodded. From instructions given by the man before him his eyes had already been opened, and ten minutes later he left the house, the Baronet's last words being:

"Remember, Jim, there's millions in this business. We mustn't lose it for the sake of that chit of a girl, however innocent and pretty she may be. Understand that!"

An hour previously Gwen Griffin, struggling slowly back to consciousness, found that, straight before her, was a square window over which was drawn a smoke-blackened, brown holland blind. The gas was still burning, although the grey wintry day had dawned some hours ago.

She was lying upon the bed in a fairly big room, still dressed, but with her clothes torn, as they had been in the desperate struggle of the previous night. Slowly and painfully she rose, and as she slipped off the bed she felt her limbs so weak and trembling that she could scarcely stand.

She caught sight of her dishevelled self in the long mirror of the wardrobe, and her own reflection startled her. All the horrors of that struggle crowded upon her. She put up her hands and pushed her thick dark hair from her white fevered brow.

"Where am I?" she cried aloud. "What will dad think?"

She staggered to the door, but found it locked and bolted from the outside. Then she went to the window and pulling aside the blind judged by the light that it must be about eleven o'clock in the morning. She tried to open the window but the sashes had been screwed together. The outlook was upon a blank wall.

Before the glass she rearranged her disordered dress, and sinking upon the side of the bed tried to recollect all that had occurred. But her head throbbed, her throat burned, and all the past seemed uncertain and indistinct.

The only fact which stood out clear in her mind as she sat there, inert and helpless, was the bitter truth which the man had spoken. The scoundrel who had represented himself to be "Captain Wetherton," the friend of her lover, had showed himself in his true colours. He had brought her there for one dastardly purpose alone—to ruin her in Frank's esteem.

She wondered what had really occurred—and while wondering, and dreading, she burst into a flood of bitter tears.

At one moment she made up her mind to batter down the door, or smash the window. But if she did that, she would, she feared, bring forth that man now so hateful to her.

She detested him. No. Rather would she starve and die there than ever look upon his blackguardly face again. The fellow was a coward, a vile scoundrel who had taken advantage of her eagerness to meet her lover, and had matched his brute strength against hers.

What should she do? How could she ever face Frank again?

She must have been carried there and placed upon that bed. She must, too, have lain for fully twelve hours in blank unconsciousness.

What had she done, she wondered, that this shameful trick should be played upon her? Alas! she had read accounts in the newspapers of how young girls had been decoyed and betrayed in our great world of London. Ah! it was no new thing she knew. Yet how long, she asked herself, was her imprisonment to continue? How long before she would be able at least to reassure her father of her safety?

For a full hour she sat in bitter tears, alone, disconsolate, and full of grave apprehension, until of a sudden she heard a footstep outside the door.

She held her breath. Horror! It was that man again.

The bolts were withdrawn, the door opened, and on the threshold stood a man, much taller, thinner and slightly older than the false "Captain Wetherton," a pale-faced man she had never seen before.

"Hullo!" he asked, looking her straight in the face. "How are you this morning, my dear? You haven't had any breakfast, I suppose?"

"I want none, sir," was her haughty reply. "I only wish to leave this place. I was entrapped here last night."

"Unfortunately, my dear girl, I know nothing about last night," replied the man. "I returned from the Continent only this morning. These happen to be my chambers, and I find they now contain a very charming tenant!"

She looked at him with her big eyes.

"I hope, sir, you do not intend to add further in suit to that which I have already received here," she said in a voice of bitter reproach, holding her torn silk blouse together with her hand.

He noticed the state of her dress, and saw what a fierce struggle must have taken place between her and Jim Jannaway.

"My dear girl," he said in a reassuring tone, "providing you are reasonable, and don't create a scene, my intention is to treat you with the deference due to every lady."

"Is that your promise?" asked the girl in breathless eagerness.

"It is my promise—but upon one condition," said the man in a slow voice. And then she detected in his closely set eyes a strange look that she had not hitherto noticed.

She asked him his condition, to which he replied in a few hard concise words, a smile playing upon his lips.

But the instant she heard him she fell wildly at his feet, and taking his hand in her trembling grasp, begged of him to show her mercy.

But the man only laughed—a laugh that was ominous in itself.

Chapter Seventeen
Contains an Expert Theory

Frank Farquhar had been at the Hotel Angleterre in Copenhagen, the hotel with the prettiest winter-garden in Europe, for four days.

They had been four days of constant activity. As guide, he had the resident correspondent of the morning newspapers of which he was one of the directors, and he had already satisfied himself that, in the Danish capital, there was but one first-class Hebrew scholar, namely Professor Axel Anderson, of the Royal University.

Copenhagen he found a bright pleasant little city full of life and movement, the shops gay and the streets thronged by well-dressed people. In ignorance of what had befallen Gwen, he was thoroughly enjoying himself, even though he saw that his visit could have no satisfactory result as far as the quest for the authorship of the mysterious document was concerned.

One morning he had called by appointment upon Professor Anderson at his pleasant house in the Norrevoldgade and sat down to chat. The Professor, a well-preserved, rather stout man of about forty-five, with a fair beard, spoke English quite well.

"As far as I am aware," he said, "there are only two professors of Hebrew in Denmark beside myself. They are close personal friends of mine, and I feel sure that neither of them entertains any unusual theory concerning the Book of Ezekiel, or they would have consulted me. Of course, we have a good many scholars come to Copenhagen to study the Northern and Oriental codices in the Royal Library here. Hence I have become acquainted with many of the chief professors of Hebrew. Have you consulted Professor Griffin in London? He is one of the first authorities upon the matter in which you are interested."

"Yes, I happen to know him," responded the young man.

"And what is his opinion?"

"A negative one."

"Ah! Then most probably this typewritten manuscript you tell me about was some baseless theory of an irresponsible crank. I would accept

Griffin's opinion before that of anybody else. There is only one other man of perhaps equal knowledge—old Erich Haupt, of Leipzig. He is a great Hebrew authority, as well as a recognised expert in cryptography."

"What is your opinion broadly upon the matter?" Farquhar asked.

"Well, candidly, I believe the theory to be without foundation," answered the Danish scholar. "I do not believe in the existence of a cipher in the Hebrew scriptures. There is nothing cryptic about the sacred record. As regards the vessels of gold and silver from Solomon's temple, they were restored by Cyrus. It is true that an ancient Talmudic tradition exists to the effect that the Ark of the Covenant, together with the pot of manna, the flask of anointing oil and Aaron's staff that budded are still hidden beneath the temple mount at Jerusalem. And my opinion is that your half-destroyed document is simply based upon this ancient tradition with which every Jew in Christendom is acquainted."

"But, Professor," exclaimed the other, "I know that you yourself are an authority upon cryptography. Have any ciphers been discovered in the original of the Book of Ezekiel?"

"Well, yes," was the Dane's answer as he stirred himself in his armchair, and reaching his hand to a bookcase took down a Hebrew-Danish Bible. Then turning to Ezekiel, he said: "There is certainly something in the Hebrew of the thirty-sixth chapter which has puzzled scholars through many centuries. It begins at verse 16: 'Moreover the word of the Lord came unto me saying, Son of man—' Now in the constant repetition of 'Son of man' certain scholars declare they have discovered a numerical cipher. In the first verse of this chapter we have, 'Son of man, prophesy unto the mountains.' In the third verse of the following one he asks: 'Son of man, can these bones live?' Again in verse 9 of the same chapter, he says: 'Prophesy, son of man, and say to the wind.' And in verse 11, still addressing him by the same title, he tells the prophet: 'Son of man, these bones are the whole house of Israel.' By the title 'Son of man' Ezekiel is so often addressed, 'Son of man' is so constantly sounded in his ears and ours, that it forces on our attention that God deals with man through the instrumentality of men, and by men communicates his will to men. Hence certain cryptographers have set to work and formed the theory of a hidden meaning in all this."

"But is the actual cipher known?" asked Frank, at once excited.

"Certainly. It was deciphered by Bamberg, of Paris, forty years ago. But the secret message had no bearing whatsoever upon the lost vessels of Solomon's temple," was the Professor's reply.

"What was the message?" inquired the young Englishman.

"Well—the alleged message which Bamberg deciphered commenced in the thirty-sixth chapter beginning at verse xvi. The passage has peculiar claims upon the attention of any one searching for cryptic writings. Addressed in the first instance to the Jews, and applicable, in the first instance, to their condition, it presents a remarkable summary of gospel doctrines, and that in a form approaching at least to systematic order. In the seventeenth verse we have man sinning: 'Son of man, when the house of Israel dwelt in their own land, they defiled it by their own way and by their doings.' In the eighteenth verse we have man suffering: 'Wherefore, I poured my fury upon them.' In the twenty-first verse man appears an object of mercy: 'but I had pity.' In the twenty-second verse man is an object of free mercy—mercy without merit: 'I do not this for your sakes, O house of Israel.' In the twenty-fourth verse man's salvation is resolved on: 'I will bring you into your own land.' In the twenty-fifth verse man is justified: 'Then will I sprinkle clean water upon you, and ye shall be clean.' In the twenty-sixth and twenty-seventh verses man is renewed and sanctified: 'A new heart also will I give you, and a new spirit will I put within you; and I will take away the stony heart out of your flesh and I will give you an heart of flesh. And I will put my spirit within you, and cause you to walk in my statutes, and ye shall keep my judgments and do them.' In the twenty-eighth verse man is restored to the place and privileges which he forfeited by his sins: 'Ye shall be my people, and I will be your God.' 'This land that was desolate is become like the garden of the Lord.' We have our security for these blessings in the assurance of the thirty-sixth verse: 'I, the Lord have spoken it, and I will do it;' and we are directed to the means of obtaining them in the declaration of the thirty-seventh verse: 'I will yet for this be inquired of by the house of Israel, to do it for them.'"

"And in these verses the French professor discovered a hidden message?"

"Yes. It read curiously, and was most difficult to decipher. But according to Bamberg it was an additional declaration of God's kindness to man. God was named as 'the God of Salvation,' and 'the author and finisher of man's faith.' It consisted briefly in an exhortation to those who discovered the cipher to read, and to believe. But as for the hiding-place of the treasure of Israel being therein designated—well, even Bamberg, whom half the scholars of Europe denounced as a crank, had never dreamed of such a thing. No, Mr Farquhar," he added, "you may rest assured that the remarkable screed never emanated from a Hebrew scholar in Denmark.

Perhaps it might have come from Gothenburg," he laughed; "more than one hare-brained theory has come from over there!" Anderson was a Dane, and the Danes have no love for the Swedes.

"You mentioned some one in Leipzig. Who is he?" asked Farquhar.

"Oh! Haupt—Erich Haupt," replied the other. "He's Professor of Hebrew at the University, and author of several well-known books. His 'Christology of the Old Testament' is a standard work. Besides Griffin in London, he is, I consider, the only other man in Europe competent to give an opinion upon the problem you have put before me."

"How can I find him?"

"You'll no doubt find him in Leipzig."

Frank felt that this German was a man to be consulted, yet he was anxious to pursue the inquiry he had started in Denmark. The man who had died in Paris, and had been so careful to destroy his secret, had been a Dane, and he felt that the originator of the remarkable theory must have been a Dane himself. Briefly this was what Farquhar explained, but Professor Anderson assured him that no such theory could have come out of Denmark without his knowledge.

"Search in Gothenburg, or in Stockholm, if you like," he answered with a smile. "My own idea is that the unfortunate man was deceived by some 'cock-and-bull' story, probably an attempt to raise money in order to carry out a scheme to recover the treasure of Solomon. He believed the story of the existence of the temple treasure, and in order that no other person should obtain knowledge of the secret destroyed it before his death."

"But who was the discoverer of the secret?" asked the Englishman.

"Who can tell," remarked the Danish professor, shrugging his shoulders. "Perhaps it was only some ingenious financial swindle. You have surely had many such in London in recent years. You call them in English, I believe, 'wild-cat' schemes."

"There are many 'wild-cat' schemes in the City of London at the present moment," Frank remarked with a laugh, "but I guarantee that none is so extraordinary as this."

"Probably not," laughed the Dane. "I confess that, to me, the whole thing seems like a fairy tale."

"Then you don't discern any foundation in fact?"

"Only of tradition—the Old Testament tradition that the treasures are still hidden in the temple mount. Yet, in opposition to this, we have another tradition to the effect that the vessels of Solomon's temple were used in Persia four hundred years after the captivity. Mention is made of this in a Persian manuscript preserved in your British Museum in London. I forget the number, but it can easily be looked up in the catalogue of Oriental manuscripts."

"You believe that statement authentic?"

"As authentic as any statement in the ancient records," was his reply. "But I would suggest that you consult Haupt. He knows more of Hebrew cryptograms and ciphers than any one else on the Continent of Europe. What does Professor Griffin think?"

"He's inclined to treat the whole theory with levity."

Professor Anderson smiled.

"Of course," he said. "Supposed ciphers in certain books of the Old Testament are many. And as you know quite well, a cipher may be invented to fit any message or record desired. Your Baconian theory in regard to Shakespeare was sufficient proof of that."

"Then in your opinion no real cipher exists in the Book of Ezekiel?" asked the Englishman.

"The Bible was inspired," was his reply. "If so, there is no cipher in it except what cryptographers invent."

Frank Farquhar was silent. His inquiries in the Danish capital had nearly carried him into a *cul-de-sac*.

The dead man was, according to his own story, a Dane. But what more natural than that he had received the extraordinary manuscript from Germany, or from Sweden?

"To me," remarked the Professor, "the situation of the man who died in Paris was this. Either he himself was the inventor of the whole story or else he had paid something for it and was trying to dispose of it to some financier or other."

"Doctor Diamond, my friend who attended him before his death, says that the man was evidently a scholar."

"Then possibly he was the inventor," remarked Anderson decisively. "But if he was a scholar he was certainly unknown to us. Therefore we may be permitted to doubt his *bonâ-fides*. My advice to you is to find Haupt."

"Yes, Professor," answered the young man, "I will."

And an hour later he sent a long telegram to the Doctor at Horsford, while that same afternoon he received a brief telegraphic message from Professor Griffin, asking him to return to London at once.

His belief was that the great expert had found some clue, and he left that same evening direct for London, by way of Kiel, Hamburg and Flushing.

Chapter Eighteen
Shows the Enemy's Tactics

The tall, thin man into whose chambers Gwen Griffin had been enticed treated the trembling girl with a certain amount of politeness. Her head reeled. She hardly knew where she was, or what had occurred.

The stipulation he had made, at the instructions left by Jim Jannaway, was that she must remain there in order to meet some person who was desirous of making her acquaintance. He did not say who this person was, but she, on her part, had a dozen times begged him to release her, or at least to telegraph to her father assuring him of her safety.

"My dear girl," the tall man had answered, "don't distress yourself. Come, do calm yourself." And he assisted to raise her to her feet again. "No harm will befall you, I assure you."

"I—I don't know you, sir," she faltered through her tears, "therefore how can I possibly trust you?"

"I can only assure you that I am acting upon instructions. As far as I'm concerned, you might walk out free—only I dare not disobey my orders."

"You dare not—and you a man!" she cried.

"There are some things that a man such as myself dare not do, miss— pardon me, but I haven't the pleasure of knowing your name."

"Griffin—Gwen Griffin is my name," and she also told him where she lived. Then she asked: "Why have I been brought here?"

"I haven't the slightest idea," was the stranger's reply. "These are my chambers, and a friend of mine has had the key during my three years' absence abroad. I returned only this morning to find you locked up in here and a note left for me, giving me instructions to keep you here until a gentleman calls to see you."

"Ah! that horrid blackguard!" she screamed. "That man who met me, and called himself 'Captain Wetherton.' He told me I should find Frank in hiding here."

"And who's Frank?" asked the stranger.

"The man to whom I'm engaged."

"H'm," grunted the other; "and he wouldn't be very pleased to find you here, with me, would he?"

"No. That is why I've been entrapped herein order to compromise me in the eyes of the man who loves me."

"Why?" asked the owner of those bachelor chambers, leaning upon the bed-rail and looking at her.

"How can I tell?" said the frightened girl. "As far as I know, I've done nothing whatever to warrant this."

"Ah! in this world it is the innocent who mostly suffer," he remarked.

"But will you not allow me to go?" she implored eagerly. "Remember that all my future happiness depends upon your generosity in this matter."

"My dear child," he replied, placing his hand upon her shoulder, "if I dare, I would. But to tell you the truth, I, like yourself, am in the hands of certain persons who are utterly unscrupulous. I tell you, quite frankly, that I couldn't afford to excite their animosity by disobeying these orders I have received."

"But who is this gentleman who desires to see me?" she demanded quickly.

"I don't know. No name is given."

"Why—for what reason does he wish to see me? Could he not have called at Pembridge Gardens, or even written making a secret appointment in Kensington Gardens or in the Park?"

"To that I am quite unable to give any reply, for I'm in ignorance like yourself."

"But is it that brutal fellow who threw me down and tore my clothes last night?" she asked. "Look!" and she showed her torn blouse.

"I think not," was his response. "But those rents look a bit ugly, don't they," he added. "Come through into the sitting-room, and see if we can't find a needle and cotton. I used to keep a travelling housewife, full of all sorts of buttons and needles and things."

So the pair passed along the short, narrow passage of the flat into the sitting-room which she so vividly recollected the night before. Before her was the couch upon which the man who had called himself "Wetherton" had flung her fainting and insensible.

After a brief search in the drawers of an old oak bureau, over in the corner, the stranger produced a small roll of khaki, in the pockets of which were all sorts of cottons, buttons, needles and odds and ends, the requisites of a travelling bachelor.

She laughed as she selected a needle and a reel of cotton, and then retired into the bedroom where, for a full quarter of an hour, she sat alone mending her torn garments.

The man remained in the sitting-room, staring out of the window into the street below, damp and gloomy on that winter's morning.

"A fine home-coming indeed!" he muttered to himself. "They've put a nice thing upon me—abduct a girl, and then leave her in my charge! Jim's afraid of being connected with the affair, that's evident. I wonder who she is, and why they want her? Devilish pretty, and no mistake. It really seems a blackguardly shame to treat her badly, and wreck her young life, as they no doubt intend. By Gad! Jim and his friends are cruel as the grave. Poor little thing!" And he sighed and, crossing the room, applied a match to the fire that had already been laid.

"Yes," he remarked under his breath. "A fine home-coming. The devils hold me in the hollow of their hands, alas! But if they dare to give me away, by Jove! I wouldn't spare one of them. These last two years I've tried to live honestly, and nearly starved in doing so. And now they bring me back by force—back to the old life, because they want my assistance. And if I refuse? Then—well, I suppose they'll compel me to act according to their instructions. Here is a specimen of the dirty work in progress. I'm holding a poor innocent girl a prisoner on their behalf! I'd let her go now—this very moment, but if I did—if I did—what then? I'd be given away to the police in half an hour. No. I can't afford that—by God, I can't. She must stay here."

Presently Gwen emerged from the bedroom with her blouse repaired, and he induced her to seat herself reluctantly in the armchair before the fire.

He lit a cigarette and, taking another chair, endeavoured to reassure her that she need have no fear of him.

Then they commenced to chat, he endeavouring to learn something from her which might give him an idea of the reason why she had been enticed there. But with a woman's clever evasion, she would tell him nothing.

He inquired about her lover, but she was silent regarding him. She only said:

"He is abroad just now. And they are evidently aware of his absence. The telegram I received was worded most cleverly. I unfortunately fell a victim to their vile conspiracy."

"Is it a plot to prevent you marrying him, do you think?"

"It must be. It can be nothing else," declared the girl quickly. "Oh, when will he return—when will I be able to see him again?"

The tall man shrugged his shoulders. He saw that she was desperate and might make a rush to escape, therefore, though he begged her pardon he kept the doors locked and the keys in his pocket.

Before his arrival, it seemed, Jim Jannaway had placed provisions in the small larder in the kitchen, for there they found bread, tinned tongues, bottled beer, tea, condensed milk and other things. Hence he had no necessity to go forth to obtain food.

This struck him that an imprisonment of several days must be intended. He felt sorry for the unfortunate girl, yet he dare not connive at her escape. He knew, alas! that he was now upon very dangerous ground.

The whole day they sat together gossiping. For luncheon they had cold tongue and bread, and for dinner the same.

The situation was indeed a curious one, yet as the hours went by and he attempted to amuse her by relating humorous incidents in his own adventurous life, she gradually grew to believe that he was devoid of any sinister intention.

Times without number she tried to persuade him to release her, but he explained his inability. Then, at evening, they sat at the fireside and while he smoked she chattered, though she told him practically nothing concerning herself.

He could not help admiring her neat daintiness and her self-possession. She was a frank, sweet-faced girl, scarce more than a child, whose wonderful eyes held even him, an adventurer, in strange fascination. And that night, when she retired to her room, he handed her the key of her door that she might lock herself in, and said:

"Sleep in peace, Miss Griffin. I give you my promise that you shall not be disturbed."

And he bowed to her with all the courtesy of a true-born gentleman.

He sat smoking, thinking deeply and wondering why the girl had been confined there. He was annoyed, for by her presence there he also was held a prisoner.

Just before midnight the bell of the front door rang, and a commissionaire handed him a telegram. The message was in an unintelligible code, which however, he read without hesitation. Then he tossed the message into the fire with an imprecation, switched off the light, and went to bed.

Next day passed just as the first, but he saw, by the girl's pale face and darkening eyes, that the constant anxiety was telling upon her. Yes, he pitied her. And she, on her part, began to regard him more as her protector than as her janitor.

He treated her with the greatest consideration and courtesy. And as they sat together at their meals, she presiding, they often burst out laughing at the incongruity of the situation. More than once she inquired his name, but he always laughingly evaded her.

"My name really doesn't matter," he said. "You will only remember me with hatred, Miss Griffin."

"Though you are holding me here against my will," she replied, "yet of your conduct towards me I have nothing to complain."

He only bowed in graceful acknowledgment. No word passed his lips.

On the third morning, about noon, a ring came, and Gwen, startled, flew into her bedroom and locked the door.

The visitor was none other than Sir Felix Challas, who, grasping the tall man's hand, said:

"Welcome back, my dear Charlie. I'm sorry I couldn't come before, but I was called over to Paris on very important business." Then lowering his voice he said: "Got the girl here still—eh?"

The other nodded.

"I want to put a few questions to her," Sir Felix said in an undertone, when they were together in the sitting-room, "and if she don't answer me truly, then by Heaven it will be the worse for her. You remember the girl of that German inventor, three years ago—eh?" he asked with a meaning smile.

The tall man nodded. He recollected that poor girl's fate because she had refused to betray her father's secret to the great financier.

And this man whom the world so firmly believed to be a God-fearing philanthropist intended that pretty Gwen Griffin, sweet, innocent and inoffensive, little more than a child, should meet with the same awful fate. He held his breath. He could have struck the man before him—if he dared.

He must blindly do the bidding of this cruel, heartless man who held him so entirely in his power, this gigantic schemer whose "cat's-paw" he had been for years.

And he must stand helplessly by, unable to raise a hand to save that poor defenceless victim of a powerful man's passion and avarice.

Alas! that the great god gold must ever be all-powerful in man's world, and women must ever pay the price.

Chapter Nineteen
Is about the Doctor

Doctor Diamond, in his long Wellington boots and overcoat, was descending the steep hill into Horsford village one gloomy afternoon with Aggie at his side.

It had been raining, and the pair had been across the meadows to Overton, a small hamlet where, from a farmhouse, they obtained their weekly supply of butter. This, the fair-haired child, her clean white pinafore appearing below her navy-blue coat, carried in a small basket upon her arm. She had been dancing along merrily at the little man's side, delighted to be out with him for a walk, when, as they came over the brow of the hill, they saw a man in a long drab mackintosh ascending in their direction.

The man raised his hand to them, but at first Diamond did not recognise him. Then, as they drew nearer, he said:

"Why—who'd ever have thought it! Here's your father, Aggie!"

"Father!" echoed the girl, staring at the man approaching. "No, dad, surely that isn't my father! You're my own father." And the child, with her fair hair falling upon her shoulders, clung affectionately to his arm.

In a few moments the two men met.

"Hulloa, Doc!" cheerily cried the man known to his intimates as "Red Mullet". "Thought I'd give you a bit of a surprise. And little Aggie, too! My hat! what a big girl she grows! Why, my darling," he exclaimed, bending and kissing her, "I'd never have recognised you—never in all my life!"

Her father's bristly red moustache brushed the child's face, and she withdrew bashfully.

"Ah! my pet," cried the tall, gaunt man, "I suppose you hardly knew me—eh? You were quite a little dot when I was here last. But though your dad travels a lot, and is always on the move, yet he's ever thinking of you." He sighed. "See here!" And diving his hand into his breast-pocket, he took out a well-worn leather wallet which contained a photograph. "That is what your other dad sent to me last year! Your picture, little one."

The child exchanged glances with the Doctor, still clinging to his arm. To her, Doctor Diamond was her father. She loved him, for he was always kind to her and always interested in her childish pleasure. True the payments made by "Red Mullet" were irregular and far between, but the ugly little man had formed a great attachment for the child, and when not at the village school she was usually in his company.

"Your wife told me the direction from which you would come, so I thought I'd just take a stroll and meet you," the tall fellow said. "Horsford does not seem to change a little bit."

"It hasn't changed, they say, for the past two centuries," laughed the Doctor. "We are quiet, steady-going folk here." And as he spoke the sweet-toned chimes rang forth from the square grey Norman tower on their left, the tower to see which archaeologists so often came from far and near.

"Well, well," exclaimed Mullet. "I had no idea my little Aggie had grown to be such a fine big girl. Very soon she'll be leaving school; she knows more about geography and grammar now than her dad does, that I'll be bound."

"Mr Holmes, the schoolmaster, is loud in her praises," remarked the Doctor, whereat the girl blushed and smiled.

"And how would you like to go back with me, and live in Paris—eh?" inquired the father.

In a moment, however, the child clung closer to Diamond, and, burying her face upon his arm, burst into tears.

"No, no, dear," declared the red-haired man. "I didn't mean it. Why, I was only joking! Of course you shall stay here, and finish your education with the Doctor, who is so good and kind to you. See—I've brought you something."

And taking from his pocket a child's plain hoop bangle in gold, he placed it upon her slim wrist. Aggie, with a child's pardonable vanity, stretched forth her arm and showed the Doctor the effect. Then at the letter's suggestion, she raised her face and kissed her father for the present of the first piece of jewellery she had ever possessed in her life.

They walked back together to the cottage, and after a homely cup of tea, "Red Mullet" sat with the Doctor in the cosy panelled dining-room, the fire burning brightly, and the red-shaded lamp upon the table.

"I'm glad you're pleased at the appearance of little Aggie," remarked the Doctor between deep puffs of his pipe. "She's quite a sweet child. Every one in the village loves her."

"I wonder, Doctor, what they'd think if they knew she was my daughter—the daughter of 'Red Mullet'—eh?" asked the red-haired man grimly.

The Doctor pulled a wry face but did not reply. Alas, he was well aware that Mr Mullet did not bear the best of reputations, and as a matter of fact he was wondering the reason why he now risked a sojourn on British soil.

"But—I—er—is that door closed?" he asked of the ugly little man as he glanced suspiciously behind him.

The Doctor rose and latched it. Then he resumed his seat.

"The fact is, I came down here to-day for two reasons—to see little Aggie and also to make some inquiries."

"Inquiries!" echoed Diamond. "What about?"

"About something that concerns you," was "Red Mullet's" reply. "About certain papers which belonged to a man named Blanc, who died in a little hotel opposite the Gare du Nord."

"I—I don't understand you. What do you mean?" asked Diamond, with a perceptible start.

"Come, my dear Doc, you may just as well be frank and open with me. You know the kind of man I am. You've got hold of papers which don't belong to you—and well, all praise to you, I say, if they're worth anything. I don't see why you shouldn't deal with a dead man's property if he deliberately wished to destroy it."

"How do you know all this, Mr Mullet?" asked the Doctor, his face pale and much surprised.

"Well, my source of information don't matter very much, does it?" remarked the other, stretching out his long legs to the warmth of the fire. "But I can tell you it's lucky for you and your friends that I've found out about it—or—well, I can only tell you something would have happened—something very unfortunate."

"I don't follow you."

"I don't expect you do," was "Red Mullet's" reply, as he laughed lightly. "Just be open with me, Doc, and I'll tell you something—something that'll interest you, no doubt. What is the purport of this precious document about which there's all this fuss?"

"It's a secret—a great and remarkable problem which, up to the present, I'm unable to solve."

"My dear old chap, there are a good many problems in this world which want solving. The first of them is Woman," laughed the other.

"Admitted. But woman doesn't concern this particular matter."

"That's just where you are mistaken, Doc," Mullet interrupted. "You live down in this rural solitude, and you don't know what goes on up in London. There is a woman in the case—a woman who is very deeply involved in it."

"Who?"

"We can leave her out of it for the present," replied Mullet. "I want to know something about the document."

Doctor Diamond hesitated. Had this man, whose reputation was so bad, and against whom he had so often been warned, come there for the purpose of levying blackmail? It seemed as though he had! "Well," he answered, "I really see no reason why we should discuss what is, after all, my own private business, Mr Mullet."

"I should not ask you if I had not a distinct object," said the other. "I may as well tell you that I've already acted in your interests, and at considerable risk to myself, too," he added.

"For which I thank you most sincerely," responded the ugly little man, now very much on the alert.

He was extremely puzzled to know by what means Mullet had learnt his secret. Surely he could not have been a friend of that man who, on his deathbed, had refused his name?

"I merely came down here to give you warning," Mullet said. "You are not the only person interested in the discovery."

"I know. I have been compelled to take certain persons into my confidence, and they will share in the profits which, we hope, will eventually accrue."

"I'm not speaking of your friends, Doc. I'm speaking of enemies— people who are working actively against you."

"Against me!" cried Diamond, starting. "Who else knows about it besides ourselves?"

"Ah!" exclaimed Mullet, smiling. "That's just the point. While you possess only a few scraps of the dead man's manuscript, those working in opposition to you have in their possession a complete copy!"

"What!" cried the ugly little Doctor, starting up. "Then the context is known! The whole document has been read!"

"Without a doubt. And I should have been in ignorance of your connection with it had it not been for a pure accident," answered Mullet.

"Who are my enemies?" demanded the Doctor. "They are powerful— but I'm not at liberty to mention their names. I can only say, Doctor, that if I can help you in secret in this affair I will. There's money in it—lots of money—that's my firm opinion."

"Then you know all about it?"

"Well—I know that the discovery is one of the most remarkable of the age, and that it seems more than likely you'll be able to locate the hidden treasure of Solomon's temple. I'm not much of a classical or Biblical scholar, but I understand that the theory has utterly staggered certain great authorities. And as a mining engineer by profession, I'm interested. I've been on more than one treasure-hunt, once in Guatemala, and again I went out with a party prospecting three years ago for those sunken Spanish galleons in Vigo Bay. We located nine of the vessels by means of that new Italian invention, the hydroscope, and got up an old cannon, several gold doubloons and silver 'pieces of eight.' According to authentic records in the Archives at Madrid, there are seventeen vessels full of gold and silver lying at the bottom of the bay, and the treasure is believed to be worth at least twenty-eight millions sterling."

Diamond smiled. Even that huge sum did not cause him dismay. The treasure of Solomon's temple would surely be worth a dozen times as much. Besides, would not he, Raymond Diamond, become one of the most noted men in the world if, by his instrumentality, the historic treasure of Israel was recovered.

"A company has been formed to work the Vigo treasure. They asked me to join them," "Red Mullet" went on. "It's a tempting business, but I have other matters to attend to just now. I wonder you don't form a syndicate to work this scheme of yours, Doctor."

"No syndicate is necessary," replied the Doctor confidently. "We can do it ourselves."

"You might—if it were not for the strong opposition against you," Mullet remarked. "No, Doc. Don't be too sure of your position. You've got others who intend to cut in before you, when the time is ripe. But," he added, "what proof have you that this treasure actually exists. I'm ignorant in these matters, you know."

"In a dozen places in the Old Testament it is referred to. Nebuchadnezzar, when he took Jerusalem, carried away over five thousand vessels of gold and silver from the temple. Yet this was only the portion which the Jews allowed to remain there. The greater part of the treasure, including the Ark of the Covenant and the tablets of the law, were hidden and have never been recovered. We learn from the Book of Ezra that when Cyrus, Nebuchadnezzar's successor, gave the Jews their liberty, that he restored to Jerusalem five thousand four hundred basons and vessels of gold and silver which the King of Babylon had taken away. Those were, no doubt, placed in the new temple which Zerubbabel erected, but of which we unfortunately possess so very few particulars. What we are in search of is not this treasure, but the vessels of Solomon's temple that were hidden by the priests before the capture of Jerusalem by the King of Babylon."

"So I understand, Doctor. But what actual statement have you that they are still concealed?"

"The plain, straightforward statement in Holy Writ," was the other's reply, as he sat huddled in the big armchair, a queer, ugly little figure. Then, reaching across to a small table whereon lay the Bible, which he now daily studied, and opening it, he said: "Now, listen to this. Jeremiah, xxvi, 19-21, reads as follows:

> "For thus saith the Lord of hosts concerning the pillars, and concerning the sea, and concerning the bases, and *concerning the residue of the vessels that remain in this city*, Which Nebuchadnezzar, king of Babylon, took not, when he carried away captive Jeconiah, the son of Jehoiakim king of Judah from Jerusalem to Babylon, and all the nobles of Judah and Jerusalem:
>
> "Yea, thus saith the Lord of hosts, the God of Israel, concerning *the vessels that remain in the house of the Lord, and in the house of the King of Judah and of Jerusalem."*

"By Jove!" exclaimed Mullet, starting up. "I didn't know of those words of the prophet. But I'm ashamed to say, Doctor, that I never was very much of a Biblical scholar. But it really looks as though there is something in the theory after all, doesn't it?"

For a long time the two men sat together, but though the Doctor was eager to learn how Aggie's father had obtained his knowledge, the latter was equally determined to tell him nothing.

"If you carry on this inquiry, Doctor," he said, "it will be a very risky proceeding—I can tell you that much."

"What! Your object then is to frighten me into inactivity, Mr Mullet—eh?" asked the little man, jumping up.

"Not at all—not at all, my dear fellow. You don't understand. You and I are friends, and—well, we'll continue to be, if you will allow me."

Raymond Diamond confessed that he did not understand the object of his visitor's presence there.

But "Red Mullet" only laughed, and taking another cigar from his case, said drily:

"Then let us drop the subject, Doctor, and talk of something else."

Chapter Twenty
The Inquisitor

The police inquiries into the whereabouts of Gwen Griffin had been futile.

The Professor, beside himself with grief and apprehension, complained most bitterly that the authorities had not treated his daughter's disappearance with sufficient seriousness. In all the interviews he had had, both at the local police-station and at New Scotland Yard, the officials had apparently taken the view that the girl had left home of her own account. He had been told on all hands that, in the end, her escapade would be found to be due to some unknown love-affair.

In frantic bewilderment he had telegraphed to Frank Farquhar at the Bristol at Copenhagen, but unfortunately he had not received the message because on arrival at the Danish capital he had found the Bristol full, and had gone on to the Angleterre. Hence he was still in ignorance of the disappearance of his well-beloved.

Those mystic figures which the Professor had found scrawled upon his blotting-pad—the same that were upon that discarded scrap of waste-paper—also puzzled him to the point of distraction. Could they have anything to do with the girl's fate? By whose hand had they been traced?

As far as they could discover, no stranger had entered the study. Yet those figures—"255.19.7"—had been written boldly in blue upon the pad. Could Gwen have done it herself? Had she left him some cryptic message which he now failed to decipher? But if so, why did those same numbers appear upon the scrap of paper discarded by the unknown man who was endeavouring to learn his secret?

After three days, during which time he puzzled over the meaning of those figures, applying to them all sorts of ciphers, he took a taxi-cab to a friend of his named Stevens, who lived at Streatham and was a Professor of Hebrew at London University.

The pair sat together for some time, Griffin having apparently called to pay a formal visit to his less illustrious *confrère*, when suddenly producing the figures upon a piece of paper he sought Professor Stevens' opinion as to their meaning.

The other stared at them through his spectacles, and after a long consideration inquired:

"Were they written by a Hebrew scholar?"

"I believe so."

"Then I think their meaning must be quite plain," replied the other coolly. "I should decipher it as the duration of the Kingdom of Israel. Did it not end after 255 years—namely from B.C. 975-721—under nineteen kings and seven dynasties, not reckoning among the latter, of course, the ephemeral usurpations of Zimri and Shallum?"

"I never thought of that!" gasped Griffin. "Those figures have greatly disturbed me, my dear Stevens. They have appeared twice in circumstances extremely strange—traced by an unknown hand."

"But the hand of a scholar without a doubt," was the other's reply. "Perhaps some crank or other who has the habit of signing himself in that manner. I have known men addicted to such peculiarities. There used to be a don at Oxford who had the humorous habit of appending his signature in most excellent imitation of that of Napoleon."

Griffin, recognising that Stevens was correct in his elucidation of the mysterious signification of those figures, became more puzzled. The man in search of the great secret was evidently a crank. That was most conclusively proved. Yet why should that mystic signature appear upon his blotting-pad?

Was it possible that Gwen and he were acquainted, and that he had actually entered the house.

The Professor was beside himself in his utter bewilderment. His daughter had slipped away, and left him without a word of farewell. Yet towards his friend Stevens he wore a mask, and only laughed heartily at the rapid solution of the problem which he had placed before him.

Was it possible, he thought many times, that Gwen, with a love-sick girl's sudden yearning, had slipped across to the Continent to join her lover? There could be no reason whatever for that, because he had never for a moment opposed their engagement. Yet girls were a trifle wild sometimes, he reflected, especially motherless girls like the dainty Gwen.

After an hour, however, he bade farewell to Stevens, and re-entering his "taxi" in King's Avenue, drove back into London, refusing his friend's invitation to remain for luncheon.

He crossed Westminster Bridge, and alighted at the British Museum to inquire if the mysterious searcher had been seen there of late.

The assistant-keeper in the Oriental room replied in the affirmative. The old gentleman had been there three days before, and had afterwards gone to the great reading-room.

Proceeding there. Professor Griffin quickly made inquiries, discovering presently that the man had given the name of Rosenberg. He was shown a slip upon which was written the titles of the two rare works he had consulted. They were:

"Cryptomengsis Patefacta (1685)," and "Kryptographik, Kluber (1809)."

These were, he recognised, the two leading works on cryptography, explaining, as they did, all the early systems of secret writing from the *scytalc* in use by the early Greeks down to the biliteral cipher of Sir Francis Bacon. It was therefore quite plain that the stranger, whoever he might be, though at Oxford he had made those calculations in order to test the existence of a numerical cipher in the Book of Ezekiel, had not yet discovered any true key.

This knowledge gave Griffin great satisfaction. The loss of that crumpled paper from his pocket was, he recognised of no import.

Inquires of the librarian showed that the stranger was not known in the reading-room as a regular reader. Yet he agreed, as indeed had other librarians and keepers of manuscripts, that the old man was undoubtedly a scholar.

This person's will-o'-the-wisp existence was most tantalising. In appearance he was described as an old white-headed man with deep-set eyes and a longish white beard, rather shabbily dressed and wearing a long black overcoat much the worse for wear. Great scholars are not remarkable for their neatness in dress. They are mostly neglectful, as indeed was Professor Griffin himself. To Gwen, her father was a constant source of anxiety, for only at her supreme command would he even order a new suit, and his evening clothes were so old and out of shape that she had, times without number, declared herself ashamed to go out to the smart houses at which they were so often asked to dine.

But genius is always forgiven its garments, and the fact that the bearded stranger was described as shabby and almost threadbare did not surprise the man who went about equally shabby himself.

If he were interested in the "Cryptomengsis Patefacta," then one thing was proved. His researches at the Bodleian had been without result.

The continued absence of Gwen, however, prevented Griffin from continuing his inquiries. Though times without number he opened the Hebrew text of Ezekiel and tried to study it, yet he was unable to concentrate his mind upon it, and always closed the book again with a deep sigh.

The house was dull and empty without little Gwen's bright smile and musical voice. This, he realised, was a foretaste of his loneliness when she was married.

Next day dragged by. The following day was cold and wet, and he spent it mostly alone in his study, after he had been round to the police-station and obtained a negative reply to his question as to whether his beloved daughter had been discovered.

That she was absent against her win he was convinced. She would never have left him in that manner to allow him to fear for her safety.

Seated alone, he brought out those large photographs of Diamond's half-destroyed manuscript, and tried to centre his mind upon them. But, alas! he was unable. Therefore, as the short grey afternoon drew in, with a sigh he rose, put on his overcoat, and telling Laura he would not be back to dinner, he went forth to wander the London streets. He could bear the dead silence of that house no longer.

Just before seven o'clock the dining-room bell rang, and the dark-eyed parlour-maid, ascending the stairs, entered the room.

"Lor', miss!" gasped the Cockney girl. "You did give me a fright! How long have you been 'ome?"

Gwen, who stood before her, pale and thin-faced and with hair slightly dishevelled, explained that she had just let herself in with the latch-key.

"The Professor's out, miss. 'E said 'e wouldn't be 'ome to dinner," the girl remarked. "Oh, we've been very worried about you, miss! The perlice 'ave searched 'igh and low for yer. We all thought something dreadful 'ad 'appened. Wherever 'ave you been all these days?"

"That's my own business," answered the Professor's daughter. "I've come back safe and sound, and I'm now going to my room. Tell my father when he comes in that I'm very tired. Perhaps he won't return till late."

"Shall I bring you up something, miss?" asked the girl.

"Yes, some tea. I want nothing else."

And she ascended to her own neat bedroom on the second floor where, after closing the door, she flung herself upon the bed and burst into tears.

Her nerves had been unstrung by the severe ordeal she had gone through. When the maid brought her tea, she dried her eyes and allowed the girl to assist her to change her dusty skirt and torn blouse, and after a good wash and a cup of tea she felt decidedly better and refreshed.

Laura lit a fire, and when it had burnt up Gwen flung herself into her cretonne-covered armchair to rest and to think.

Since she had last sat in that cosy well-remembered room of hers there had been hideous happenings. The past seemed to her all like a bad dream. She shuddered as she recalled it. Even the events of that day hardly seemed clear and distinct. Her recollection of them was hazy, so agitated and anxious had she been. Why she had been so suddenly released from that hateful bondage was also to her a complete mystery.

She was recalling that first interview with the coarse, red-faced man whose name she had not been told: with what little consideration he had treated her, and how he had compelled her to come forth from her stronghold in order to speak with him.

He had asked her many curious questions, the purport of which she could not discern. Some of them concerned her father's recent actions and movements; some of them concerned the man she loved.

But she was independent, and refused point-blank to answer anything. She defied that man who, in turn, jeered at her helplessness, and so insulted her that the flush of shame rose upon her white cheeks.

"You shall answer me these questions, young lady," cried the pompous man in firm determination, "or it will be the worse for you!" he added with a look, the real meaning of which she was unable to disguise from herself.

Yet she stood defiant, even though she was helpless in his hands.

"My father's business does not concern you," she had cried, "and if you think his daughter will betray him into the hands of his enemies you are mistaken, sir!"

The bloated, red-faced brute blurted forth a quick imprecation, and would have struck her had not the tall man who was her janitor interfered, saying:

"No, don't. She'll reconsider her refusal, no doubt."

"If she does not tell me everything—everything we want to know—and if she does not consent to do our bidding and bring to us whatever we desire, then she need not look for mercy. She is ours, and we shall treat her as such. The man who called himself 'Wetherton' shall come back to her.

He'll very soon overcome her scruples and cause her to reflect!" the man had laughed hoarsely.

"Give her time," suggested the tall man.

"We want no more of these heroics about her betraying her father," the other sneered. "If so, she'll regret it. You know, Charlie, what I mean: how more than one girl has bitterly regretted her defiance."

Gwen fell suddenly upon her knees, imploring to be allowed to go free. But her tormentor only repeated his threats in terms which left no doubt as to what he intended should be the poor girl's fate, and laughing he took up his hat and strode forth.

From that moment the tall man addressed as Charlie, though he would give no explanation whatever as to the reason those strange questions had been put to her concerning her father and her lover, treated her with the greatest consideration, yet at the same time kept constantly expressing a fear that, if she still refused, the danger threatened would certainly befall her.

Again, on the following day, the fat red-faced inquisitor came and put those questions to her. But he still found her obdurate. She recognised that those people were her father's enemies, therefore she had determined to say nothing.

Ah! would she ever forget all the horror of those dramatic interviews—the dastardly threats of that blackguard who laughed at her unhappiness and who uttered words which caused her face to burn with shame.

And then came the final scene, just as suddenly as the first.

The inquisitor came again, and after another violent scene left, declaring that the false "Wetherton" should return and become her janitor in place of the man she knew as Charlie.

The latter seemed pained and very anxious after the red-faced man had gone. She inquired the reason, but he only sighed, declaring that the man under whose power they both were would most certainly carry out his threat towards her.

Half mad with anxiety and grief, she had then confided in the tall man, telling him a brief disjointed story of the half-burned manuscript, in the course of which she had mentioned the name of a man whom she had never met—Doctor Diamond, of Horsford. Her lover, she explained, was the Doctor's friend.

The man had put to her a few rapid questions to which she had replied; then, as though with sudden resolve, he had risen from the table where he had been sitting, and clenching his fists poured forth a flood of execrations upon some person he did not name.

She was surprised at the action, and her surprise increased when, a few minutes later, he had halted before her saying:

"Though I risk my own liberty in assisting you, Miss Griffin, I will not keep you here, the innocent victim of that heartless blackguard and his sycophants. I have a daughter of my own—a little daughter who is all in all to me. 'Red Mullet'—that's my name, Miss—may bear a pretty bad reputation, but he will never lift a finger against a defenceless girl, nor will he act in opposition to a man who has stood his friend. My only stipulation is that you will say nothing. We will meet again ere long."

And then, five minutes later, having given her solemn promise of secrecy, she had left the house, wandering the dark streets until she had found herself in Oxford Street, where she had hailed a cab and driven home.

Over all this she sat thinking, gazing thoughtfully into the dancing flames and wondering.

But from her reverie she was awakened by the re-entry of the maid, who said:

"Both the Professor and Mr Farquhar are downstairs, miss. Will you please go down to them at once?"

She started quickly. A cold shudder ran through her.

With that vow of secrecy upon her, the vow given to the man who had been her protector, what explanation of her absence could she give to Frank.

She rose slowly from her chair, her great dark eyes fixed straight before her.

Chapter Twenty One
The Falling of the Shadow

Gwen stood before her father and her lover, a pale, wan, trembling figure, evasive in all her answers.

With the seal of silence upon her lips what could she say?

As Professor Griffin had entered the door with his latch-key a hansom had drawn up at the kerb, and Frank, who had come straight from Charing Cross, after dropping his kit at his rooms, sprang out and ran up the steps to the porch to meet the elder man with a merry greeting.

His first inquiry had been of Gwen, but the Professor's face told him that something was wrong, and they entered the hall together. Next moment, however, the maid rushed forward exclaiming: "Miss Gwen's come home, sir. She's upstairs."

"Tell her we are here," said her father, "and we'd like to see her at once."

Then the two men walked into the dining-room, where, in a few brief sentences, the Professor explained to young Farquhar his daughter's sudden disappearance.

Frank was quick to notice that the girl he loved had scarce dared to raise her eyes to his as she entered the room. The grey gown she wore, unrelieved by any touch of colour, served to accentuate the deadly pallor of her soft countenance. A change had been wrought in her—a great astounding change.

"Why, Gwen dear!" gasped her father. "What's the matter? What has occurred?"

"Nothing, dad," faltered the girl.

"That's quite absurd, my child," cried the elder man. "You've been absent from home all these days, and sent me no word! Something unusual must have occurred."

"Nothing, dad dear—at least, nothing that I can tell you."

Frank started, staring straight at her, utterly amazed at her response.

"But, Gwen," he exclaimed, "you surely can explain where you've been. The police, it seems, have been searching for you everywhere."

Her eyes were cast quickly around the room, as though seeking means of escape from that cross-examination. Then she answered:

"I really don't see what my business concerns any one—so long as I am at home again."

"This is scarcely like you, Gwen," exclaimed the grey-haired man reproachfully. "You are usually so very thoughtful for me, and careful not to give me cause for a moment's anxiety."

"It was quite inevitable, dad," she replied. "I would not have remained silent intentionally—as you well know."

"But surely," interrupted Frank in a voice which showed that his suspicions were already aroused, "surely you can at least allow us the satisfaction of knowing where you've been, dear!"

"No harm has befallen me, has there? Therefore, why trouble about my absence?" she asked. To utter those words required all her self-control. She knew in what an awkward position she was now placing herself.

"Well, you seem to regard very lightly all the anxiety you have caused me, my child," protested Griffin sharply.

"I am very sorry—truly sorry, dear dad," was the pale-faced girl's reply, "but my silence really was not my own fault."

"At least you might be frank with us now, Gwen!" declared her lover. "You surely have nothing to hide!"

"Nothing whatever," she said, smiling bitterly, "only I am, for certain reasons, compelled to regard my recent whereabouts as a secret."

"Why?"

She was silent. What could she say! What indeed? The man Mullet, who had been her protector, and who had treated her with such kindness and consideration, making her confinement much the less irksome than it would have been; the man who had stood between her and her brutal, red-faced inquisitor, and who, just at the moment when a grave peril threatened her, had opened the door and allowed her to escape, and laid upon her a solemn vow of secrecy. His words rang distinctly in her ears: "Remember, Miss Griffin, if you tell your friends what has happened to you it will result in my ruin. Our enemies will avenge themselves by giving me over to the police. Therefore, I beg of you to remain silent—at all hazards—for my sake!" And she had promised.

Could she break that pledge, given to the man who had saved her from shame and dishonour?

By her hesitation, grave suspicions had gathered within the minds of both her father and her lover. Ignorant of the true facts, they both misjudged her.

Frank's quick jealousy had been fired by her determination not to make explanation. Yet he had tried to suppress the bitter thoughts growing within him, hoping that it was her father's presence which prevented her from telling him in confidence what had occurred.

"I cannot see why you should make such a great mystery of the affair, my dear child," remarked the Professor, clearly annoyed.

"Well," and she laughed nervously, "perhaps I may tell you something some day, dad. But please excuse me now, dear. I—I'm tired and—and very upset."

The old man recognised from her pale, hard-drawn features that she was not herself. Her highly strung nerves were at their greatest tension. And, perhaps, after all, he thought, it was injudicious of him to submit her to that cross-examination in Frank's presence.

Indeed, both men desired to speak with her alone, both believing that they would then induce her to tell the truth.

Little did they dream that the truth could never issue from her lips— that the vow she had made was to a man to whom the exposure meant loss of his liberty.

Her own position was a ghastly one. She had already realised that. She shuddered at the recollection of those hideous insults of that fat, brutal tormentor—and of the fate which he had marked out for her because she would not satisfy him concerning either her father or her lover.

Her sole thought was of "Charlie"—Mr Mullet, or "Red Mullet" as his friends were in the habit of calling him. She smiled at the humour of the appellation. It fitted him so well on account of his red hair and bristly red moustache.

Half an hour later the subject of her absence having by mutual consent, been dropped, the Professor went to his study to write some letters, while Gwen and her lover strolled into the big drawing-room, gaunt and cheerless without a fire.

When they were alone he took her white, trembling hand, and, looking steadily into her eyes, begged her to afford him the satisfaction of knowing the truth about her absence.

She had been dreading that moment, and she only shook her head.

"But, dearest!" he urged, "surely I have a right to know!"

"I thought you said only the day before your departure for Copenhagen that you could always trust me, Frank," she answered, in a voice full of quiet reproach.

"I said so, I admit. But almost immediately I had gone it seems that you slipped out of the house without a word, and have only just returned. You will make no explanation, therefore what am I to think? What can I think!"

"You must think as evil of me as you may, Frank," was the girl's calm reply.

"No, no," he cried. "Come darling, tell me all about it—in confidence. I won't say a word to any living soul."

"I cannot tell you," was her faint response, standing rigid, with her eyes fixed straight before her. "Please do not ask me again."

"Do you refuse, even me?"

"Yes, Frank—even you."

He was silent. What ugly incident could she have to hide from him? He knew that before their first meeting she had, like many a young and pretty girl, been a sad flirt; that men had hovered about her continually, attracted by her sweet beauty and charming daintiness. He was not her first love. On the contrary, she had more than one little serious affair of the heart; first with a young Italian officer of infantry at Florence, where she had spent a winter with her father, and again with the son of a north country ironmaster while staying at the Empire at Buxton. She had confessed to those, and others. Indeed, hitherto she had never withheld from him any secret concerning her past. Therefore, why should she now refuse to give any account of her mysterious absence!

He was puzzled—puzzled by her attitude and puzzled by her determination to evade his questions. And, as was but natural, there sprang up in his breast the burning fire of jealousy.

The amazing, horrifying thought occurred to him that she, the sweet-faced girl he loved with his whole heart and soul, had, while he had been absent abroad, met some secret lover, an old "flame" most probably, believing that she could excuse herself to her indulgent father and induce him to make no mention of the affair to him upon his return. He, however, had returned to London a day too early—returned to learn the bitter and astounding truth.

Time after time, still holding her tiny white hand in his, and looking into those dark timid eyes, he urged her to give him some satisfaction. But she steadily refused, declaring:

"I am unable, Frank. And even if I were able, you would never believe me—never!"

"Why are you unable?" he inquired, suspiciously.

"Because secrecy has been imposed upon me."

"By one who is in fear of certain consequences—eh?" he asked furiously.

"Yes," was her faltering response.

"Then is it not right that I, your future husband, should be acquainted with what has occurred, Gwen?" he demanded quickly. "By your silence, you are only arousing suspicions within me that may be cruel and unjust towards you."

"I regret, Frank, that it must remain so. I have given a pledge that I cannot break—even at your request."

"Ah! then your love for me is not so strong as I believed it to be!" he cried reproachfully, letting her hand drop. "How many times have you placed your arms about my neck and declared your affection for me?" he asked bitterly.

"I do love you, Frank—I swear I love you as much as I have always done!" she cried wildly, stretching forth her arms to him in her despair.

"Impossible. You have made a solemn pledge to another—a man. Do you deny that it is a man?"

"No. I deny nothing that is the truth," she whispered hoarsely, "I dare not tell you the truth for—for that man's sake!"

"You apparently think a great deal of him!" exclaimed Farquhar, with rising anger.

"He is my friend—my best friend, as you will some day learn."

"And you actually tell me this, Gwen!" he cried, staring at her. "You—whom I've loved so truly!"

"I am telling you the truth," she replied, in a voice again strangely calm. "You need entertain no jealousy of him. He is my friend—my devoted friend—nothing more."

"And you stay from home for days, and on returning tell me this!" he exclaimed, his brows contracted in fierce anger. "What is this fellow's name?" he demanded.

"I am not at liberty to tell you," she responded, "believe me if you will— if not," —and she shrugged her shoulders without concluding her sentences.

"I have a right to know," he blurted forth.

She realised the effect her words had had upon him. She saw his fierce jealousy and his dark suspicion. Yet what more could she say in the hideous circumstances. She was now the innocent victim of a silence imposed upon her by the man who had been her protector. How could she betray him into the hands of his enemies? Ah! her situation was surely one of the most difficult and maddening in which a girl had ever found herself.

To tell Frank Farquhar the truth would be to rouse his mad jealousy to a great pitch. He would seek out Mr Mullet, face him, and create a scene which must inevitably bring down upon her friend and protector the vengeance of those who held him so helpless in their unscrupulous hands.

Hence she foresaw the inevitable. It was as plain as it was tragic. Her refusal to give satisfactory replies to Frank's most natural questions had aroused his darkest suspicion. He, on his part, discerned in her determination a deliberate attempt to mislead him. During his absence she had changed towards him, changed in a most curious way that held him mystified.

"You appear, Gwen, to be utterly unconcerned and careless as to whether I believe you or not," he said gravely, after a few moments' silence. "Well, I would like now to speak quite plainly and openly."

"Speak," she said, "I am all attention." She was struggling valiantly with herself.

Her coolness was feigned. Ah! what would she give if she were at liberty to tell Frank the whole strange and ghastly truth!

"I have put to you a question which you refuse to answer," he said in a low, hard voice. "You have admitted that, by this silence of yours, you are protecting another man. Well—in that case I can only say that I must leave you in future to your friend's protection. I hope he loves you better—better than I!"

"Leave me!" she gasped in a hoarse whisper. "You—you will leave me! Ah! no—no Frank," —she shrieked in her despair, "you can't mean that— you won't let—"

But her lover had already turned upon his heel, and without further words he left the room—and the house.

She heard the front door slam, and then with a sudden cry of despair she flung herself upon the couch and buried her head among the silken cushions sobbing.

Chapter Twenty Two
Increases the Mystery

The morning was foggy, damp and dark in London, one of those to which dwellers in the Metropolis are so accustomed in the short December days.

In "Red Mullet's" sitting-room off Oxford Street—that same room in which Gwen Griffin had endured her imprisonment—he and Doctor Diamond were seated.

A fortnight had passed since the red-haired man's visit to Horsford, but in accordance with a promise made he had, late the previous evening, telegraphed to the hunchback, and in response to the message the latter had left Peterborough by the up-express at nine o'clock that morning.

"Well, Doc," the tall man was saying as he lay stretched lazily in his chair smoking a cigarette. "I'm giving away my friend in order to oblige you, and I've had a lot of difficulty, as you may imagine. My friends are a pretty tough crowd, as you know. But I've fulfilled the promise I made to you, and all will be well providing that young lady, Miss Griffin, only holds her tongue."

"Then you've really obtained a copy of the document for me—eh!" interrupted the ugly little man, his face brightening quickly.

"Yes. I was very nearly caught in the act of taking it. It was kept in a safe, and I had to get hold of the *key* by a ruse. I kept it a day, and got a typed copy made. Then I retained it to its place."

"By Jove, Mr Mullet, you're a real friend!" cried the Doctor, starting up. "As you know, we've been handicapped hitherto by not knowing the context of the document. Ours has been all guesswork."

"Well, it needn't be any more," remarked the red-haired man with a light laugh, "for here's a complete copy. You'd better read it out. It's a very remarkable statement." And he produced a typewritten manuscript which the Doctor, after clearing his throat, eagerly read as follows:

"THE TREASURE OF ISRAEL.

"Revealed by a Hebrew Cipher in the Old Testament.

"I, Peter Holmboe, graduate of Helsingfors University, in Finland, late Professor of Hebrew at St. Petersburg University, and now resident at Langenfelder Strasse, 17, Altona, Germany, make oath and declare as follows:

"Curious, and perhaps improbable as it may at first appear, I claim to have discovered the actual whereabouts of the hidden treasure of the Jewish Temple, which includes among other things the Ark of the Covenant, the Tablets of moses, and the enormous treasure of gold and silver known to exist before the capture of Jerusalem by Nebuchadnezzar, King of Babylon.

"*The Secret.*

"The secret of the place of concealment is contained in a cipher which runs through certain chapters of the Book of Ezekiel, and which clearly relates the whole story and gives absolute and most complete directions with measurements by which the spot is indicated. And not only this. The same story, in a much more abbreviated form, is, curiously enough, also repeated in the same cipher in certain chapters of Deuteronomy.

"It is a historical fact that when Nebuchadnezzar seized Jerusalem nearly the whole of the treasure of the Temple had disappeared, and it would seem that into the Book of Ezekiel the secret was incorporated, so that the treasure, which formed the war-chest of the Jews, could be recovered at the coming of the Messiah.

"Many points are, of course, highly interesting and curious. Perhaps my discovery—which, by the way, was by pure accident—will create much controversy and arouse great excitement among scholars and archaeologists. Nevertheless the cipher exists, as I am ready, under certain conditions and on certain financial considerations, to indicate its existence to any competent Hebrew scholar who may be appointed to investigate my discovery.

"*The Cipher.*

"For many years I had been greatly interested in the various astronomical, astrological and cabalistical signs and cycles so apparent in the chronology of the ancient peoples. In the Bible, and more especially during the five hundred or so years before Christ, I found evidences of the astrology that was used in the division of time, and therefore set to work, using the comparing method in order to obtain an insight into the different ciphers most universally used, and also into the methods of concealing secret messages and statements. Many of the ciphers used were highly ingenious and most difficult to decipher. The Jews in Jerusalem used them, so did the Jewish Greeks in Alexandria and the Buddhists in India, as well as the Gnostics, etc.

"I had been studying certain curious expressions in the 'Mischna,' which seemed to me to contain certain hidden meanings, when one day, in studying the Book of Ezekiel in the original, I was amazed to come across an expression which, habituated as I was to the presence of ciphers, told me at once that a hidden message was contained there.

"After countless failures through several years, I one day applied one of the earlier known cabalistic ciphers—which, by the way, is so complicated and ingenious that the whole message must be deciphered before the first word becomes apparent—and, to my intense astonishment, on making the complete decipher I found myself able to read a clean declaration (extending through nine chapters) of the secret hiding-place of the Great Treasure of Israel!

"The cipher declaration opens with an intimation of 490 years before the arrival of the Messiah, and continues as follows:

"*The lapse of years are nearing its filling. The relief of the Doom will come in spite of all. The people's right is nearing. The Period of the Blood-Debts and that of the Suppression will lose its power.*"

"It is then stated that Moses' tablets, the archives of the Temple, the Ark of the Covenant and 'the Chair of Grace between two cherubims of fine gold,' 'the insignias Urim and Thummim with two rubies of extraordinary size surrounded by a multitude of other precious stones,' the 'written archives of the earliest period of the Jews' till about B.C. 600, 'the great treasures of the Temple, gold and silver vessels, coined gold, and precious stones of every description' were all *'concealed beneath the earth in a dry-room in connection with which is a series of water-tunnels.'*

"The secret declaration goes on to give the most complete details of how the treasure may be reached. It is stated that there are three entrances, one of which is impossible as it is inaccessible, being closed up by masonry in a labyrinth of caves; the second is also too difficult. But the third is accessible by draining the water and will not present much difficulty.

"The cipher continuing, declares:

"The tablets shall remain in their hiding-place till the arrival of the Messiah, who alone may open their place of concealment, in order that He may furnish proof of the faith, and if necessary the treasure shall provide a war fund when the Messiah conquers the world and establishes his residence in Jerusalem."

"The cipher concludes by declaring:

"Six curses, yea! sixty times six curses, shall be upon the head of any one who dare to attempt to violate the treasure-house."

"That the messages, each identical, run through both Ezekiel and Deuteronomy is indisputable, and I am quite ready to explain them, provided my secret is properly protected.

"Among the many curious and interesting features which go far to prove that the treasure is still lying undisturbed, I may perhaps indicate the Biblical fact that, after the Babylonian imprisonment, the tablets of Moses were never again exhibited in the Temple. Yet did not Nehemiah convince himself that they were intact and in good condition?

"We know that Nebuchadnezzar received certain vessels from the Temple at Jerusalem (Ezra, i, 7-11) but no mention is made of the tablets, of the Ark, or of any other of the things mentioned in the cipher!

"Again, when Titus destroyed Jerusalem he did not obtain the Ark. On the Arch of Triumph still existing in Rome are representations of the candlesticks, but there is no representation of the Ark.

"Through the whole prophecy of Ezekiel I can point out many evidences of the existence of the treasure.

"And, finally, it is extremely curious that the Crusaders searched actively for it, but mostly in the neighbourhood of Engeddin.

"Whether the treasure of Israel still exists or not, the cipher declaration stands out in black and white, one of the best known and most difficult of all the various modes used by the ancients for concealing messages.

"I claim that it is a most amazing discovery which must be of deepest interest to the whole civilised world, and should be at once investigated. I have not, of course, space to give complete Biblical references, etc. These I will supply later on, if necessary.

"Any Jew who may be consulted will no doubt scorn the idea of the existence of the treasure. He will do so because he will argue that no cipher can exist in a book inspired. Again, he may declare that all the treasure was all carried off to Babylon. This is, I maintain, disproved by historical facts.

"Again, there may be considerable argument as to whether the Books of Ezekiel and of Deuteronomy were written about the same period. According to the latest theory, Deuteronomy was, written before Ezekiel, nevertheless this discovery of the same cipher record in both now conclusively proves that they were written at very nearly the same time.

"Further, I am aware of the Talmudic tradition which states that the treasures I have enumerated, with the addition of Aaron's staff, the pot of manna and the flask of anointing oil, are hidden beneath the Temple Mount. But the cipher in question shows plainly that they are not concealed upon the site of the Temple, which is now occupied by the Mosque of Omar, but at some considerable distance away.

"*The Key.*

"As regards the key to the cipher and the manner in which to decipher it, I have, believing my existence to be now short-lived—for alas! I am suffering from a disease that I am told is incurable—placed the key, with such directions as are necessary to read it, in a place where it will remain hidden until such time as I have arranged with a capitalist or syndicate of financiers to despatch an expedition to secretly purchase the land in question and excavate for the holy relics. To them alone it will be revealed.

"The key, which will disclose a statement that must cause the whole world to be surprised and thrilled, is divided into two parts, the one useless without the other. One part now lies in one city and another in a second. Therefore, for any person to attempt to discover the truth without first entering into business relations with me will be utterly impossible. And even if both keys were illegally obtained, the requisite knowledge could not then be ascertained without a third direction, that can be supplied by myself alone.

"If I live, then I hope to search and recover the sacred objects. If, however, Providence wills my death ere my task is done, none shall complete it; for none shall ever profit by the secret which the Unseen Power has revealed unto us, a statement of which I have herein written and signed by my own hand.

"(Signed) Peter Holmboe, *Professor of Hebrew.*"

The following note, with the impression of a rubber stamp, was appended in German:

"Sworn before me, Karl Weizel, notary public at 38, Neuer Junugferustieg, in the Free City of Hamburg, on the eighth of July, One thousand Nine hundred and Seven."

Chapter Twenty Three
His Ugliness at Pembridge Gardens

An hour later the Doctor called upon Frank Farquhar in Half Moon Street, and excitedly showed him the precious copy of the document which "Red Mullet" had secured for him.

Frank was highly interested, of course, but refused to accompany the hunchback to Pembridge Gardens. As his reason, he gave that he had a directors' meeting down in Fleet Street which he was bound to attend. Sir George was absent and he was therefore compelled to be in his place. The truth was that he had no desire to meet Gwen.

The girl had written him several pitiful and reproachful letters during the past fortnight, but to these he had made no response, except by one brief note in which he had repeated his very pointed question.

"No, Doctor," he said, "go yourself to Pembridge Gardens. The Professor will, I'm sure, be delighted to meet you, and you can discuss the matter thoroughly with him. I'll see him this evening."

Therefore Diamond had taken a cab out to Notting Hill Gate, and on inquiring for Griffin and giving his name, was shown at once upstairs to the study.

The Professor, with his usual courtesy, expressed his pleasure at the meeting, though if the truth were told he had not expected to see a man of the little Doctor's extreme ugliness. Then, when his visitor produced the precious copy of the dead man's manuscript, the great scholar sat down and breathlessly read it through from end to end.

"This is exactly what I surmised from the burnt fragments," he remarked, taking off his glasses as he turned to where the Doctor was sitting. "But the great and fascinating problem we have to solve is the whereabouts of the two keys to the cipher. One thing seems clear from the document, namely, that the dead man was Holmboe, the discoverer of the hidden secret."

"Exactly. He knew the uncertainty of his life. Indeed he told me so when he had his first attack," replied the little man, "the initials 'P.H.' were also upon his clothing."

"He told you he was a Dane. But in all probability he was a Russian or a Finn," remarked Griffin slowly turning over the leaves of a reference book before him. "Yes—here he is—Peter Holmboe, Professor of Hebrew at St. Petersburg, University, appointed four years ago. He apparently occupied a very high post for so young a man. He made the declaration in Hamburg, I see, therefore he had, no doubt, resigned his professorship in order to devote his time to finding capital to exploit the remarkable secret he had discovered."

"Yes. But what's the use of the secret without the key to the cipher?" queried the Doctor.

"None whatever. We must work to discover the key," Griffin replied. "If I close study, discover the key myself."

"Farquhar's journey to Copenhagen was utterly fruitless. We were led there upon a wild goose chase," the Doctor said. "The unfortunate fact is that others are also in search of the secret."

"I am aware of that. But how did you discover it?"

"I was told by my friend—the man who secured for me this copy—an old friend named Mullet. He knows more than he will tell me!"

While the Doctor was speaking, Gwen had opened the door and entered the room.

She heard the visitor utter the name of her protector, and became instantly interested.

"This is Doctor Diamond, dear," explained her father. "You have heard Mr Farquhar speak of him."

The little Doctor jumped to his feet and bowed, while the girl, in dark skirt and clean white blouse, graciously acknowledged his greeting.

She was anxious to learn what connection this dwarfed man could have with her mysterious protector.

"I heard you speak of a Mr Mullet, Doctor," she remarked. "Is that a man known as 'Red Mullet'?"

"Yes, Miss Griffin. He is a friend of mine."

"Or rather you are a great friend of his, I have heard—eh?"

"Then you know him!" exclaimed the Doctor, much surprised. "You met him abroad, I suppose?" The girl did not reply. She was puzzled at the curious connection between the red-haired man who had been her janitor and the ugly little Doctor who was Frank's friend.

"I know him," she said at last. "And being a friend of yours, he is a friend of ours."

"That's so," declared the Doctor, laughing. "Some people say ill things of him, but I have known him for some years, and he has always acted straight and honourably towards me."

"Well," exclaimed the Professor with some impatience. "Leave us, child. We want to get on with the examination of this paper which Doctor Diamond has just brought me."

"Does it concern the Treasure of Israel, dad?" inquired the girl, walking up to his table.

"Yes, dear. It is a copy of the complete document, so you may imagine how deeply I'm interested in it."

"Has Frank seen it?" she asked quickly, to which the Doctor replied in the affirmative.

Then when the girl had, with some reluctance, left them together, they resumed their discussion.

"We can discover nothing tangible without a knowledge of the cipher," remarked Griffin very gravely. "And in my belief, though it is here stated that the key is concealed in two separate cities, at the time of Holmboe's death he had it in his possession. That was a portion of it which you rescued—the one folio in manuscript. The typewritten document was evidently prepared to place before a financier with a view to the equipment of an expedition to Palestine. But the additional manuscript was evidently a record of the cipher, together with its key. Have you a copy of it?"

"Yes," replied the Doctor, taking from his breast-pocket some papers from among which he took a copy he had made in his own handwriting. "As far as I could judge, the manuscript of which this is one folio, consisted of about seven folios. I recollect quite well noticing, as I placed it in the stove, that certain characters in Hebrew were written upon it."

"Well," exclaimed Griffin, spreading the copy of the half-destroyed leaf before him, "that the cipher is a numerical one is quite apparent. It seems that it is based upon the wâw sign, or sixth letter of the Hebrew alphabet. Six is the sign of evil. Nevertheless I have turned up the reference to Ezekiel, xli, 23, but cannot find anything unusual in the Hebrew text."

"Because we do not possess the key," remarked the hunchback with a sigh.

"Admitted. But we have the basis of the calculation—the regular occurrence of the letter 'w' or 'v' in the text. For days, nay, weeks, I have been trying to solve that problem, using each of the known cabalistic ciphers of the ancients, but without the slightest success."

"It is an unknown cipher, without a doubt—even though you recognise the basis."

"Numerical ciphers are always most difficult," Griffin declared. "Yet was it not Edgar Allen Poe who declared that human ingenuity could not invent a cipher which human ingenuity could not solve. I have tried my calculations upon the earliest known text, that preserved in St. Petersburg—but in vain."

"What do you think of the dead man's statement that the key is divided into two parts—one portion being concealed in each city?"

"I don't accept that as genuine," declared the Professor. "I regard it as a mere embellishment of facts, in order to prevent any one from trying to unriddle the message. The unfortunate man ordered you to destroy the directions for reading the message, together with the statement itself."

"I rather wish I had disobeyed," remarked the Doctor with a grin. "The fact that it was in manuscript and not in typing shows that he would not trust any one with sight of it."

"Which goes far to prove the truth of my argument. There is a key number, depend upon it. When once you have that, and we ascertain at what point to start, then the secret record will soon be revealed."

"But how can we obtain it—that's the question," the Doctor said. "I would like to know how far the inquiries of our enemies have advanced. This copy was obtained from the complete copy in their possession."

"Who are our enemies? Do you know them?" asked the Professor, starting forward quickly.

"No. My friend, though he had supplied me with this, refuses all information concerning them, except to say that they are both powerful and wealthy."

"What do they know concerning the key?"

"Not so much as ourselves. They do not possess even the few words concerning it that we do."

"But will not your friend divulge the identity of our enemies?" asked Griffin, "not if we take him into partnership with us, and allow him to share in the huge profits which must accrue if anything is actually recovered?"

"I thought that your opinion upon the whole story was a negative one," remarked the Doctor with a strangely wily look.

The Professor, bent upon writing a learned article in the *Contemporary*, giving a story that should startle the world, held his breath for a moment. But only for a single instant.

"Well," he answered without hesitation, "at first I was, it is true, inclined to regard it as an amazing piece of fiction, but after certain researches and study I have now come to the conclusion that there may be more truth in it than would at first appear. I, of course, regard it from a scholar's point of view, and not from that of a financier."

"I believe in money," declared the ugly little man frankly. "It should be put forward, when ripe, as a sound financial proposition—just as, no doubt, its discoverer, Peter Holmboe, intended to put it forward."

"Then if so, why will not your friend Mullet join forces with us? It would surely be to his advantage!"

"Because he's tied to the other side."

"If it has not prevented him from supplying us in secret with this copy of the document, it surely would not prevent him assisting us further, and placing us upon our guard regarding the actions of our enemies. Have you no idea, Doctor, how these other people obtained a copy of Holmboe's statement? It surely could not have been kicking about the streets, having in view the fact that he was so careful to destroy it before his death."

"I haven't any idea how they obtained it, or even their names. My friend will tell me nothing."

"Who is this man Mullet? Have you any objection to telling me?"

"The man whom your daughter was discussing—the man known to his friends as 'Red Mullet'—is a cosmopolitan who lives mostly on the Continent, and, between ourselves, has the reputation of being an adventurer."

"And a friend of my daughter!" the elder man exclaimed in surprise. "She seems to meet very undesirable people sometimes. The latitude allowed to girls nowadays, Doctor, is very different from that of thirty years ago—eh?"

"What can we expect in this age of the 'New Woman' and the Suffragette?" laughed the other, holding up his hands.

"But could we not induce this Mr Mullet to help us—or at least to reveal to us in what direction our enemies are working? They have with them a very clever and ingenious scholar, of that I have already satisfied myself."

"Ah!" sighed Diamond. "If we only could get 'Red Mullet' with us. But I fear that there are certain circumstances which entirely preclude such an arrangement. At least, that is what I suspect."

"I wonder what my daughter can know of the man?" remarked Griffin, ignorant of the fact that Gwen's curiosity had got the better of her, or that the door being ajar she had heard the Doctor's statement.

"It certainly does seem a rather curious fact that they are acquainted," remarked the Doctor. "But, Professor," he went on eagerly, "I suppose you now have no doubt that there is more in the remarkable story than mere surmise."

Griffin was again silent for a few moments.

"Providing that the sacred relics remain still hidden—and there certainly seems nothing against that belief, even though some have declared that Solomon's golden vessels were afterwards used in Persia—then we have, of course, precise knowledge of certain of them," he said with great deliberation. Opening the Hebrew-English Bible at 2 Chronicles, iv, 19, he said: "Listen to this as an example," and he read as follows:

"'And Solomon made all the vessels that *were for* the house of God, the golden altar also, and the tables whereon the shew-bread *was set*;

"'Moreover the candlesticks with their lamps, that they should burn after the manner before the oracle, of pure gold;

"'And the flowers, and the lamps, and the tongs, *made he of* gold, *and* that perfect gold;

"'And the snuffers, and the basons, and the spoons, and the censers, *of* pure gold; and the entry of the house, the inner doors thereof for the most holy *place*, and the doors of the house of the temple, *were* of gold.'

"Concerning the Ark of the Covenant, which the cipher says still lies hidden, we have in the next chapter, commencing at verse 7:

"'And the priests brought in the ark of the covenant of the Lord unto his place, to the oracle of the house, into the most holy *place, even* under the wings of the cherubim:

"'For the cherubim spread forth *their* wings over the place of the ark, and the cherubim covered the ark and the staves thereof above.

"'And they drew out the staves *of the ark* that the end of the staves were seen from the ark before the oracle, but they were not seen without. And there it is unto this day.

"'There was nothing in the ark save the two tables which Moses put *therein* at Horeb, when the Lord made *a covenant* with the children of Israel, when they came out of Egypt.'

"The gold, of course, came from the ancient Ophir," remarked the Doctor, "and curiously enough the site of this El Dorado has only recently been established by Dr Carl Peters as having been at Zimbabwe, and the surrounding region in south-eastern Mashonaland."

"Yes," remarked the Professor. "There is, I think, no question that Solomon obtained his gold from that district. The old workings are said by Hall and Neal to number seventy-five thousand, and hundreds of thousands of tons of gold ore must have been dug out during the Himyaritic era. The Kaffirs still call the place 'Fur.' and the Arabs 'Afur.' It was from there that Solomon's ships brought the four hundred and twenty talents of gold mentioned in 1 Kings, ix, 26-28, and in 2 Chronicles, viii, 17-18. Again, we are told that in one year Solomon obtained six hundred and sixty-six talents of gold—each talent being worth eleven thousand pounds of our money—from the same region, most of which was used in the manufacture of the vessels for the temple."

"Some of which we hope to recover, Professor," laughed the ugly little man.

"We certainly might," sighed the other, "if only we could discover the solution of this most fascinating yet tantalising problem."

Chapter Twenty Four
A Page in Piccadilly

A long, grey, hundred-horse-power racing motor-car with its two glaring head-lamps drew suddenly up in the falling darkness before the big house in Berkeley Square, and from it stepped Sir Felix Challas in his heavy fur coat, cap and goggles. He was a motor enthusiast, and declared that his runs on his high-power racer cleared the cobwebs from his brain, and braced up his nerves.

He had started forth soon after breakfast, lunched at the Mermaid at Wansford, eighty miles away up the Great North Road, and was now home again, just as darkness had set in.

He had sat beside his chauffeur in silence while being whirled along the great northern highway, for he always thought out the most ingenious of his schemes while travelling thus.

Ere he had ascended the steps of the house, the splendid car, which only a few weeks before had made a record on the Brooklands track, moved off to the well-appointed garage, where he kept his three other cars.

On entering his own luxurious little den on the left of the hall, he found Jim Jannaway comfortably ensconced before the fire, smoking one of his choicest cigars and with a whisky and soda at his elbow.

"Hulloa!" exclaimed Sir Felix surprised. "I thought you were on your way out to the East? You were to have left this morning, weren't you?" And he threw off his heavy coat and stood with his back to the fire.

"Yes. But I've remained, because I've discovered something," replied the other. "I've found out the reason why that girl Griffin got away."

"Oh! Why?" asked Challas quickly. "It was a great misfortune for us. She's evidently discovered who we are, and why we wanted the information."

"Well—he played us false."

"Who—Mullet?"

"Yes. The girl appealed to his honour, and all that, and he found out that she was a friend of that Doctor Diamond, the fellow who attended Holmboe before he died and got hold of a portion of his papers. This man, it appears, had befriended Mullet in some way—so he, like a fool, let her go."

"Fool—idiot!" cried Challas. "Then the brute's betrayed us!"

"Absolutely!"

"By letting the girl go, he's exposed us. Griffin now knows that we are working against him. And he is, according to old Erich, the only man we have to fear."

"Except that man Farquhar, partner with Sir George Gavin, the newspaper owner."

"Ah! I forgot him. But surely he doesn't count?"

"Yes, he does," protested Jannaway. "He's in love with the girl. Hence we must see that he turns his back upon her, or there may be further trouble. I foresee pretty awkward complications in that direction."

"Very well, my dear boy, all that I leave to you," answered Sir Felix, with a heavy, thoughtful look.

"But it does not lessen our danger. If we're not careful we'll lose the thing altogether," Jannaway pointed out. "I've been a full fortnight making careful investigations. The Doctor called on Griffin the day before yesterday, and what's more, the girl has written to Charlie, asking him to meet her."

"How have you found that out?"

Jim Jannaway smiled.

"No matter," he laughed. "Except that Laura, the parlour-maid at Pembridge, is a friend of mine. I took her to the Tivoli last Thursday. Told her I was a lawyer's clerk."

"By Jove, Jim," exclaimed the Baronet, "you're always ingenious when you've set your mind on worming out a secret."

"A little love costs nothing," laughed the nonchalant adventurer, "and very often does a lot."

"Well, we must know what's going on between them, that's quite plain," remarked Challas. "I never expected Charlie to give us away."

"Bah! he always was chicken-hearted where women were concerned. He must have been in love once, I fancy, and hasn't got over the attack yet."

"We must be very watchful, Jim."

"That's why I didn't leave for Constantinople, as you suggested," was the other's reply, as he tossed the end of his cigar into the fire and lazily rose from his comfortable chair. "My own idea, Felix, is that Charlie is growing far too scrupulous. One day we shall have him in a fit of remorse making some nasty confession or other, taking the consequences, and putting us both into a confounded hole. Think what it would mean for you!"

"By Jove, yes!" gasped the other, turning pale at the very suggestion of exposure. "We can't afford to risk that."

"I maintain that if Charlie lets the girl escape us and give us away, as he has done, then he'll do something worse before long," exclaimed the crafty man with a curious glance at the Baronet, whose back was at that moment turned to him.

Challas was silent. He clearly saw the drift of the man's argument.

"Well?" he asked at last, lowering his voice. "What do you suggest?"

"Suggest? Why there's only one course open, my dear fellow," replied the other, glancing apprehensively at the door. "Get rid of him while there's yet time."

"He might retaliate."

"Not if he's arrested over in France," Jannaway exclaimed. "The French police won't bother over any information that he may give concerning us. Your reputation stands too high. They'll only regard him as a type of gentlemanly blackmailer such as every wealthy man has to contend with. If we don't do that, then good-bye to all our hopes concerning Holmboe's secret," he added.

"I fear I must agree with you, Jim," said the other, very slowly. "He was a fool for not allowing you to force the truth from the girl. I had intended that she should assist us, and—"

"And by Heaven! she shall do so, even now, if you will only leave matters to me," interrupted the clever, good-looking adventurer, leaning his back easily against the table.

"I leave them entirely to you," the Baronet answered quickly. "Act just as you think fit, only remember there must be no exposure. I can't afford that!"

"The secret discovered by that fellow Holmboe shall be ours," declared Jim Jannaway, slowly and determinedly.

"It might be, if only Erich could discover the key to that infernal cipher. He told me yesterday that he suspected Professor Griffin had already solved the problem."

"If he has, then I'll compel the girl to obtain it for us. You understand!" he exclaimed quickly.

"Even though Charlie has become a weak fool, moved to penitence by some tub-thumping revivalist perhaps, I intend to carry through the scheme I devised. The secret of the treasure of Israel shall be ours, my dear Felix. You shall be the great benefactor to the Jewish race, and discover the sacred relics so long concealed."

"Benefactor!" echoed the red-faced man with a short dry laugh. "Oh yes, I'll show the Jews how I can repay them in their own coin. Only be careful—do, I beg of you. Charlie is not the man to take a blow lying down, you know."

"You ought to know me well enough to be fully aware that I never act without consideration," the younger man protested. "Jim Jannaway is no fool at a game of checkmate, I think."

"There was that affair in Bordeaux," remarked the Baronet in a rather hard voice.

"You believe that Red Mullet knows something of that!" laughed Jim, admiring the fine diamond ring upon his finger. "Bah, he is in entire ignorance. It was an unfortunate incident, I admit. But under the circumstances couldn't be helped. But there—why need we recall it? You're so fond of dwelling upon unpleasant themes," he laughed. "You gave an extra five thousand to the Hospital Saturday Fund as a conscience-soother, didn't you?"

The Baronet turned upon his heel, and walked to his writing-table, whereon stood an electric lamp shaded with green silk. Then, after turning over some letters, he asked suddenly:

"When does that girl meet Charlie?"

"To-night."

"At her request?"

"Yes."

"Very well. I leave everything to you," Sir Felix said with a mysterious smile. "It would not be against our interests—if—well, if we had her in our hands again."

Jim Jannaway nodded. He understood the suggestion perfectly.

"Charlie ought, I think, to be sent back to the Continent, don't you agree?" he asked. "A timely warning that the police had learned of his return here, and he'd skip across by the next Channel service. Once over there, matters would be quite easy. The Leleu affair has never been cleared up, you know!" he added in a lower voice.

"I leave it entirely in your hands," declared the plutocrat whom the public believed to be a high-minded philanthropist. "Whatever you do must be on your own responsibility, recollect."

"But with your money. I want a couple of hundred."

"Ah! hard up again, Jim," sighed the other. But unlocking the safe opposite, the safe that contained the typed copy of the dead man's document, the Baronet took out some banknotes and handed them to his cat's-paw.

They were French notes. They were safer than English to give to persons like Jannaway, for the numbers could not be traced in cases of inquiries, while they could always be at once exchanged at any of the tourist offices. Sir Felix Challas, though compelled to employ men of the racing-tout stamp like Jim Jannaway, and unscrupulous concession-hunters like "Red Mullet," was ever upon his guard.

He trusted his men, but in "Red Mullet" he had confessed himself sadly disappointed.

"Revivalists and missionaries have a lot to answer for," was one of his pet phrases.

Jim Jannaway, slipping the notes into his pocket-book without troubling to count them, put on his smart overcoat and well-brushed silk hat, and wishing his employer an airy "good-evening," strolled out into the damp chilliness of Berkeley Square, where he hailed a hansom and drove away.

He had given the man an address in Knightsbridge, but as the cab was turning from the misty gloom of Berkeley Street into the brightness of Piccadilly several persons were waiting at the left-hand kerb in order to cross the road.

Among them he apparently recognised somebody, for in an instant he drew back and turned his head the other way.

Next second the cab had rounded the corner and was on its way along Piccadilly. Yet he knew that he had sat there for several moments in the full glare of the electric lights in front of the Ritz Hotel, and he felt convinced that he had been recognised by the very last person in the world that he desired to encounter.

Jannaway sat there breathless, staring straight before him into the yellow mist, his eyes glaring as though an apparition had arisen before him.

He tried to laugh away his fears. After all, it must be only fancy, he reflected. Somebody bearing a strange resemblance. It could not be she! Impossible. Utterly impossible.

But if it had been she in the flesh—if she had in that instant actually recognised him! What then!

He huddled himself in the corner of the cab, coward that he was, and shuddered at the recollections that crowded through his mind.

Would he ever have entered that hansom if he had known that it would carry him into such exposure—and worse?

But from Jim Jannaway's lips there fell a short bitter laugh. Was not his life made up by narrow "shaves?" Had not he been in hundreds of tight corners before, and with his wonderful tact and almost devilish cunning wriggled out of what would have meant ruin and imprisonment to any other man.

He had been a born adventurer, ever since his day as a stable-lad down at Newmarket, and he had the habit of laughing lightly at his own adventures, just as he was laughing now.

Would he have laughed, however, if he had but known how that chance encounter was to result?

Chapter Twenty Five
The Girl and the Man

Gwen Griffin had appointed half-past eight as the hour to meet her mysterious friend "Red Mullet" outside the "Tube" station at the corner of Queen's Road, Bayswater.

Immediately after dinner she had slipped up to her room, exchanging her silk blouse for a stuff one, and putting on her hat and fur jacket, went out, leaving her father alone in the study. He was—as now was his habit every evening—busy making those bewildering calculations, as he tested the various numerical ciphers upon the original Hebrew text of Ezekiel.

Through the damp misty night she hurried along the Bayswater Road, until she came within the zone of electricity around the station, where she saw the tall figure of her friend, wearing a heavy overcoat and dark green felt hat, awaiting her.

"This is really a most pleasant surprise, Miss Griffin," he cried cheerily, as he raised his hat, and took her little gloved hand. "But—well, we can't walk about the street in order to talk, can we? Why not drive to my rooms? You're not afraid of me now—are you?" he laughed.

"No, Mr Mullet," was her quick answer. "I trust you, because you have already proved yourself my good friend."

Truth to tell, however, she was not eager to go to that place where she had spent those anxious never-to-be-forgotten days, yet, as he suggested it, she could not very well refuse. One thing was quite certain, she was as safe in his hands as in her own home.

Therefore, he hailed a "taxi" from the rank across the way, and they at once drove in the direction of the Marble Arch.

Hardly, however, had they left the kerb, when a second "taxi" upon the rank, turned suddenly into the roadway and followed them. Within, lolling back and well-concealed in the darkness, sat Jim Jannaway.

A quarter of an hour later, Mullet let himself in with his latch-key, and the girl ascended those carpeted stairs she recollected so well.

In his own warm room Mullet stirred the fire until it blazed merrily, and then helping the girl off with her jacket, drew up a chair for her, taking one himself.

Her sweet innocent face, frankness of manner, and neatness of dress charmed him again, as it had when he had been forced against his will to keep her prisoner there. As he gazed across at her, he, careless adventurer that he had been for years, a man, with a dozen *aliases* and as many different abodes, recollected their strange *ménage*.

"Well," he said with a smile, "I was really delighted to get a note from you, Miss Griffin. You said in it that you wished to consult me. What about?"

"About several things, Mr Mullet," answered the girl, leaning her elbow upon the chair arm and looking straight in his face. "First, I am very unhappy. My position is an extremely uncomfortable one."

"How?"

"I have kept the promise of silence I gave you, and as a consequence Frank Farquhar, the man to whom I was engaged, has left me."

"Left you!" he echoed. "He suspects something wrong—eh?"

She nodded in the affirmative.

"That's bad, Miss Gwen—very bad!" he said with a changed countenance. "I know well what you must suffer, poor girl. You love him—eh?"

"Very dearly."

"And I am the cause of your estrangement," he remarked in a low sympathetic tone.

"Ah! it was not your fault, Mr Mullet," she cried, "I know that. Do not think that I am blaming you. The real blackguard is that red-faced man and his accomplice—the man who enticed me here on such a plausible pretext."

"I am also to blame. Miss Gwen," replied the big fellow with the bristly red moustache. "A deep game is being played, and, alas! I am compelled to be one of the players. It is being played against your father."

"I know that," she said. "I overheard Doctor Diamond telling my father how you had furnished him with a copy of that document describing the remarkable discovery of Professor Holmboe."

"Hush!" cried Mullet quickly, glancing at the door that stood slightly ajar. "There's nobody here, for the man who usually does for me is ill. Yet we'd better not discuss that action of mine, Miss Gwen. I only did it in order to repay in part a great service the little Doctor has rendered me. So," he added, "the Doctor took the copy to your father?"

"Yes. He had previously, through Mr Farquhar, consulted my father regarding the half-burnt fragments in his possession. But the other day he came, bearing the full document, which they discussed for a couple of hours or more. Now, Mr Mullet," she said, "you have been a very good and kind friend to me; therefore, I'm wondering if you would render us a further service?"

"Anything in my power I will most willingly do," replied the *blasé* man, seeking permission to light his cigarette.

"I first want to know," she exclaimed, "who is that blackguard who came here and demanded to know my father's business?"

"He's a person of whom you need have no concern," was his evasive reply.

"But he possesses a copy of the statement by Professor Holmboe?"

"He does. And he has instituted an active search in which three of the greatest scholars on the Continent are assisting, in order to ascertain the key to the cipher alleged by the Russian professor to exist in the prophecy of Ezekiel."

"But does he possess any manuscript of the Professor's relating to the cipher?" inquired the girl, eagerly.

"Ah! that I do not know," was his answer, "as far as I'm aware, he does not."

"Nothing definite has yet been ascertained, I suppose?"

"Nothing actually definite," he said. "But you can tell your father that Erich Haupt believes that at last he has struck the right line of inquiry."

"Haupt!" she repeated. "Who is he?"

"Your father will know him as the great professor of Leipzig. He is now staying at the Waldorf Hotel."

"But—well, Mr Mullet," she said with some hesitation. "Pardon me for saying so, but your friends seem a very unscrupulous and remarkable lot."

"And they are just as influential as they are unscrupulous," he laughed. Then growing serious next moment, he added with a sigh, "Ah! Miss Gwen, if you only knew all, you'd realise how very delighted I'd be to cut myself adrift from such a rascally association."

"Why don't you?" she asked, looking straight into his eyes. "This business of the treasure of Israel is surely a big and lucrative one. Why don't you leave them, and join my father, Mr Farquhar, and Doctor Diamond?"

"Well—shall I tell you the truth, Miss Griffin?" he asked, blowing a cloud of smoke from his lips as he contemplated the red end of his cigarette, "Because—well, because I dare not!"

"Dare not?"

"No," he said in a strained voice. "You see my part has not been an altogether blameless one. Need I explain more than to say that very often, for my very bread, I have to depend upon these persons who are working against your father."

The girl sighed, a painful expression crossing her brow.

"I wish I could help you, Mr Mullet," she said seriously. "Can't you possibly disassociate yourself from those scoundrels?"

He shook his head sadly.

The next instant she turned towards the door exclaiming:

"Hark! What was that? I heard a noise!"

"Nothing," he laughed. "The window of the next room is open a little, and the wind has blown the door to."

By this, she was reassured, even though she feared that the horrid red-faced man whose name he refused to tell her, might again reappear there as her inquisitor.

"It seems to me," she said, "that your friends, whoever they are, are dishonourable men whose bread you are compelled to eat. Surely you are in a position quite as wretched as I am?"

"Yes," he admitted. "But do me one favour, Miss Gwen. Never breathe to a soul that I've handed the copy of that document to the Doctor. If they knew that, they would never forgive me."

"I will remain silent, and I'll tell my father also to regard your action as confidential."

"Tell Mr Farquhar also," he urged.

"Ah!" sighed the girl. "Unfortunately I never see him now. He always meets my father at the Royal Societies Club—in order to avoid me."

"Then there is an actual breach between you?"

"Yes," she replied hoarsely. "He asked me certain questions, to which I could not reply without betraying you."

"And you risked your love for a worthless fellow like myself!"

"Well? And did you not risk your liberty for my sake?" she asked. "Did you not protect me from that blackguard who would have struck me because I refused to answer his questions?"

"Oh, that was nothing, Miss Gwen. I am thinking of you."

"Can you—will you assist my father?" she urged. "For myself I care nothing. But for my father's reputation—in order to enhance it, and also that through him Israel shall recover her sacred relics, I am ready to sacrifice anything. Disassociate yourself from these men, and assist us, Mr Mullet. Do."

"That is, alas! impossible," was his slow response. "It would mean my instant ruin. Would it not be better if I remained in the enemy's camp? Reflect for a moment."

"I wish you could meet my father," she said.

"Well, if he'd really like to see me, perhaps I might call upon him."

"He wants so much to know you. He was only saying so when we sat together last night after dinner."

"But you know, Miss Gwen, I'm not the sort of man that he would care to associate with."

"You have been my friend and protector, Mr Mullet, and surely that is sufficient I have always found you a gentleman—more so than many others who pose as honest men."

"Well," he said. "I don't pose. I've told you the simple truth."

"And I admire you for it. You once said you'd tell me all about your own little daughter."

He was silent for a moment, and she saw she had touched a tender chord in his memory.

"I'll tell you about little Aggie one day; not now, please, Miss Griffin."

"Well, tell me, then, why your friends are so antagonistic towards my father?"

"For several reasons. One is that the man you don't like—the one with the red-face—is a fierce hater of the Jewish race. His own avarice knows no bounds, and he has sworn to recover the treasure of Israel if it still exists and when recovered he will break up and melt the sacred vessels and destroy the sacred relies in order to exhibit to the Jews his malice and his power."

"Why, it would be disgraceful to desecrate such objects—even though he is a Gentile."

"Certainly. But your father's known leaning towards the Jews—his friendship with certain Rabbis, and the assistance he has once or twice rendered the Jewish community in London, have aroused the ire of this man, who is now his bitterest and most unscrupulous opponent."

"Then you can assist us, Mr Mullet—if you will."

"I fear that is impossible—certainly not openly," was his reply. "Personally, I would not lift a finger to help one whose fixed idea is despoliation and desecration of the sacred objects. My sympathies, my dear Miss Gwen, are entirely with you in your own unfortunate position, and with your father in his strenuous efforts to discover the key to this cipher, and afterwards place the expedition to Palestine upon a firm business basis, the most sacred treasures to be handed over to their rightful owners, the Jews."

"Why does this man, whose name you refuse to tell me, so hate the Jews?"

"Because, in certain of his huge financial dealings, they have actually ousted him by their shrewdness combined with honesty," he answered. "It has ever been, and still is, the accepted fashion to cast opprobrium upon the Jews. Yet, in my varied career, I have often found a Jew more honest than a Christian, and certainly he never hides dishonesty beneath a cloak of religion in which he does not believe, as do so many of your so-called Christians in the City."

"Then you are, like my father, an admirer of the Hebrew race?" she said, rather surprised.

"I am. In them as a class I find no cant or hypocrisy, no humbug of their clerical life as we have it, alas! apparent so often in our own churches, while among the Jews themselves a helpful hand is outstretched everywhere. They settle their own quarrels in their own courts of law and they adhere strictly to their religious teaching. Of course, there are good and bad Jews, as there are good and bad Christians. But with the anti-Jewish feeling so apparent everywhere throughout Europe, I have nothing in common."

"And because of that, Mr Mullet, you will assist us—won't you?" she urged.

The red-haired adventurer hesitated.

Chapter Twenty Six
In which a Desperate Game is Played

"To serve you, Miss Gwen, and to return a favour to my friend the Doctor, I'll keep you informed of what transpires on our side," he promised at last. "I'd like to call and see your father. When's the best time?"

"He will be pleased to see you at any time you may appoint! Why not ring me up on the telephone—if you are not able to make an appointment now?"

"Very well," he replied, "I will."

He saw that she wanted to ask him something, but was hesitating, as though not daring to put her question.

At last she asked:

"Mr Mullet, will you not reveal to me in confidence who it is who is thus working against us?"

"A person of highest reputation as far as financial reputation in London goes, and of enormous influence. He has at his service every power that wealth can command."

"And is he nameless?"

"Alas! he must be," was "Red Mullet's" decisive answer. The truth was that he feared to tell the girl, lest her surprise might lead her to expose the secret, which must at once reflect upon herself. He was glad that she had not recognised Challas from the many photographs which so constantly appeared in the illustrated papers.

A door somewhere in the small flat clicked again, but neither took any notice of it, attributing it to the wind from the open window.

They had no suspicion of an eavesdropper who had silently entered after them with the latch-key he possessed, and had just as silently left again, and crept down the stairs.

"Miss Gwen," exclaimed her friend a few moments later, "I would really urge you to have a care of yourself. Your enemies evidently mean mischief. You have, by a blackguardly ruse, been parted from the man you love—hence you are defenceless."

"Except for you—my true friend."

"I may have to leave London suddenly, while at any moment, you may, if you are not careful, fall again into the net they will, no doubt, spread and cleverly conceal. They fear your father and his friends, and from him will demand a price for you—a price for your honour, most likely."

"What do you mean?" she cried, starting, and staring at him.

"I am compelled to speak frankly, Miss Gwen; please forgive me," he said. "I know these men, remember. I know they will hesitate at nothing in order to gain their dastardly ends. They will compel your father to pay the price—and it will be the relinquishing of the struggle, and the leaving of it to them."

"We will never relinquish it!" declared the girl. "But do have a care of yourself," urged the man with the bristly moustache in deep earnestness. "If you again fall into the hands of these two men, you will not, I fear, escape without disaster."

"I know that, alas! only too well. I owe everything to your kindness and the pity you had for me. How can I ever sufficiently repay you?"

"You are now repairing me—repaying me with all you love most dearly. Your silence has cost you your lover."

She sighed, and hot tears rose to her splendid eyes. He was quick to notice her sudden change, and deftly turned the conversation into a different channel.

Then, when he had smoked another cigarette, chatting the while, he reminded her to tell her father of Erich Haupt, and to say that he, "Red Mullet", would call on the following day.

At last they descended together into the street, and at the corner of Oxford Street entered into a taxi-cab in which they drove back to Notting Hill Gate station.

There he raised his hat as she descended and hurried across into Pembridge Gardens, while he gave the man directions to return to his own chambers.

"By Jove!" he exclaimed, aloud, as they went along the Bayswater Road with the horn "honking."

"The whole situation is now a terribly complicated one. To throw in my lot with the Professor and his daughter would mean a 'stretch' for me, without a doubt. Challas is vindictive, because I allowed her to escape from his infernal clutches. He meant to serve her the same as he did that poor young German girl! Hang me! I may be an outsider, but I'm not going to stand by and see another woman fall a victim. Now what is the best game to play in the interests of Griffin and Diamond? Stand by, watch old Erich, and if he gets hold of anything tangible, give it to them at once. That's the only way that I can see. Yet—yet I may already be suspected of playing a double game—and if I am, it means that I'll be given away to the police at the first opportunity. No," he added with great bitterness, "in this game Felix Challas and Jim Jannaway hold all the cards. Money talks here, and it does always," he sighed.

And he sat back in his cab in a deep reverie. Already he was tired of London, though he had not set foot in it for three years. He was too near Challas. When absent on the Continent, he simply obeyed orders, and led the easy-going life of the cosmopolitan concession-hunter, always well-dressed, always apparently flush of money, always merry and prosperous-looking, and always outwardly, at least, presenting the appearance of a gentleman.

Here, in London, however, he was simply the cat's-paw of an unscrupulous parvenu who cloaked his evil doings beneath the remarkable sanctity and generous philanthropy.

"It's a blackguardly shame that poor little Gwen, a smart little girl and yet sweet and innocent as a child, should be parted from her lover like this!" he went on, still murmuring to himself. "No doubt this man Farquhar, whoever he is, doubts her. I'd do the same if the girl to whom I was engaged ran away from home, stayed away a few days, and then on her return refused to give any account of herself. Frank Farquhar isn't a fool, and I admire him for that. I'm to blame for the whole thing," he added with a bitter imprecation, "because I'm a coward and fear nowadays to face the music. Yes," he went on, "Red Mullet is in fear of his enemies! It's no good denying it. Hitherto he's always defied them, even at the muzzle of a gun! But recently they've become just one too many for him!"

He paused and lit a cigarette. Then with a sudden gesture of despair he asked himself aloud: "How can I assist the little girl to get back her lover? Frank Farquhar is a good fellow, I've discovered. And he's devoted to her. How can I compel him to believe in her?"

When he entered his chambers, he flung himself again into the armchair in which Gwen had sat.

"It would be a cursed shame if ever the sacred relics of Israel fell into the hands of such a blackguardly hypocrite as Challas. What does he care for their antiquity, or their religious significance? Nothing. The gold he'd melt down and sell at its market value per ounce, while the sacred objects of the Holy of Holies he would wantonly destroy, in face of the Jews and in order to laugh them to scorn. He shan't do that! By Heaven! he shan't. If the treasure is still there it shall be recovered by the Doctor and Griffin. I'll help them, and I'll still remain little Gwen's protector, even if it costs me my liberty to do so. Besides—"

His fierce words of determination were interrupted by a ring at the front door bell, and he went along the small hall to open it.

Jim Jannaway, in a light overcoat and crush hat, stood upon the mat.

"By Jove, Charlie!" he cried, "I'm jolly glad you're at home, old chap!"

"Why?" asked Mullet admitting him, and closing the door.

"Well, my dear fellow," he said in a breathless voice. "Something ugly has happened. You've been given away. Somebody has recognised that you're back in London!"

"Who?" gasped the red-haired man.

"Ah! that we don't know yet. The 'boss' has just sent me round to tell you to clear out at once—this instant!"

"H'm," remarked "Red Mullet." "Now that's deuced funny! Why didn't he keep his fears to himself, and let me take the consequences—eh?"

"Why, of course he wouldn't do that. He never lets us down—you surely know him too well for that," remarked the other.

"And he gives me the tip to clear out!" said Charlie Mullet. "It's really very kind and considerate of him."

"Well, my dear fellow. You don't seem to appreciate his kindness very much."

"I never appreciate the solicitude of my enemies, my dear Jim," he replied with perfect nonchalance. "It's my failing, I suppose."

Jannaway disregarded the sarcasm, and said:

"I was with him only half an hour ago round in Berkeley Square, and he told me to come along at once to you, and urge you to get away. He gave me these for you," and from his pocket he produced three thousand-franc notes.

"My dear Jim, both you and Felix seem to take me for a silly mug," laughed Red Mullet defiantly, "but you must please remember that I've been mug-hunting too long to be bluffed like this. The exemplary Baronet is desirous that I should leave London, and sends you, his emissary, to give me timely warning. Well, my dear boy. I want no warning," he said, for he was now on his mettle. "I shall simply remain here. If they send anybody from Scotland Yard—well, here's a drink for them," and he indicated the tantalus and glasses upon a side table.

"But surely you don't wish to remain here, and give the whole game away!" cried Jannaway, anxiously, standing in the centre of the room, his hat pushed slightly to the back of his head.

"What does it matter to me? I never move without just cause. I'm growing rather sceptical in my old age. What proof have I of this extraordinary *contretemps*?"

"What proof do you want? I'm here to warn you. Are you a fool, Charlie?"

"Yes. Until I know why this warning has been given me. How does Felix know?"

"He has a pal down at Scotland Yard—a sergeant whom he helped 'over the stile' a few years ago. He gives him valuable tips sometimes. One of them is that you've been recognised, and that the warrant has been given for your arrest to-night."

"Ah, my boy," replied "Red Mullet," lighting a fresh cigarette without turning a hair, "that's really interesting. And if I go down to Bow Street depend upon it I shan't go alone. So you can just go back to Berkeley Square, and tell Felix what I say."

"Why—what's the matter with you to-night, Charlie?" asked the other, looking at him in surprise.

What could the man know, he wondered? He seemed to scent the betrayal intended as soon as he was across the Channel.

"Matter?" he echoed. "Why, my dear Jim, I merely keep my eyes skinned, that's all."

"And you refuse to heed Felix's warning?"

"Yes, I'm very comfortable at home here—and here I mean to stay. Let the police come along if they like and I'll entertain them with a very interesting story. They re fond of hearing stories from men like myself, Jim."

"What the devil is the matter with you!" cried Jannaway, turning upon him fiercely.

"Nothing, I'm only surprised to find you such a fool, Jim. I thought better of you," was the other's calm response. "Do you know," he added, "you people who live in London want the moss scraped off you. We boys on the Continent are a lot sharper. We see the word danger written up, even when it's beyond the horizon and the detective is still off the map. You people here deliberately run your heads into nooses."

"How?"

"Well, you and Felix have arranged the little loop for yourselves in this affair, my dear boy. So do go home and sleep on it," he laughed merrily.

"You're a fool!" declared the other, turning from him impatiently.

"Of course. I'm a fool for not falling into the very clever trap which Sir Felix Challas and his sharp 'cat's-paw', Jim Jannaway, have laid for me," he answered, looking the fellow straight in the face.

"Bah! All this quarrel arises over a girl—a little chit of a girl who, after all, hasn't much of a reputation to lose."

"And to whom do you refer, pray?" asked Charlie, indignantly.

"To Griffin's girl, of course—the girl who was with you so long in these chambers, and whom you pretended to regard with such paternal care," he sneered.

"You cast a slur upon the poor girl who was your victim!" cried the red-haired man angrily.

"I cast no slur. I speak the truth."

"Then you're an accursed liar!" cried Mullet, angrily. "Having failed to entrap her, you come here to-night to try and have me! But your ruse is a little bit too thin! Let the police come and learn from me the truth concerning our beautiful Birthday Baronet! I'll welcome them. So first go back with my compliments to Berkeley Square."

"Then your intention, now you're in danger, is to give us away—eh?" exclaimed Jannaway, now flushed and excited. And in a second he had snatched up a heavy bronze ornament from the mantelshelf, intending to bring it down upon the other's head with a blow that must have crushed him.

In an instant, however, Mullet was on his guard. He was not a man to be taken by surprise.

"Now put that down at once, Jim, and clear out of my rooms," he cried, and Jannaway found himself looking down the plated barrel of a serviceable-looking Smith-Wesson revolver.

"Curse you!" cried the man, and he cast the ornament heavily upon the floor.

"My dear Jim," said the other, "the best place for you would really be on the Continent. You would learn wisdom, and would never attempt a bluff on a pal like this. You can't attempt a four-flush with me, you know. So first go back to the 'Birthday Money-Spinner' and tell him 'Red Mullet's' decision is to remain in London, and if necessary—to tell Scotland Yard the tale!"

"But—"

"Curse you! There are no buts!" cried Red Mullet, his eyes now flashing with anger while he held his revolver straight at his enemy's head. "Out of my rooms with you, or by Gad! I'll plug you! I see through your clever little game. Once I'm over there, then you'd send me to prison without the least compunction—because I let the girl slip through your blackguardly fingers. But no more gas. I mean business to-night. Out you go—and quick!"

"You wouldn't say this if I had a gun!" remarked Jannaway between his teeth.

"I care less for your gun than I do for you, my dear boy," laughed "Red Mullet;" "go back to Challas, and tell him that to-night he's tried to bluff the wrong man, and that he'll have to pay heavily for losing the game."

"You talk like an idiot."

"And you've acted as one. Out and begone!"

And the man who, when he had entered, believed that he held all the honours in the game, was compelled to walk slowly out beneath the threatening muzzle of the weapon, cowed and vanquished.

"And now, Jim Jannaway!" Mullet cried, when he was on the threshold, "send your detectives along as soon as you like, for I'll go to bed in an hour, and if they come afterwards I shan't admit them. Understand that? Good-night and bad luck to you!" And with a laugh he slammed the door.

Then he held his breath, and stood staring straight before him, wondering whether that bold action had not been his own undoing.

Chapter Twenty Seven
Explains Frank's Attitude

Christmas had passed, the New Year had been welcomed, its advent quickly forgotten, and London now lay dark and fog-bound in the yellow gloomy days of mid-January.

As far as Professor Griffin was concerned, little had occurred. His surprise when Gwen had told him of Erich Haupt being interested in the investigation of the secret was unbounded, and he had taken a cab at once to the Waldorf Hotel. He was anxious to meet the great German scholar, but was disappointed to learn that he had suddenly left the hotel on the previous night for the Continent.

Once again was he prevented from meeting the man who was working in opposition to him, even though he was now aware of his identity.

It puzzled him, as it also puzzled Diamond and Gwen, to know who was behind the German scholar. That there was some one was evident from what the girl had admitted. But his identity was still kept a profound secret.

Gwen had expected to be rung up on the telephone by Mullet, but having waited for three anxious days, found his number in the telephone directory and rang him up. She did so on four different occasions, but on each the response from the exchange was the same. "No reply."

What could have happened?

Was it possible that he could have left hurriedly for the Continent? She recollected how he had told her that perhaps he would be compelled, by force of circumstances, to leave London, and leave her alone. She wrote him a brief note, and posted it, hoping that it might be forwarded to him.

Then she had waited — for nearly four long weeks.

Doctor Diamond came up from Horsford on several occasions, but the interviews he had with the Professor carried them no further. The key to the cipher was still an enigma which none could solve.

Griffin's one thought was of Erich Haupt. He had returned to the Continent. Perhaps he was hot upon a solution of the tantalising problem.

In those four weeks, with the interval of a dreary Christmas spent alone with her father, nothing startling had occurred. The estrangement had driven Frank Farquhar to distraction. Jealousy had caused him to think ill of the girl he so dearly loved, and in order to try and forget, he had gone South for a week or so at Monte Carlo. But as soon as he stepped inside the Hotel de Paris, he had longed to be back again at Gwen's side in Pembridge Gardens. The smart women he saw in their white serge gowns, golden chatelaines, and picture hats, all nauseated him. Of the lilies of France, none were half so fair as his own sweet English rose. Christmas he had spent with a big and merry house-party up in the Highlands, but the gaiety of it all bored him to death, and at last, when he returned in the New Year, he had, after a severe struggle with himself, driven down to Notting Hill Gate, and again bowed over the soft little hand of the girl whose wonderful eyes held him in such complete fascination.

For Gwen, that evening was a never-to-be-forgotten one.

She was seated by the fire at the further end of the study buried in the big saddle-bag chair with a book, while her father was busily writing, when the maid announced the young man's arrival.

She held her breath. Her heart gave a great bound, and then stopped and she sat rigid, her face blanched, her hands grasping the arms of the chair.

She heard his well-known voice, and rising slowly, faced him without a word.

And he, without a word also, took her hand, bowing gallantly over it.

Then, with a half-timid look into her pretty face, he stammered:

"I—I've been wondering, Gwen, how you've been all this time. I've been away, first at Monte Carlo and afterwards up in Scotland. How did you spend your Christmas?"

"Well—it was not very exciting," she laughed, "was it, dad?"

"No, my dear," replied the old man, "I fear it was a very very dull time for you."

Her lover glanced at her, and she saw by the expression of his eyes that he was full of genuine regret. That absence had, indeed, caused both their hearts to yearn for each other. He had, alas! been too hasty, he declared within himself. Would she ever forgive him? Would she ever allow him to kiss her again upon the lips?

Before her father his greeting was, of necessity, a somewhat formal one; besides, he was compelled to sit and discuss with him the present situation, and ask his opinion as to the next move in the game.

"The possession of a complete copy of Holmboe's statement has carried us a good deal further. Professor," he said, "but how are we now to act?"

"I really don't know, my dear Farquhar," was the elder man's response, as he rubbed his big round glasses.

"I only wish this man Mullet would tell Diamond a little more," he sighed. "We ought to discover who is directing the opposition against us."

"That's just where we are so completely handicapped. We're handicapped in two directions," said the Professor. "First, we remain in ignorance of the identity of our enemy, and secondly we are at a loss to discover the key to the cipher. We now know the truth concerning the Russian's discovery, and naturally we are beckoned on to see what more may be added to the mental outfit of our religion and our civilisation, by recovering the sacred treasures that yet remain. The occasional excavations scattered through the last two centuries in Palestine, Egypt, Rome and Assyria, have shown but a fraction of all that has to be done. Such a prospect is most attractive, and if we could but find the key to the cipher the interest of the whole Jewish race would instantly be stimulated, and we should certainly not lack funds for the expedition, the purchase of the land in question, and the necessary excavations. It would be a great undertaking of international co-operation, but no loophole must be allowed for vandalism and wrecking, of which we have so much evidence in the past few centuries. Such wrecking is, alas! by no means unknown, even down to our day. The Department of Antiquities in Egypt, for instance, at the present moment, sells the right to dig up and destroy all the Roman buildings in Egypt at so much per thousand bricks removed by the speculators! We must allow no such sort of speculation with the treasures of Israel."

"I take it, Professor, that our opponents are anti-Semitics of the most pronounced type," said Farquhar. "At least, so the Doctor informs me. Once it is in their hand their chief object will be to destroy the sacred relics, and melt down the golden vessels. Diamond says, that according to his information, those working against us are rich, and have no need of gain. The whole of their energies are directed towards an anti-Semitic demonstration—one that would convulse the whole civilised world."

"We will not allow it, Farquhar!" cried the old Hebrew scholar, bringing his hand down heavily upon his writing-table. "I am not a Jew, but while it remains within my power I will never allow the sacred relics of Israel to be desecrated."

"If they exist," added Gwen from the depths of her armchair.

"They do exist!" exclaimed her father, "of that I now feel quite convinced. At first I was very sceptical, but I have spent many weeks in close and ardent study, and my first opinion is now greatly modified."

"And you anticipate that we shall one day gain a knowledge of the mode of reaching that cipher record?" asked Frank, eagerly.

"I fervently hope so," was the elder man's response. "I hope so in the interests of the Hebrew race. As soon as I write my article in the *Contemporary* or in the *Jewish Chronicle*, the world will instantly be agog."

"But until you have read the hidden message for yourself you will write nothing?" remarked Farquhar.

"Of course not. We must closely preserve the secret for the present. Not a soul must know, or Holmboe's discovery will most certainly get to the ears of some enterprising journalist. Why, we'd be having one of your papers, Frank, sending out an expedition in search of the Ark of the Covenant!" he laughed. "And that would surely be fatal."

Farquhar held his breath for a few seconds.

"Why fatal, Professor?" he asked, for it was at the bade of his head to suggest to Sir George the advisability of despatching an expedition when the time was ripe.

"Fatal to the scheme as well as to the newspaper," was the elder man's response. "Even you modern journalists cannot make money by exploiting sacred relics of such importance."

"No, but we could investigate for the benefit of the Hebrew race. We sorely would not lose prestige by that?"

"Yes, you would. No Jew, or even Christian for that matter, would ever believe that a newspaper defrayed the cost of an expedition out of pure regard for the interests of the Hebrew faith." He laughed. "The public know too well that a 'boom' means to a newspaper increased circulation, and, therefore, increased income. Before these days of the yellow journalism, the press was supposed to be above such ruses; but now the public receives the journalistic 'boom' with its tongue in its cheek."

"You're quite right, Professor, quite right!" remarked Frank, for the first time realising that to "work" the treasure of Israel as a "boom" for his group of newspapers and periodicals was impossible. "I've only regarded it from the business side, and not from the sentimental. I see now that any newspaper touching it would be treading dangerous ground, and might at once wound religious susceptibilities."

"I'm glad you've seen it in that light!" replied the old scholar, stroking his grey hair. "As far as I can discern, the best mode of procedure—providing of course, that we can discover the key number to the numerical cipher—is for me to write an article in the *Contemporary* with a view to obtaining the financial assistance of the Jewish community. I know the Jew well enough to be confident, that all, from the Jew pedlar in the East End to the family of Rothschild itself, would unite in assisting to discover the sacred treasures of the Temple." And for half an hour or so they chatted, until Frank was able to slip away with Gwen into the drawing-room where, without a single word, he clasped her in his arms passionately and kissed her upon the lips.

He held her closely pressed to his breast, as he stroked her soft hair tenderly, and looked into those wide-open, trustful eyes. Surely that frank expression of true and abiding love could not be feigned! There is, in a true woman's eyes, a love-look that cannot lie! He saw it, and was at once satisfied.

In a low voice he begged forgiveness for misjudging her, repeating his great and unbounded affection. She heard his quick strained voice, and listened to his heartfelt words, and then, unable to restrain her joy at his return, her head fell upon his shoulders, and she burst into tears.

She was his, she whispered, still his—and his alone.

And he held her sobbing in his strong arms, as his hand still stroked her hair and his lips again bent until they touched her fair white brow in fierce and passionate caress.

Chapter Twenty Eight
Describes certain Curious Events

Has it never struck you that this twentieth century of ours is the essential age of the very young girl?

Supreme to-day reigns the young woman between the age of—well say from sixteen to twenty—who dresses her hair with a parting and a pigtail, wears short skirts, displays a neat ankle, and persists in remaining in her teens. Grumpy old fossils tell us that this species is a product of an advanced state of civilisation which insists that everything must be new, from a dish of *pêches à la Melba* to the tint of that eternal hoarding in front of Buckingham Palace. One can only suppose that they are correct. Ours is a go-ahead age which scoffs at the horse, and pokes fun at the South-Eastern Railway, which forsakes Saturday concerts for football, yet delights in talking-machines.

Is it any wonder therefore that the statuesque beauty and the skittish matron of a year ago no longer finds herself in demand for supper-parties, Sandown or Henley? No, she must nowadays stand aside, and watch the reign of her little sister who dashes off from the theatre to the Savoy in a motor-brougham still wearing her ribbon bow on her pigtail, much as she did in the schoolroom.

The young of certain species of wild fowl are termed "flappers," and some irreverent and irascible old gentleman has applied that term to the go-ahead young miss of to-day. Though most women over twenty-one may attempt to disguise the fact, it is plain that the young girl just escaped from the schoolroom now reigns supreme. Her dynasty is at its zenith. She is the ruling factor of London life. Peers of the realm, foreign potentates, hard-bitten soldiers from the East, magnates from Park Lane all hurry to her beck and call. The girl in the pigtail and short skirt rides over them all roughshod. And what is the result of all this adulation upon the dimple-faced little girl herself? In the majority of cases, I fear it results in making her a stuck-up, *blasé* and conceited little prig, for she nowadays takes upon herself a glory and exalted position to which she is entirely unsuited, but which she has been taught to consider hers by right.

Gwen Griffin was a perfect type of the very young girl, courted, petted and flattered by all the men of her acquaintance. Having no mother to forbid her, she was fond of going motor-rides and fond of flirtation, but through it all she had, fortunately, never developed any of those objectionable traits so common in girls of her age. She had managed to remain quite simple, sweet and unaffected through it all, and six months before, when she had found the man she could honestly love, she had cut her male friends and entered upon life with all seriousness.

A week had gone by, and Frank had called every evening. Once he had taken her to dine at the Carlton, and on to the theatre afterwards, for now they had, by tacit though unspoken consent, agreed that all bygones should be bygones.

Often he felt himself wondering what had been the real cause of her mysterious absence from home, yet when such suspicions arose within him, he quickly put them aside. How could he possibly doubt her love?

The Doctor was back again at Horsford, leading the same rural uneventful life as before, but daily studying everything that had any possible bearing upon the assertion of Professor Holmboe.

Frank came down to visit Lady Gavin one day, and as a matter of course was very soon seated with the ugly little man in his cottage home.

Diamond, over a cigar, was relating the result of his most recent studies, and lamenting that they were still as far from obtaining a knowledge of the actual cipher as ever.

"Yes," murmured the young man with a sigh, "I'm much afraid that old Haupt will get ahead of us—even if he has not already done so. How is it that you can't get your friend Mullet to assist us further?"

"He has left London, I believe. He disappeared quite suddenly from his rooms, and curiously enough, has sent me no word."

"You hinted once that he's a 'crook.' If so, he may have fled on account of awkward police inquiries—eh?"

"Most likely. Yet it's strange that he hasn't sent me news of his whereabouts."

"Not at all, my dear Doctor," responded the other. "If a man is in hiding, it isn't likely that he's going to give away his place of concealment, is it?"

"But he trusts me—trusts me implicitly," declared Diamond.

"That may be so. But he doesn't trust other persons into whose hands his letter might possibly fall. The police have a nasty habit of watching the correspondence of the friend of the man wanted, you know."

"Perhaps you're right, Mr Farquhar," said the Doctor, with a heavy expression upon his broad brow. "The more I study the problem of the treasure of Israel, the more bewildered I become," he went on. "Now as regards the original of the Old Testament, it is not all written in Hebrew, I find. Certain parts are in Aramaic, often erroneously called Chaldee. (From Daniel, ii, 4, to vii, 28; Ezra iv, 8, to vi, 18; vii, 11 to 26; and Jeremiah x and xi.) Again, we have a difficulty to face which even Professor Griffin had never yet mentioned to me. It is this. On the very lowest estimate, the Old Testament must represent a literary activity of fully a thousand years, and therefore it is but reasonable to suppose that the language of the earlier works would be considerably different from that of the later; while, on other grounds, the possible existence of local dialects might be expected to show itself in diversity of diction among the various books. But, curiously enough—though I am handicapped by not being acquainted with the Hebrew tongue—all the authorities I have consulted agree that neither of those surmises find much verification in our extant Hebrew text."

"I've always understood that," Frank remarked. "Yes. I've been reading deeply, Mr Farquhar. Curiously enough the most ancient documents and the youngest are remarkably similar in the general cast of their language, and certainly show nothing corresponding in the difference between Homer and Plato, or Chaucer and Shakespeare. Though we know that the Ephraimites could not give the proper (Gileadite) sound of the letter *shin* in *Shibboleth*, (Judges, xii 8) yet all attempts to distinguish dialects in our extant books have failed."

"I think," said Farquhar, "that such remarkable uniformity, while testifying to the comparative stability of the language, is in part to be explained by the hypothesis of a continuous process of revision and perhaps modernising of the documents, which may have gone on until well into our era."

"Exactly," remarked the Doctor, "yet in spite of this levelling tendency there appear to remain certain diversities, particularly in the vocabulary, which have not been eliminated, and these serve to distinguish two great periods in the history of the language, sometimes called the gold and silver ages, respectively, roughly separated by the return from the exile. To the former belong, without doubt, the older strata in the Hexateuch, and the greater prophets; to the latter, almost as indubitably, Chronicles, Ezra, Nehemiah, Ecclesiastes and Daniel, all of which use a considerable mixture of Aramaic of Persian words. Then, the great question for us is whether the ancient text of Ezekiel preserved in St. Petersburg is an original, or a modernised version. If the latter, much of the cipher, perhaps all, must have been destroyed!"

"I quite follow your argument, my dear Diamond," Farquhar replied, "but has not Holmboe established to his own satisfaction that the cipher still exists in the manuscript in question? He has, therefore, proved it to be an exact copy of the original—if not the original itself."

"Experts all agree that it cannot be the original," declared the Doctor. "It is quite true that Holmboe alleges that the cipher exists, and gives quotations from it. Yet now that I have been reading deeply I have become a trifle sceptical. I'm anxious for Griffin to discover the key number, and prove it for himself. Personally, I entertain some doubt about the present text of Ezekiel being the actual text of the prophet."

"That can only be proved by the test of the cipher," was Farquhar's reply. "If you accept any part of the dead man's declaration, you must surely accept the whole."

"I have all along accepted the whole—just as Griffin accepts it."

"Then why entertain any doubt in this direction? The Professor has never mentioned it, which shows us that there is no need why we should query it."

"Yes, but may not the fact of the text having been modernised be the reason of Griffin's non-success in discovering the key number?"

"Holmboe discovered it," remarked the other, "therefore, I see no reason why Griffin—with Holmboe's statement before him and in addition that scrap of manuscript which evidently relates to the key—should not be equally successful."

"Ah!" sighed the ugly little man whose fidgety movements showed his increasing anxiety, "if we could but know what the old German was doing—or in what direction he is working."

"He's not back at his own home. I received a telegram from our Leipzig correspondent only yesterday. His whereabouts is just as mysterious as that of your friend Mullet. By the way—would he never tell you who were the principals in this opposition to us?"

"No, he has always steadily refused."

"Some shady characters, perhaps—men whom he is compelled to shield, eh?"

"I think so," answered the Doctor. "I wanted him to stand in with us, but he's a strange fellow, for though he promised to help me, he refused to participate in any part of the profit."

"Has some compunction in betraying his friends, evidently," laughed Frank. "I'm very anxious to meet him. He promised to call on Griffin, but has never done so."

"He's been put on his guard, and cleared out, that's my candid opinion. 'Red Mullet' is a splendid fellow, but a very slippery customer, as the police know too well. He's probably half-way across the world by this time. He's a very rapid traveller. I've sometimes had letters from him from a dozen different cities in as many days."

"To move rapidly is always incumbent upon the adventurer, if he is to be successful in eluding awkward inquiry. He never writes to the child, I suppose?" Frank asked, as Aggie at that moment passed the window.

"Oh, yes, very often. But he always encloses her letter to me. He never gives his address to her, for fear, I suppose, that it should fall into other hands. I wired to his rooms in Paris a week ago, but, as yet, have received no response. His rooms in London are closed. I was up there on Thursday. Why he keeps them on when he's away for years at a time, I can never understand."

"Probably sub-lets them, as so many fellows do," Farquhar suggested, "yet it's unfortunate we can't get into touch with him."

"Miss Griffin is acquainted with him—I wonder if she knows his whereabouts?" remarked Diamond quite innocently.

"She knows him!" Frank echoed in surprise. "Are you quite sure of that?"

"Quite. She told me so."

"How could she know a man who is admittedly an outsider?" asked Frank.

"My dear Mr Farquhar," he laughed, "your modern girl makes many undesirable acquaintances, especially a pretty go-ahead girl of Miss Griffin's type."

Frank bit his lip. This friendship of Gwen's with the man Mullet annoyed him. What could she possibly know of such a man? He resolved to speak to her about it, and make inquiry into the circumstances of their acquaintance.

He must warn her to have nothing to do with a man of such evil reputation, he thought. Little did he dream that this very man whom the world denounced as an outsider had stood the girl's best and most devoted friend.

He walked back along the village street to the Manor, and dressed for dinner, his mind full of dark forebodings.

What would be the end? What could it be, except triumph for those enemies, the very names of whom were, with such tantalising persistency, withheld.

Half an hour after he had left the Doctor's cottage the village telegraph-boy handed Aggie a message which she at once carried to her foster-father.

He tore it open, started, read it through several times, and then placed it carefully in the flames.

Then he hurriedly put on his boots, overcoat and hat, and went forth, explaining to his wife that he was suddenly called on urgent business to London.

That evening, just before ten o'clock, a short dark figure could have been seen slinking along by the railings of Berkeley Square, indistinct in the night mist, which, with the dusk, had settled over London.

The man, though he moved constantly up and down to keep himself warm, kept an alert and watchful eye upon the big sombre-looking mansion opposite—the residence, as almost any passer-by would have told the stranger, of Sir Felix Challas, the anti-Semitic philanthropist.

Over the semicircular fanlight a light burned brightly, but the inner shutters of the ground floor rooms were closed, while the drawing-room above was lighted.

Time after time the silent watcher passed and repassed the house, taking in every detail with apparent curiosity, yet ever anxious and ever expectant.

The constable standing at the corner of Hill Street eyed the dwarfed man with some suspicion, but on winter nights the London streets, even in the West End, abound with homeless loafers.

The Doctor, wearing a shabby overcoat several sizes too large for him and a felt hat much battered and the worse for wear, watched vigilantly and with much patience.

He saw a taxi-cab drive up before Sir Felix's and a rather tall, good-looking man in opera hat and fur-lined coat descend and enter the house. The cab waited and ten minutes later the visitor—Jim Jannaway it was—was bowed out by the grave-faced old butler, and giving the man directions, was whirled away into Mount Street, out of sight.

"I suppose that's the fellow!" murmured the ugly little man beneath his breath, as he stood back in the darkness against the railings opposite. Hardly had the words escaped his lips when a hansom came from the direction of Berkeley Street, and pulling up, an old, rather feeble white-bearded man got out, paid the driver, and ascending the steps rang the bell.

He was admitted without question, and the door was closed behind him.

"Erich Haupt, without a doubt," remarked the Doctor aloud. "Why has he returned to London? Has he made a further discovery, I wonder. The description of him is exact."

For half an hour he waited, wondering what was happening within that great mansion.

Then Jim Jannaway suddenly returned, dismissed his "taxi," and was admitted. All that coming and going showed that something was in the wind.

"Red Mullet" had given him due warning from his hiding-place. His telegram had been despatched from Meopham, which he had discovered was a pleasant Kentish village, not far from Gravesend. He was evidently in concealment there.

Just before eleven o'clock another hansom turning out of Hill Street in the mist, pulled up before the house, and he watched a dark figure alight from it.

Notwithstanding the dim light he recognised the visitor in an instant. The figure was that of a tall, dark-eyed girl.

"Good Heavens!" he gasped, staring across the road, rigid. "Mullet was right! He was not mistaken after all! By Jove—then I know the truth! We are betrayed into the hands of our enemy!"

And as the Doctor stood there he was entirely unaware that he, in turn, was being watched from the opposite pavement—and by a woman!

Chapter Twenty Nine
Which Solves a Problem

That day had been an eventful one at Pembridge Gardens. Indeed, the event of the great scholar, Arminger Griffin's life had occurred.

It happened in this way. The January morning had been so dark that he had been compelled to use the electric light upon his study table, and during the whole morning he had been engaged upon that same futile task—the problem of the cipher.

With the Hebrew text of Ezekiel open before him, and sheets of manuscript paper upon the blotting-pad, he had been absorbed for hours in his cabalistic calculations which, to the uninitiated, would convey nothing. They appeared to be elementary sums of addition and subtraction—sums consisting of ordinary numericals combined with letters of the Hebrew alphabet.

And curiously enough, in a back bedroom in the Waldorf Hotel, in Aldwych, the white-bearded old German, Erich Haupt, who only the previous night had returned from the Continent, sat making almost similar calculations. Before him also he had a copy of the Hebrew Bible, and was taking sentences haphazard from Ezekiel xix, the lamentation for the Princes of Israel under the parable of the lion's whelps taken in a pit.

Early in the morning he had rung up Sir Felix on the telephone beside the bed, announcing his arrival, and obtaining an appointment for later in the day.

Both scholars, unknown to each other, were busy upon the same problem, each hoping for success and triumph over the other.

Through weeks and weeks Griffin, seated in his big, silent, rather gloomy study, had tried and tried again, yet always in vain. He was a calm, patient man, knowing well that in cryptography the first element towards success is utmost patience.

It was noon. The fog had not lifted, and Bayswater was plunged in the semi-darkness of the London "pea-souper."

Gwen was out. She was trying on a new evening frock at Whitley's—a dainty creation in pale blue chiffon ordered specially for a dance which Lady Duddington was giving in Grosvenor Street in a few days' time.

Alone, his grey head bent on the zone of shaded light upon the big writing-table, the Professor had ever since breakfast time been putting a new cipher theory to the test.

All the thirty odd numerical ciphers known to the ancients he had applied to certain chapters of the Book of Ezekiel, but each one in vain. The result was mere chaos. The ancients employed numerous methods of cryptography besides the numerical cipher, among them being the use of superfluous words where the correspondents agreed that only some of the words, at equal distances apart, was necessary to form the message; by misplaced words; by vertical and diagonal reading; by artificial word grouping; by transposing the letters; by substitution of letters; or by counterpart tabulations with changes at every letter in the message, according to a pre-arranged plan.

All these, however, he had, in face of the reading of the scrap of the manuscript of the dead discover of the secret, long ago dismissed.

He held the firm opinion—perhaps formed on account of that crumpled paper found at the Bodleian—that the cipher was a numerical one, and based upon some variation of the numerical value of the "wâw" sign, or the number six.

He now fully recognised how very cleverly old Erich Haupt had endeavoured to put him off the scent. The German was a very crafty old fellow, whose several discoveries, though not altogether new, had evoked considerable interest in academic circles in Europe. He was author of several learned studies in the Hebrew text, as well as the renowned work upon the Messianic Prophecies, and without a doubt now that he had possessed himself of the dead professor's discovery he intended to take all the credit to himself. Indeed it was his intention to pose as the actual discoverer.

Continuing his work in silence and without interruption Griffin had been making a long and elaborate calculation when, very soon after the little Sheraton clock upon the mantelshelf had chimed noon, he started up with a cry of surprise and stared across at the long old-fashioned bookcase opposite.

Next moment his head was bent to the paper before him, as he rapidly traced numerals and Hebrew characters, for he wrote the ancient language as swiftly as he wrote English.

"Yes!" he whispered, as though in fear of his own voice. "It actually bears the test—the only one that has borne it through a whole sentence! Can it be possible that I have here the actual key?" For another half-hour he remained busy with his calculations, gradually evolving a Hebrew character after each calculation until he had written a line. Then aloud he read the Hebrew to himself, afterwards translating it into English thus:

"...the house of Togarmah, of the north quarters..."

The old man rose from his chair, pale and rigid, staring straight through the window at the yellow sky.

"At last!" he gasped to himself. "Success at last! Holmboe's secret is mine—*mine!*"

He was naturally a quiet man whom nothing could disturb, but now so excited had he become that his hand shook and trembled and he was unable to trace the Hebrew characters with any degree of accuracy.

He walked to the window, and looked out into the foggy road below.

He, Arminger Griffin, though Regius Professor, had, in the course of that brief hour, become the greatest Hebrew scholar in Europe, the man who would announce to the world the most interesting discovery of the age!

He gazed around that silent restful room, like a man in a dream. His success hardly seemed true. Where was Haupt, he wondered? Would his ingenuity and patience lead him to that same goal whereby he could read the hidden record?

Pausing at his table he recalculated the sum upon the sheet of paper. No. He had made no mistake. There was the decipher in black and white, quite clear and quite intelligible!

He stretched his arms above his head, and standing upon the hearthrug before the blaring fire, reflected deeply.

The declaration of the dead professor was true, after all. The cipher did exist in Ezekiel, therefore there was little doubt that the treasure of Israel would be discovered through his instrumentality.

Haupt fortunately did not possess any of that manuscript which was evidently a written explanation of the mode of deciphering the message.

Hence he would not be aware that the "wâw" sign formed the basis of calculation necessary. But he, Arminger Griffin, had elucidated a problem of which bygone generations of scholars had never dreamed, and Israel would, if the secret were duly kept, recover the sacred relics of her wonderful temple.

His face was blanched with suppressed excitement. How should he act?

After some pondering he resolved to make no announcement to Diamond or to Farquhar, both of whom he knew were away in the country, until he had made a complete decipher of the whole of the secret record.

He intended to launch the good news upon them as a thunderclap.

"They both regard me as a 'dry-as-dust' old fossil," he laughed to himself. "But they will soon realise that Arminger Griffin has patience and ability to solve one of the most intricate problems ever presented to any scholar. We can now openly defy our enemies—whoever they are. Before midnight I shall be in possession of the whole of the secret record contained in the book of the Prophet, and if I do not turn it to advantage it will not be my fault. That man Mullet evidently fears to call upon me. Ah! his friends little dream that I have solved the problem—that success now lies in my hands alone."

Crossing again to the table he slowly turned over the folios of the text of Ezekiel which he had been using, glancing at it here and there.

Then he touched the electric bell, and Laura, the tall, dark-haired parlour-maid, answered.

"Is Miss Gwen in?" he inquired.

"No, sir. She's not yet returned."

"When she comes, please say I wish to see her at once."

"Very well, sir," was the quiet response of the well-trained maid who, by the expression upon her master's face, instantly recognised that something unusual had occurred.

She glanced at him with a quick interest, and then retired, closing the door softly after her.

The Professor, reseating himself at his table, pushed his scanty grey hair off his brow, and again readjusting his big round spectacles settled down to continue his intensely interesting work of discovery.

"Holmboe says that the cipher exists in nine chapters," he remarked aloud to himself. "I wonder which of the forty-eight chapters he alludes to! Now let's see," he went on, slowly turning over the leaves of the Hebrew text, "the book of Ezekiel's prophecy is divided into several parts. The first contains chapters i-xxiv, which are prophecies relating to Israel and Judah, in which he foretells and justifies the fall of Jerusalem. The second is chapters xxv-xxxii, containing denunciations of the neighbouring nations; the third is chapters xxxiii-xxxix, which gives predictions of the restitution and union of Judah and Israel, and the last, chapter xl-xlviii, visions of the ideal theocracy and its institutions. Now the question is in which of those parts is hidden the record?"

The few words of the cipher which he had been able to read were continued in chapter xxiv, beginning at verse 6; "Wherefore thus saith the Lord God; Woe to the bloody city, to the pot whose scum is therein, and whose scum not gone out of it! bring it out piece by piece; let no lot fall upon it. For her blood is in the midst of her; she set it upon the top of a rock; she poured it not upon the ground, to cover it with dust," etc, down to the end of verse 27. If those twenty-two verses only contained eight words of the hidden record, then it was apparent that the Professor had a greater task before him than he imagined.

Gwen, in emerging from Whiteley's into Westbourne Grove, had met a young naval officer she knew. He was home on leave, therefore she had strolled leisurely with him down Queen's Road and along Bayswater Road, in preference to taking a cab. A couple of years before, when she was still a mere girl and he only an acting sub-lieutenant, they had been rather attached to each other. He was, of course, unaware of her engagement to Frank Farquhar, and she did not enlighten him, but allowed him to chatter to her as they walked westward. His people lived in Porchester Terrace, and he had lately been at sea for a year with the Mediterranean Fleet, he told her.

The yellow obscurity was now rapidly clearing as, at the corner of Pembridge Gardens, he raised his hat and with some reluctance left her.

Then she hurried in, just as the luncheon gong was sounding, and had only time to take off her hat and coat to be in her place at table. Her father was most punctual at his meals. He believed in method at all times, and carried method and the utmost punctuality into all his daily habits.

When he entered the dining-room the girl saw, from his preoccupied expression, that something had occurred.

She, however, made no inquiry before the servant, while he on his part, though bursting with the good news, resolved to keep his information until they had had their meal and retired into the study together.

Then he would explain to her, and show her the amazing result.

Therefore she chatted merrily, telling him how sweet her new gown looked, and gossiping in her own sweet engaging way—with that girlish laughter and merriment which was the sunshine of the old scholar's otherwise dull and colourless existence.

Little did she dream, he thought, as he sat at table, of the staggering announcement which he was about to make to her.

He had solved the problem!

Chapter Thirty
Closed Doors

"Will you come up with me into the study, dear?" asked the Professor, in as quiet a voice as he could, when they had finished luncheon.

"I have a letter to write, dad," replied the girl in excuse. "I'll come in and sit with you before tea."

"But I want to speak to you, dear," he said. "I want to tell you something. Come with me now." Rather surprised at her father's somewhat strained and unusual demeanour, the girl ascended the stairs to the book-lined room, and when the door was closed the old man crossed to where she stood, and said:

"Gwen, congratulate me, child."

"Upon what, dad?" she said, looking into his face, surprised.

"I have discovered the key to the cipher!"

The girl started. Then with a wild cry she threw her arms about her father's neck, kissed him passionately, and with tears of joy welling in her eyes, congratulated him.

"What will Frank say!" she exclaimed breathlessly. "How delighted he'll be! Why, dad, we shall discover the position of the hiding-place of the sacred relics, after all!"

Her enthusiasm was unbounded. Her father who had worked so hard by night and by day upon those puzzling cryptic numericals, was at last successful.

"Can you really read the cipher?" she asked quickly.

"Yes, dear," was her father's response. "I have already deciphered part of the extraordinary statement."

"Then we must telegraph to Frank," she said. "He is down at Horsford, visiting his sister and seeing Doctor Diamond at the same time."

"No, not yet, my child," he replied quietly. "Let me complete the work before we announce the good news to our friends. I have told you, because I knew you would be gratified."

"Why, of course I am, dad," replied the girl eagerly. "It will greatly enhance your reputation, besides preserving the sacred relics to the Jews. Our opponents had other intentions. Their efforts are directed towards causing annoyance and bringing ridicule upon the Hebrew race. But," she added, her arm still affectionately around his neck, "how did you accomplish it, dad?"

"Sit down, dear, and I'll explain to you," he said, pointing to the armchair near his writing-table, while he took his writing-chair, and drew towards him the open Hebrew text of Ezekiel.

"You see," he commenced, "for some weeks I have been applying all the known numerical ciphers to this text, but without result. More than once I was able to read a couple or three words, and believed that I had discovered the key. But, alas! I found it to fail inevitably before I could establish a complete sentence. I was about to relinquish the problem as either impossible of solution, or as a theory without basis, when this morning, almost as a last resource and certainly without expecting any definite result, I applied a variation of the Apocalyptic Number, which though appearing in the Book of Revelation, (Revelations, xiii, 13) was no doubt known at a much earlier period. In the text of Ezekiel xvii, the first and second verses: 'And the word of the Lord came unto me, saying, Son of man, put forth a riddle and speak a parable unto the house of Israel;' I had long recognised certain signs by which I had suspicion that there was a hidden meaning, and again in verses 14, 16 and 16, ending with the words 'even with him in the midst of Babylon he shall die.'

"To my utter amazement I found, by applying the numbers 666—the Hebrew 'wâw' sign three times repeated, that I could read an intelligible sentence which was nothing less than a portion of the cipher exactly as quoted by Holmboe! Since my discovery I have been hard at work, and have deciphered many ominous sentences."

"Then there is no doubt whatever now that the cipher record exists in the writings of the prophet?"

"Not the slightest."

"But I don't quite understand how you arrived at the key, dad?" she said. "Explain to me, for, as you know, I'm all curiosity."

"Well, as you don't know Hebrew, dear, I'll try and explain it as clearly as I can," he said. "Each Hebrew letter has its own numerical value, as you know, *A-leph* representing 1, *Bêth* 2, *Gi-mel* 3, and so on to *Yodh* 10, and the nine tens to 100, or *Qoph*, to 400, represented by the last of the twenty-two consonants, *Tâw*. The fact that Holmboe mentioned '*wâw*,' or the number 6, in his manuscript, first caused me to believe that he did so as a blind, because this also signified 'hook' and was the sign of evil. I applied it diligently in nearly two hundred places in the Book of Ezekiel, but without a single success. I used other numbers, indeed most of the combinations of the twenty-two consonants, especially the one of three and thirty-three which was one of the earliest numerical ciphers. You know well how diligently I worked, and how unsuccessful I have been until to-day."

"I know, dad," exclaimed the pretty girl, "but I confess I can hardly follow you, even now."

"Well, listen," he said. "The Apocalyptic Number is 666, and its interpretation rests upon the fact that in Hebrew, as well as in Greek, the letters of the alphabet did service for numbers. Hence, a writer, while avoiding a direct mention of some person or thing, could yet indicate the same by a number which was the sum of the various values comprising the name. First establishing the point where the actual message commences, which I may as well explain is at Ezekiel, x, 8; 'And there appeared in the cherubim the form of a man's hand under their wings,' I took the first 'wâw' or 6 sign, then the eleventh letter, being the sixth of sixty-six, then the sixty-sixth letter, and afterwards the six hundred and sixty-sixth letter. Following this, I made the additions which are known to the Greeks and also to the Hebrews, working it out thus: The fiftieth letter, the two-hundredth letter, the sixth letter, the fiftieth letter, the hundredth letter, the sixtieth letter and the two-hundredth letter—making in all six hundred and sixty-six. The Hebrew signs of each I wrote down in a line, and having divided them into words, I found to my amazement, that I was reading the secret record alleged by the dead professor!"

"But, surely, dad, that is a most ingenious cipher!" remarked his daughter.

"Most intricate, I assure you. By sheer good fortune I discovered the starting-point."

"What led you to it?"

"A slight, almost unnoticeable deviation of the present Hebrew text from the St. Petersburg codex. I had never before noticed it, and it only arrested my attention because I was studying the subject so very closely."

"And after making the additions of 666, how did you proceed?" urged the girl.

He paused for a few seconds as though in hesitation.

"By starting at the first 'wâw' sign and repeating my key. Sometimes, in a whole chapter, there is not a word of cipher, but following the numbers with regularity it reappears in the next. It is a most marvellous and most cunningly concealed record accounting, of course, for the number of superfluous and rather incongruous words in the writings of the prophet."

"Was it written in the text—or placed there afterwards?" she asked.

"Placed there afterwards, without a doubt," was the Professor's quick reply. "Holy writ was inspired, of course, but some temple priest, an exile in Babylon probably, worked out the cipher and placed the record in the text in order that it might be there preserved and the existence of the treasure be known to coming generations of Jews who would be then aware of the existence of their war-chest."

"It really is a most amazing discovery, dad dear," declared the girl much excited. "When you publish it the whole world will be startled!"

"Yes, my dear," was the old fellow's response, as he ran his fingers through his scanty grey hair. "We have here before us," and he placed his hand upon the open Hebrew text, "a secret explained which is surely the greatest and most remarkable of any discovered in any age."

The girl, rising from her chair, saw upon the manuscript paper on her father's blotting-pad, a number of lines of hastily-written Hebrew words.

"Is that part of the deciphered record?" she inquired, greatly interested.

"Yes, dear."

"Oh, do read them to me, dad," she cried, "I'm dying to learn exactly the purport of this message hidden through so many generations!"

"No, Gwen," was the old man's calm response, "not until I have worked out the whole. Then you shall, my child, be the first to have knowledge of the secret of Israel. And remember it is my wish that you write nothing to Farquhar regarding it. We must keep our knowledge to ourselves—very closely to ourselves, remember. Erich Haupt must have no suspicion of my success. Otherwise we may even yet be forestalled."

"I quite see the danger, dad," remarked his daughter, "but I'm so interested, do go on with your task and show me how it is accomplished."

"Very well," he said, smiling and humouring her. "You see here, at this mark," and he showed her a pencilled line upon the Hebrew text, "that is where I halted for luncheon. Now we go on to the next sign of six. See, here it is—in the next line. Now we count the eleventh letter," and he wrote it down in Hebrew. Then he counted the sixty-sixth, the six hundredth and sixty-sixth, the fiftieth, the two-hundredth, and so on until he had a number of Hebrew signs ranged side by side. Presently he said, pointing to them:

"Here you are! The English translation to this is '...yourselves, and wonder, for unto thee, O children of Israel...'"

"Really, dad!" exclaimed the girl, highly excited. "It's most remarkable!"

"Yes," he admitted. "I confess that until now I held the same idea that every Jewish Rabbi holds—namely that no secret cipher can exist in our inspired writings."

"But you have now proved it beyond question!" she declared.

"Yes. But startling as it may be, we must preserve our secret, dear. There are others endeavouring to learn the trend of my investigations, recollect. We may have spies upon us, for aught we know," he added in a low tone, glancing at her with a significant look.

"How long do you expect it will take before you are in full possession of the whole of the secret statement?" she asked.

"Many hours, my dear. Perhaps many days—how can I tell. Holmboe says it runs through only nine chapters. Therefore it should end with chapter xxvi. But as far as I can gather I believe I shall find further cryptic statements in the later chapters. There are certain evidences of these in chapter xxxvii, 16, in chapter xxxix, 18, 19 and 20, and again in chapter xliv, 5. Therefore, I anticipate that my task may be a rather long one. The counting and recounting to ensure accuracy occupies so much time. The miscounting of a single letter would throw everything out and prevent the record being recovered, as you will readily foresee. Hence, it must be done with the greatest precision and patience."

"But, dad—this is most joyful news!" declared the girl excitedly, "I'm most anxious to telegraph to Frank."

"Not until the secret is wholly ours, my dear. Remember we must keep the key a most profound secret to ourselves."

"Of course, dad," the girl answered, "I quite see that this information must not be allowed to pass to our enemies."

Little did father or daughter imagine that, within their own quiet household, was a spy—the maid Laura, suborned by Jim Jannaway.

When the pair had entered the study she had crept silently up to the door, and listened intently for the one fact which Jannaway had instructed her to listen—the means by which the cipher could be unravelled.

She was a shrewd, intelligent girl, and the inducement which the good-looking adventurer had held out to her was such that the Professor's explanation to his daughter impressed itself upon her memory.

She recollected every word, and still stood listening, able to hear quite distinctly, until there seemed no further information to be gathered. Then she descended the stairs, and made certain memoranda of the text at which to commence, and the mode by which the decipher could be made.

Half an hour later she made an excuse to the cook that she wished to go out to buy some hairpins, and then despatched a telegram to the name and address which her generous and good-looking "gentleman" had given her.

Meanwhile Gwen still sat with her father at his writing-table watching him slowly taking from the text of the Book of Ezekiel the full and complete record that had been hidden from scholars through all the ages—the record which was to deliver back to the house of Israel her most sacred possessions.

The light of the short afternoon faded, the electric light was switched on, tea was served by the faithless maid-servant, and dinner had been announced.

But the Professor worked on, regardless and oblivious of everything. He was far too occupied, and Gwen was also too excited to dress and descend to dinner. Therefore, Laura served the meal upon a tray.

All was silence save the Professor's dry monotonous voice as he counted aloud the letters of the Hebrew text, recounted them to reassure himself, and then set down a Hebrew character as result.

Thus from after luncheon until midnight—through the time indeed that Diamond was so patiently watching the big house in Berkeley Square—the work of solving the problem went slowly on.

Gwen sat and watched her father's Hebrew manuscript grow apace, until it covered many quarto pages. Now and then she assisted in counting the letters, verifying her father's addition.

Then at last, just after the old-fashioned clock upon the mantelshelf had chimed twelve, the old scholar raised his grey head with a sigh, and wiping his glasses, as was his habit, said:

"Sit down, dear, and write the English translation at my dictation. I think we now have it quite complete."

Chapter Thirty One
Exposes the Conspiracy

While Professor Griffin had been so busily engaged deciphering the concluding portion of the secret record, a strange scene was in progress at Sir Felix Challas's, in Berkeley Square.

First, Jim Jannaway had arrived and had held a short consultation in the library with the red-faced Baronet, afterwards quickly leaving. Then, from the Waldorf Hotel, summoned by telephone, came old Erich Haupt, bustling and full of suppressed excitement.

Soon afterwards, the well-dressed Jim had returned, and had waited in momentary expectancy, ready to dart out into the hall on hearing the sound of cab wheels.

At last they were heard and the man-servant opened the door to Laura, tall, dark-haired and rather good-looking parlour-maid at Pembridge Gardens.

In the well-carpeted hall she recognised the man who had taken her out to dinner and the theatre on several occasions, and advanced excitedly to meet him.

"Oh! Laura!" he cried. "I'm so glad you've come. I had your 'wire,' and you got my message in reply, of course? You must see the gov'nor. This is his house, and I want you to tell him how the Professor is solving that puzzle." Then, lowering his voice, he added. "There's a pot of money in it for both of us, dear, if you keep your wits about you. You recollect what I promised you last Tuesday, don't you?"

The girl sniggered and nodded. She was a giddy young person, whose head had been turned by the admiration of that good-looking man who called himself "Miller," and who said he was a lawyer's clerk. He had promised to become engaged to her and to marry her, provided they could get only a good round sum from "the gov'nor" for the information she could, with such ease, supply.

This had placed the girl upon the constant alert, with the present result.

Her nonchalant admirer led the way across the hall to the library, pushed upon the door, and introduced her to the two men therein—Challas, fat and prosperous, and Haupt, white-bearded and bespectacled.

Then, when the door was closed and she had seated herself, Challas—or "Mr Murray," as he had been introduced—asked:

"I believe you're Laura, and you are parlour-maid at Professor Griffin's, aren't you?"

"Yes, sir," replied the girl, timidly, picking at her neat black skirt.

"Well, sir," explained Jim, bearing out his part of lawyer's clerk, "some time ago I explained to my young lady here, what we particularly wanted to know, and she's kept both eyes and ears open. To-day she's learned something, it seems."

"What is it?" inquired old Erich, in a deep tone, with his strong German accent.

"Let the young lady explain herself," urged the man introduced as "Murray," and they all sat silent.

"Well, sir," the girl faltered, a moment later. "You see it was like this. After luncheon to-day the Professor, who'd been very hard at work as usual all the morning, took Miss Gwen up to the study to speak to her privately; I listened, and I heard all their conversation. He told her how he'd solved the problem of the cipher."

"Solved it!" ejaculated the old German, staring at her through his spectacles.

"Yes, sir," the girl went on. "He told Miss Gwen that he'd tried and tried, but always failed. But he had taken the—well, sir, I think he called it the apoplectic number."

The German laughed heartily.

"I know," he said. "You mean the Apocalyptic Number, *fräulein*—the number 666."

"That's it, sir," she said, a little flurried, while Jim exchanged significant glances with Challas. "He commences at the tenth chapter of Ezekiel, eighth verse, and—and—" Then she fumbled in her pocket, producing a piece of crumpled paper to which she referred. "He takes the first sign of 6," she went on, "then the eleventh letter, the sixty-sixth letter, and the six hundred and sixty-sixth letter. After this, the fiftieth letter, the two-hundredth letter, the sixth letter, the fiftieth letter, the hundredth letter, the sixtieth letter, and the two-hundredth letter—making six hundred and sixty-six in all.

He writes down each of the Hebrew letters, and then reads them off like a book."

"Wait—ah! wait!" urged the old German. "Let us have that again, *fräulein*," and crossing to Sir Felix's big mahogany writing-table, he opened the Hebrew text of Ezekiel upon it. "Where do you say the Professor commences—at the tenth chapter, eighth verse—eh? Good!" and he hastily found the reference. "Now?"

"Just tell this gentleman," urged Jim, "tell him exactly what you heard."

"Well, starting with the eighth verse, he commences with what he termed the first 'wâw' sign."

"Zo! that's the equivalent of the number 6," Haupt remarked.

"Then the eleventh letter."

The old professor counted and wrote down the letter in question in Hebrew characters.

"The sixty-sixth," said the girl.

The old man counted sixty-six, while Sir Felix and Jannaway watched with intense, almost breathless interest. Here was the secret, snatched from their dreaded opponent, Arminger Griffin!

"And now the six hundred and sixty-sixth," the girl went on, apparently thoroughly at home with the strangely assorted trio.

This took some time to count, but presently it was accomplished, and the girl time after time gave the old professor directions—the fiftieth letter, the two-hundredth letter, and so on.

"Well?" asked Challas, a few moments later, unable to repress his excitement any longer. "Do you make anything out of it?"

The old man was silent. He was carefully studying the Hebrew characters he had written down.

"Yes!" he gasped. "It is the secret—the great secret!" And he started up, exclaiming, "At last! at last—thanks to *fräulein* here—we have the key!"

"And we can actually read the cipher?" cried Challas.

"Most certainly," responded the old scholar. "The secret is ours! Marvellous, how Griffin discovered it."

"Confound Griffin!" exclaimed Jim Jannaway. "We have to thank Laura, here, for our success! She ought to be well rewarded."

"And so she shall," declared the man, whom the girl knew as "Mr Murray."

"It's late to-night, and we want Erich to get on at once with the decipher. Besides, the young lady, no doubt, wishes to get back home. Bring her to me to-morrow, or next day—and she shall be well rewarded."

"Thank you very much, sir," was the silly girl's gratified reply, as she looked triumphant into the face of the cunning man who had declared his love for her.

The truth was that, having obtained that most valuable information, the trio wanted to get rid of her as soon as possible. Therefore, with excuses that the household at Pembridge Gardens would be suspicious if she returned too late, they bundled her almost unceremoniously outside, Jim hailing a hansom for her, paying the man, and telling him to drive to Notting Hill Gate Station.

Then, when he re-entered, he exclaimed with a laugh to the Baronet, "That was a cheap 'quid's' worth of information, wasn't it—eh?"

"Cheap, my dear boy? Why, it's placed us absolutely on top. The treasure, if it still remains there, is ours!"

"Ah! not too hasty! Not too hasty!" exclaimed the old German in his deep guttural voice, and raising his head from the table. "Up to a certain point, it is all right, but—"

"But what?" the others gasped, in the same breath.

"Well, there's something wanting, alas! Or else the girl has made a great mistake. After the addition of the numbers to 666, all goes entirely wrong!"

"Goes wrong!" they echoed breathlessly, with one accord.

"Yes. The further reading is quite unintelligible," he declared, speaking with his strong Teutonic accent.

"The girl seemed quite certain about it!" exclaimed Jim, exchanging glances with Challas.

"Quite," the other remarked, blandly.

"Well, my dear sirs!" exclaimed Haupt, pointing to his lines of hastily-written Hebrew. "The commencement of the record is here, plain enough. It commences, 'Remember and forget not, O Israel. Not for thy righteousness—' But after taking the two-hundredth letter I can discover nothing. Commencing again at six only results in nothing, while a repetition of the fiftieth and the consequent addition is equally futile. No! The confounded girl has made some mistake—and we are once more at a standstill. You see that one false number throws out the whole. The cipher is one of the most ingenious ever conceived."

"But, my dear Haupt, you know the basis, and where it commences! You will surely succeed!" Challas cried, frantically.

The old man shook his head very dubiously.

"As I have already told you," he responded in his deep voice, "a single misplaced number throws it all out. We are again at an absolute deadlock — and must remain as ignorant as we were before."

"But have you made every possible effort?" asked Jim Jannaway, with eager face, as he bent over the old man's shoulders.

"I have tried all the combinations of the Apocalyptic Number, but they are futile!" replied the old German, laying down his pen, and blinking through his glasses.

"Then the girl has failed us after all," remarked Challas in a low, hard voice. "Griffin has deciphered the record and we're absolutely 'in the cart.'"

"I won't give up!" declared Jannaway. "I'm hanged if I will! This may be one of Charlie's tricks, remember! He may have learnt the truth and got hold of Laura to put us on the wrong scent."

"He may — curse him!" muttered Sir Felix. "Why didn't he take my warning and get away abroad?"

"Because he's quite as cute as we are. He knows full well that while he remains in England circumstances will continue to be propitious. So he lives quietly down in Kent, with both eyes very much open."

Already Jim Jannaway's ingenious mind was active; already he was devising a way out of the awkward *cul-de-sac* in which they now found themselves.

"What are we to do?" inquired Sir Felix, with his dark brows knitted at this sudden failure of all his elaborate plans.

"Leave it to me," replied the good-looking scoundrel, with the utmost confidence. "Let Erich remain quietly within reach — not, however, at the Waldorf — and allow me to carry out the scheme in my own way."

"I cannot think why the girl made such a mistake," Challas remarked very disappointedly. "I admit the solution was complicated, but you saw that she was clever enough to write it down."

"She listened behind a closed door. She may have misunderstood," Jim remarked.

"Or, what is much more likely," remarked the German, "Griffin, who has the reputation of being a very shrewd man, does not trust his daughter, and purposely misled her in explaining his secret."

"No, I don't think that," said Jannaway. "Griffin trusts the girl, even though she's quite young, absolutely and implicitly."

And thus the three desperate schemers agreed to leave matters in the hands of the most daring and unscrupulous of men, Jim Jannaway, unconscious that the exterior of the mansion was being watched independently by two persons, Doctor Diamond, and a thin-faced, ill-clad woman, who, noticing the Doctor's keen interest in the place, glanced at him full of surprise and wonder.

Chapter Thirty Two
Reveals the Cipher Record

In the study at Pembridge Gardens, the silence only broken by the solemn ticking of the little Sheraton clock, Professor Griffin's calm, even voice was slowly dictating to Gwen the translation from the Hebrew of the cipher record into English.

The girl, as her father's amanuensis, had long ago become quite an expert with the typewriter, and in order to make a clear copy she had seated herself at the machine, her slim, white fingers deftly touching the keys.

"If you are ready dear, we'll begin," said the old man, drawing his folios of scribbled Hebrew towards him.

"I'm quite ready, dad," she assured him, pulling her skirt around her at the little table by his side upon which the typewriter was fixed.

"Very well, then. I'll translate slowly. Forgive me if I hesitate, child, for some of it may perhaps be difficult to put into intelligible or Biblical English. It is really a most astounding statement by a scribe of the Temple."

Then, after a brief pause, he began to dictate to her the hidden record, which was as follows:

"*Remember and forget not*, O Israel. *Not* for thy righteousness, or for the uprightness of thine heart, dost thou go to possess thy land, but for the wickedness of these nations the Lord thy God shall drive them out before thee.

"*Thou shalt love* the Lord thy God and keep His charge, His statutes and His commandments.

"*And* know ye this day why this secret record is written, that it may be preserved unto the just... *The* lapse of years are nearing its filling. *The* relief of the Doom will come, in spite of all. *The* people's right is nearing. *The* period of the Blood-debts, and that of the Suppression will lose its power, and Israel shall be restored (here follow seven words undecipherable).

"*...As* the Lord God was against Gog, the land of Magog, the chief prince of Meshech and Tubal, Gomer and all his bands, the house of Togarmah, of the north quarters, so shall He be against all the enemies of Israel that spread over the land. *For* He will make His Holy name known in the midst of His people Israel, and will not let them pollute His Holy name any more; and the heathen shall know that He is the Lord, the Holy One in Israel...

"And the desolate places of the Land shall become populated, Jerusalem the city shall be restored, the sanctuary shall be set up, and the children of Israel shall be gathered there from the four corners of the earth where they will be found scattered.

"Be thou prepared, and prepare thyself, for the Lord God will make a covenant of peace with His chosen people; it shall be a peace everlasting and His tabernacle shall be set in the midst of them for evermore, even upon Mount Moriah.

"Stay yourselves, and wonder, for unto thee, O children of Israel, are the greater treasures of Solomon's Temple still preserved. *And* thus it is therein written in a book that is sealed, so that the wicked of Babylon and the enemies of Israel shall not know. *Verily* I say unto you the Ark of the Covenant, and the tablets, and the rod of Aaron, and the other sacred objects which Solomon placed in the house of the Lord are still with thee, O Israel, until the wastes be builded, the cities inhabited and the Lord God cometh again unto the mountains of Jerusalem... for your own ways— and the Lord will build up the ruined places—

"Know ye the truth concerning the sacred treasures of Israel, the vessels out of the house of the Lord. *In* the third year of Jehoiakim, King of Judah, cameth one night into Jerusalem one Hashbbiah, a secret messenger from Antioch, who seeking Zeruiah, the high priest, told him in private that Nebuchadnezzar of Babylon, had advanced upon the hosts of Pharaoh-Necho at Carchemish and defeated him, and that the King of Babylon had taken from the river of Egypt unto the river Euphrates all that pertained unto the King of Egypt.

"Now Zeruiah, a man full of learning, remembered the prayer of Solomon, and saw that the prophecy of the fall of Jerusalem was to be fulfilled, and that Judah was to be led into captivity by the Babylonians... *And* he went out upon the mountain alone and prayed unto the Lord. *And* the Lord directed him to take counsel of six priests, of whom one was the prophet Ezekiel, to decide how the sacred things of the house of the Lord should be held from the hands of the despoiler.

"And to one of the priests, Uzziah, son of Haziah who came from Gaza, was revealed a hiding-place outside the gates of Jerusalem, beyond the valley of Jehoshaphat, where the treasures could be concealed beneath the

earth in a dry-room, in connection with a series of water-tunnels, which could be emptied only by those who knew the secret gate of the waters.

"*And the ears of Zeruiah* the high priest, heard a voice behind him saying: 'This is the way, walk ye in it. Place the treasures of the house of Jehovah therein, and seal them with the waters, so that no man shall know.'

"*So* at night he went with Uzziah onto the place that was revealed, which is on the side of the mount.

"*And* he saw that it had been used by thieves in the days when Rehoboam was king, and that its entrance had since been unknown to any man.

"*And returning to* the inner court of the Temple in darkness of night he went into the Holy Place and called unto him Baruch, the son of Neriah, Sherebbiah, the scribe, Ezekiel the priest, and the five other priests. *And* together both that night and the next and through many nights did they carry forth the most treasured objects of the Temple down into the valley, letting no man know that they were being taken from the house of the Lord.

"*For since the beginning* of the world men have not seen such great treasure as was in the darkness removed from the house of Jehovah, from the defenceless city upon which the judgment of God was set. *Woe* unto Jerusalem for Nebuchadnezzar was hastening upon the City of Judah, and the hour of her destruction was approaching.

"*And they took from* the Holy of Holies the Ark of the Covenant, together with the stone tablets which Moses put there at Horeb, the pot of manna and the staff of Aaron and the two cherubims of fine gold, the Urim and Thummim with two rubies of great size and a multitude of other gems set around them... And of the other treasures of the house of the Lord did they bring forth; of basons of pure gold made by Solomon which Shishak, Ging of Egypt had restored, three thousand and forty; of the chargers of gold eight hundred and two; of the candlesticks of gold from the oracle four; of the lamps of gold six hundred and ten, of the tongs of gold six hundred, and of the smaller tablets of gold four score and five; of spoons of gold two thousand; of censers of gold one thousand and forty-six, and of the bowls which Solomon commanded to be made of the gold of Ophir two thousand and seventy... *Furthermore* of the gems and precious stones of Solomon they took seven ox-loads of fine gold, three talents together with the archives of the Temple in secret; so that of the vessels of gold there remained only about six thousand and these Nebuchadnezzar afterwards carried off to Babylon, where they were dedicated unto his god Belus—

"*It came even to pass* that when the King of Babylon and his host searched for the other holy vessels of the Temple they found them not, for they knew not their hiding-place, and none knew save the priests and the two scribes. *Wherefore* afterwards in my captivity in Babylon, I, Michaiah the scribe, invented this secret writing by which the place of concealment of the tablets of Moses should not be lost. Secure shall they remain, with the great treasure, the war-chest of the house of Israel, until the coming of the Messiah, who alone may open their place of concealment, in order that He may furnish proof of the faith. *He* hath chosen Jerusalem that His name may be there.

"*And be it now known* unto you in what place to seek for the chamber of the sacred Ark. *At* the lower platform of the brazen altar of the Temple turn thy face to the southward, and measure four reeds and thirty-three legal cubits, unto the north end of the Pool of Siloh. *Thence,* to the sunrise, measure one thousand and fifty cubits unto the highest point on the mount of Solomon's idolatry. *Face* unto the south-west, and measure ten-score cubits and four, down to the hillside to the face of stone. *From* the cleft fifteen cubits.

"*Moreover, at the gate* of the Priests at the north-west corner of the sanctuary, face the south-east, and pace four hundred and three cubits unto the centre of the tomb in the Valley of Jehoshaphat, and thence to the south nine reeds and three-score cubits, which bringest thee unto the same wall of rock, fifteen cubits from the cleft.

"*And the distance* from En-rogel is, to the north-east, of cubits three hundred and ninety-four, where the entrance faceth directly the bend of the Valley of Hinnom.

"*Of the three entrances,* two are impassable. Know ye therefore that the third is in the face of the rock, concealed from the sight of all men at the point where the valleys converge, at the base of the mount, from the cleft fifteen legal cubits.

"*To learn* the whereabouts of the secret chamber of the Ark, O ye Israel, measure from the hidden entrance up the face of the rock and over the mount with thine eyes set to the east two reeds and fourscore cubits and three, till thou comest to the gate of stone set in the rock which, when opened, will let forth the flood to admit thee from the Valley of Jehoshaphat.

"*O hear me,* ye enemies of the Lord! Curses, yea, sixty times six curses shall be upon the head of any who dare to attempt to violate the sacred treasure-house of Israel.

"*Moreover the Lord* hath performed the word that He spake, and Judah remaineth beneath the heel of the oppressor.

"Now therefore these acts are not written in the book of the chronicles of Israel lest thine enemies search to recover the holy things.

"Hearken O Lord God of Israel to the supplications of Thy servant. If Thy people be put to the worse before the enemy, because they have sinned against Thee, and shall return and confess Thy name, then hear Thou from the heavens and bring them again unto the land which Thou gavest to them and to their fathers.

"Wherefore I beseech Thee to stay Thine hand, and seek not to discover what is hidden until the Lord have given rest unto your brethren, as well as unto you, and until they also possess the Land, which the Lord your God hath given them.

"For he who entereth therein shall be accursed. Cursed shalt thou be in the city, and cursed shalt thou be in the field. Cursed shalt thou be when thou comest in, and cursed shalt thou be when thou goest out *The* Lord shall send thee cursing, vexation and rebuke, in all that thou settest thine hand unto for to do, until thou be destroyed, and until thou perish quickly; because of the wickedness of thy doings. *Fear* the Lord thy God.

"These words am I commanded by Zeruiah the high priest to write in our captivity in secret script, that only those of the faith shall know and shall understand."

And when the girl had finished typing, she raised her head, and stared at her father in abject wonder. Here was the complete solution of the problem! The truth was written there!

Chapter Thirty Three
In the Night

Laura, the parlour-maid, had been let in at the area-door by the cook, to whom she had made her excuses for the lateness of the hour, and had crept up to her room, fully satisfied at having assisted her good-looking lover. She was, of course, in utter ignorance that "Mr Miller" was the person to whom Miss Gwen's mysterious absence from home had been due. Otherwise she certainly would not have fallen into the trap.

Meanwhile, in the study, with the typed folios of the cipher before him, the old Professor sat making certain explanations to his daughter and answering her eager questions.

"We ought to telegraph to Frank the first thing in the morning, dad!" she cried, when she had recovered from her excitement at learning the secret.

"I have not yet decided upon my course of action, dear," was his slow, deliberate answer. "To-night we are dealing with this astounding record of the authenticity of which there seems not the slightest doubt. I have been using the exact copy of the St. Petersburg text of Ezekiel—the oldest known manuscript. It is evident from the word of Michaiah the scribe, that, having invented the cipher, he altered certain words of the original text of Ezekiel with Ezekiel's knowledge and consent, in order to include in the book this secret record."

"It agrees entirely with Biblical history, does it not?" asked the girl.

"Yes. Several hitherto uncertain facts are here explained. For instance, it is now made quite clear that Shishak, King of Egypt, restored to the Temple certain of the basins of gold made by Solomon. Again, Michaiah shows that none of the sacred vessels secreted were afterwards used in the Temple. Those used in the second temple were certainly those carried away by Nebuchadnezzar and restored by Cyrus."

Then rising he took from a cupboard a large roll-map of the environs of Jerusalem issued by the Palestine Exploration Fund, and both studied it very closely.

"What is meant by the mount of Solomon's idolatry?" asked Gwen.

"It is now known as the Mount of the Offence," he answered. "Here it is—about half a mile almost due south of the temple mount. Sometimes it is called the Mount of Scandal, for upon it Solomon and some of his successors built high places, altars to Moloch, to Ashtoreth, and to other strange gods. (1 Kings xi, 5-7.) I recollect the hill quite well. On the summit is now a Benedictine Monastery, while the slopes are occupied by a Jewish cemetery. The Turks call it Baten el Hawa (Bottle of the Winds). The measurements given seem to be most explicit, the entrance to the chamber being on the west side of the extreme south of the mount, facing the sudden bend in the Valley of Hinnom. See, here," and he pointed to the spot upon the map. "And at the east side, at some spot to be determined by measurements, are the secret flood-gates by which the waters can be released. The 'dry-room' is evidently situated above the water-tunnels, at such a height that the waters never rise there."

"And can those ancient measures be worked out to modern measures?"

"Yes. We practically know almost exactly what was the reed, and what was the legal cubit of the days of Jehoiakim as compared with the ordinary cubit. Surveyors will have no difficulty in finding the exact spot indicated."

"You do not think, dad, that after the restoration and rebuilding of the Temple that the treasures were recovered?"

"Certainly not. If so, we should certainly have had some record in Holy Writ of the Ark of the Covenant and the tablets. But there is none. Since a few days before Nebuchadnezzar's hosts entered Jerusalem, the Ark has never been seen. My firm belief is that it is still in its place of concealment as stated by Michaiah the scribe."

"And what shall you do now, dad?" inquired the girl, her elbows upon the table, as she looked up into his face. "You have solved a problem that will startle the whole world!"

"Yes, dear," he sighed, passing his hand across his brow. "It is so remarkable that I hardly know how to act. I must, of course, see Diamond and Farquhar, and consult with them. One thing is quite certain; for the present we must keep this matter a most profound secret. If our enemies were to gain wind of it, they would send out at once and purchase the land for themselves."

"But they can't know, dad."

"Ah, dear! I'm—I'm suspicious. With such enormous possibilities before us, who knows that our secret enemies may not have bribed our servants," he said. "For that reason, Gwen dear—and please forgive me—fearing that there might be eaves-droppers, I purposely, when explaining to you the cipher this afternoon, rearranged and omitted some of the second portion of it, so that our secret could not possibly leak out."

"But surely, dad!" cried the girl. "You don't suspect Laura or Mullingar, or Kate, being in the employ of our enemies, do you?"

"My child, it is best to be always wary in a matter such as this. As your friend Mr Mullet has already told you, they appear to be most unscrupulous."

"I wonder where Mr Mullet is—why he doesn't write or telephone to me, as he promised."

"Don't distress yourself about him," urged the old Professor. "We hold the secret, and for to-night at least that is sufficient."

And then, after gathering the typed sheets together he put a fastener through them and locked the precious decipher carefully in one of the drawers of his writing-table. Then a few moments later, it already being two o'clock in the morning, they both ascended to their rooms.

When upon the landing, the old man kissed his daughter tenderly on the brow as was his habit, saying:

"Good-night, my child. I fear you must be very tired. But think!— we have completed our task. We alone know the great secret which will convulse the whole civilised world!"

In her own pretty room Gwen threw herself into the cosy chintz-covered armchair before the fire, and pondered deeply.

She was thinking of Frank—ever of him. Though she had been fond of flirtation, and though perhaps she had committed grave breaches of the *convenances* before she had known young Farquhar, yet all had now changed. She would give her very life for him—for was she not his, and his alone?

Over her spread the thought of the man who had posed as Frank's friend—that man who had laughed defiance in her face, the man who was in league with her father's enemies. Who was he? What was he? she wondered. Then there rose before her the recollection of the man Mullet, the man with the ugly past, as he himself had admitted, yet nevertheless devoted to his little daughter, and a gentleman. She longed to see him again—to introduce him to her lover, and to tell the latter the whole strange truth.

To her, it seemed as though Mullet feared the man who had so cleverly entrapped her, just as he was the "cat's-paw" of the bloated red-faced man who had raised his hand to strike her.

Who were these people? she wondered. Why did Mullet fear them?

Having exchanged her dress for an easy *robe-de-chambre*, she sat before the fire plaiting her long dark tresses, her eyes fixed upon the fire, now fast dying away.

She had knowledge of that marvellous secret—the whereabouts of the bewildering treasure of Israel. Yet how would it all end? Why had her father suspicion of spies in their own home? What could he suspect?

She wondered, as she had often wondered, what conclusion her father had formed regarding her mysterious absence from home, and often, in her moments of reflection, she found herself puzzled and pondering regarding her unconsciousness on that never-to-be-forgotten night when she had found herself alone and helpless in the hands of the man who had laughed at her innocence and dismay.

She dare not tell Frank. It was her secret—a dark secret which she had resolved to keep at all hazards—one that he should never know.

"But he is mine again!" she murmured to herself, a sweet smile of contentment playing about her lips. "I have been a fickle girl, I know, but, after all, every girl is entitled to have one good time in her life. I've had mine, and I have found Frank. I love him, and he loves me. I know he does. And to-morrow dad will 'wire' him, and I shall see him again. Ah! what will he say, I wonder—now that dad has discovered the secret. Dear old dad! He deserves all the *kudos* he'll get from the great discovery, for he's worked hard—worked night and day almost. And the ugly little Doctor? I wonder how he'll take it? One thing is plain, that we have outwitted that red-faced scoundrel and his friends. We know the truth, while they are still in ignorance."

For a long time she sat, her pretty head, with its two long plaits secured by blue ribbons, pillowed upon the muslin-covered cushion in the low comfortable armchair, her bare feet thrust into slippers, and upon her sweet countenance an expression of calm content.

The little clock upon her mantelshelf, chiming the half-hour—half-past three—aroused her from her reverie, and she shivered, for the fire had died away and the room had now become chilly. So preoccupied had she been that she had not noticed that the fire was already out.

As she stirred herself, she suddenly recollected that, downstairs in the study, she had left her book in which she was greatly interested, and which she wanted to continue when she awoke in the morning. It was a heavy work of one of the German philosophers which she was studying, for since leaving school she had done a vast amount of reading, especially French and German literature. She was highly educated and cultured, and, unlike the average young girl of our twentieth century, she had not put aside her books with her ankle-skirts.

In her long trailing robe of pale *eau-de-nil* she crossed the room, and seating herself at her writing-table scribbled a note to her dressmaker, which she had forgotten. Then having put a stamp upon it, she quickly opened her door, crept softly past her father's room, fearing to wake him, and down the thickly carpeted stairs where her slippered feet fell noiselessly.

She had no candle, but she knew her way about the house quite well in the dark, and also knew where to put her hand upon most of the electric switches.

Creeping softly down, afraid every moment that the stairs would creak—for stairs always have a horrid habit of creaking in the silence of the night—she carried the letter in her hand for the purpose of placing it in the rack in the study which Laura always cleared when she went to the room in the morning, and Kate took the letters to the post-office down at the corner.

Reaching the landing she crossed it to the study-door, but as she did so she saw, to her surprise, a light issuing from the crack beneath.

Her father had evidently returned there to continue his work, as he sometimes did when unable to sleep.

For a second she hesitated whether she should enter, but making up her mind suddenly, she placed her fingers upon the handle and opened the door.

Next instant, however, uttering a low cry, she stood upon the threshold, rigid as one petrified.

Chapter Thirty Four
"Silence for Silence!"

"*You!*"

It was the only word which the girl uttered, but its tone showed her horror and indignation.

The green-shaded light was, she saw, switched on at the writing-table, and as she entered, there before her, seated in her father's chair, was the man who had posed as Frank's friend, "Captain Wetherton!"

As she had slowly opened the door he had raised his head, pale and startled. But only for a second. When he recognised who it was, he rose and, bowing, smiled with perfect *sangfroid*.

He had entered the house with the false latch-key which he had had made from the wax impression he had taken of the key which Gwen had carried on that night of the false assignation. His only fear had been, however, a meeting with the girl Laura.

Now that he saw that it was not she, he only smiled triumphantly.

"Yes," he said simply. "It's me! Are you very surprised?"

Instantly she recognised that, upon the blotting-pad, was lying open the precious document which she herself had typed. He had opened the drawer, abstracted it, and read it.

He, her enemy, knew their secret!

"By what right, pray, are you here, sir?" she demanded, advancing into the room boldly, and facing him.

"I have no right. I'm here just by my own will," was his quick, defiant response.

"This is my father's house, and I shall alarm him," she said determinedly. "You have no right thus to pry into his private affairs!"

"I have to decide that, Miss Griffin," he said, as over his dark face spread that evil smile she remembered so well.

Having risen from the chair, he had now advanced closely to her. She noticed that he wore thick woollen socks over his boots, so as to muffle his footsteps, while upon his hands were a pair of grey *suède* gloves which appeared too large for him. Jim Jannaway had been a man of many precautions, ever since his finger-prints had been taken on a certain memorable day at Ipswich police-station, prior to his conviction.

"But," he laughed, examining her from head to toe, "you really look charming, my dear little girl—even better than when in your walking kit. Why!" he exclaimed, pointing across the room. "Why—what's that—over there?"

She turned suddenly, taking her eyes off him for an instant, but saw nothing. His ruse succeeded, for that instant was sufficient for him to slip behind her and close the door, turning the key in the lock.

"I must apologise for doing this in your own house, Miss Griffin, but I fear that we may be overheard," he said. "Now I want to have a very serious chat with you."

"I wish to say nothing to you, sir," she replied drawing herself up haughtily, the train of her pretty gown sweeping the floor. "I only demand to know what you are doing here, reading my father's papers."

"And suppose I refuse to tell you—eh?" he asked, raising his brows.

"Then I shall scream, and alarm the household. They will hand you over to the police."

"And if you were so ill-advised as to do that, Miss Griffin," answered the fellow impudently, advancing a step nearer to her, and looking straight into her face. "Well—you would suffer very severely for it. That's all."

"I'm prepared to take all the consequences," was her calm reply.

"Take care!" he said threateningly, in a low hoarse voice. "I'm a desperate man when driven into a corner."

"You mean rather that you're a coward when cornered," she said coldly. "I am glad to have this opportunity of meeting, in order to repay you for the gross injustice which you have done me."

"You're a little fool!" he said in a hard tone. "Keep quiet, or somebody will hear you."

"You entrapped me in that place. I have now entrapped you—in my own house," she exclaimed, with a look of triumph.

"Not for long," he said determinedly. "Do you know that I could strangle you where you stand, and still get clear. Even though you screamed.

I already have a rope on the balcony yonder, down into the street. But don't be alarmed. I have no wish to injure you, my dear little girl—not in the least. We will just make an arrangement, and cry quits."

"What do you mean?"

"Well, listen. You've discovered me here, and you could give me away. But I want to buy your silence."

"Buy my silence!" she exclaimed, staring at him. "Yes. Why not? You must buy mine. Shall we not then be quits?"

She regarded him with a puzzled air. He was her bitterest foe, and she was wondering what was the true meaning of the suggestion. She was undecided, too, whether not to alarm the house, instead of parleying further. She had caught the fellow in her father's room wearing the apparel of the modern burglar, therefore the police would, without doubt, arrest him as such.

Suddenly her mind was made up, and with a quick movement she rushed across to the electric bell beside the fireplace.

He gave vent to a short dry laugh of triumph, the reason of which was next second plain. The little porcelain push had been broken, and the contact disarranged.

Jim Jannaway always took precautions. He was a cool and calculating scoundrel.

She turned upon him in quick anger, and he saw that she intended to scream for help.

"One moment, if you please, Miss Griffin," he cried in a low voice. "Just hear my suggestion before you raise the alarm and compel me to depart hurriedly through the window. A word now will save both of us a great deal of unnecessary bother afterwards. You're a very brave little girl, and I admire you for it. Most other girls, on seeing me here, would have gone into hysterics, or fainted. But you're a little 'brick.'"

"Thank you, this is really no time for compliments," was her cold, resentful reply. "Please say what you have to say, and quickly."

She had managed to cross the room half-way, and from where she now stood she could see that the precious document she had typed lay open at its last page. The fellow had evidently read it all!

"Well," he said, in that easy-going manner of his that she found so extremely irritating. "As far as I can at present discern, Miss Griffin, the game is a drawn one. I can quite—"

"I consider it blackguardly impertinence on your part to enter my father's house at night, and read his private papers," she protested, her face pale and determined.

"My dear girl, to me your opinion of my actions really doesn't matter," he laughed. "I wanted to discover something, and have adopted the easiest means of doing so."

"Even at risk of being arrested?"

"Oh, I shan't be arrested," he laughed. "Don't think I'm afraid of that. Why, my dear girl, perhaps you wouldn't believe it, but this isn't the first time I've been in this very room. I know what's in all those drawers yonder, and even the balance in your father's banker's pass-book."

"You've been here before!" gasped the girl astounded. "How did you get in?"

"Why, with your own key. It was easy enough. Your servants never bolt the front door. They really ought to be more careful, you know," he laughed.

She hesitated for a moment, and in that slight hesitation he, crafty malefactor that he was, recognised that he had triumphed.

"I may presume, I suppose, that you've read that document upon the writing-table?" she asked a moment later.

"I have—every word of it," he replied, with a polite bow.

"That is why you came here?"

"It was. I really expected to experience greater trouble in finding it. I opened only three drawers before coming across it."

"Probably you'd like a copy of it," she said, with bitter sarcasm.

"Thank you, no. I have a very excellent memory, and can recollect all I require. Besides, I've taken a few notes," was the bold and defiant answer, "All I would request of you, my dear girl, is to keep a still tongue in your head, go up to bed, and forget all about this unexpected meeting. Such a course will be much the best for you, I assure you."

"You—my enemy, are trying to advise me as a friend—eh? This is really amusing! I tell you quite frankly that I intend to give you over to the police. You cleverly entrapped me, and now from me you may expect no clemency."

"I want none," he laughed. "But if I'm arrested, your friend, 'Red Mullet,' shall also see the inside of a prison again. I promise you that."

"He is innocent of this burglary," she said.

"But he isn't innocent of certain other little matters about which Scotland Yard will be only too delighted to know," replied the fellow, with an evil grin. "So if you don't want him to go to 'quod'—and he's been pretty good to you, I think—you'd better remain silent about to-night. And there's the other matter—the—"

And he paused, and looked straight into her face, without concluding.

"Well?" she asked in a hard voice, holding the train of her robe with one hand, and still facing him boldly. "And what is the other matter, pray?"

"I wish to tell you quite plainly that if you choose to be a little fool, you'll take the consequences. They'll fall on you, and pretty heavily too. Trust me to escape them."

"And I tell you that I intend to be a little fool, as you so politely put it," was her fearless response. "It is my duly to my father to go at once and tell him of my discovery. And I will!"

"Very well," he answered quite calmly, his evil eyes still fixed upon hers. "Go. You are perfectly at liberty. To me, it is of no great consequence, but to you it will mean both the ruin of your reputation and the loss of your lover!"

"How?" she gasped quickly, her face in an instant as pale as death.

"How?" he echoed in a fierce low whisper, advancing until he was close to the girl. "Cannot you see that I shall tell Frank Farquhar the truth of your absence from your home—that you met me, and stayed with me in those rooms!"

"You scoundrel!" she cried, drawing away from him, her cheeks flushed with sudden anger. "You threatened this before—you despicable coward, to thus try and take advantage of a woman's good name! You destroyed that false telegram, so that I should not have it to show as proof!"

"You could get a copy from the post-office, I daresay," he laughed airily. "But I merely make plain what is my intention, and that's why I've come to the conclusion that the game between us is a drawn one."

"Your threats have no terror for me!" she exclaimed, turning fiercely upon him. He saw that in her big eyes was determination and defiance, and was surprised.

"Then shout away, my dear girl—scream the house down, if you like," he laughed coolly, as though with utter unconcern. "But just let me put things straight again first." Then walking to the writing-table he took the translation of the decipher, replaced it in its drawer, and relocked it with a key he drew from his pocket.

His coolness was amazing, his cunning, extraordinary. The long window leading to the balcony over the portico was ajar. He had fixed a thin silken rope to the railings ready for escape to the street in case of necessity.

"Your conduct is abominable!" she ejaculated. "What harm have I done you that I should deserve this?"

"My dear girl, my conduct is only abominable of necessity, I assure you," he argued with an impudent smile. "Our compact is simple enough. You do not wish to lose the man you love. Indeed, why should you?"

"Ah! why indeed?" she cried. "I have you alone to thank for all the evil suspicions cast upon me."

"You have told them nothing—of course. You're far too clever for that—eh?" he remarked, standing easily before her with his hands in his pockets. "Besides, what could you say?"

"I could say nothing," she replied bitterly. "I only know that you lied to me, by posing as Frank's friend."

"My dear little girl," he answered with an arrogant laugh. "I was compelled to tell you a fairy-story, because—well, shall I tell you the truth?—because I was so very anxious for the loan of your latch-key."

"Then why was I kept there a prisoner? Why did that red-faced blackguard come to me, and threaten me?"

"I had nothing whatever to do with that. I was not there," he protested.

"You enticed me into the hateful place by saying that Frank was in hiding there," she replied firmly.

"For the reason I have already explained. I apologise. Can I do more, Miss Griffin?"

"Apologise!" she echoed in a hoarse whisper. "You apologise! I wish for no apology!"

"But you desire your own happiness, and can secure it, providing I am silent," he said in a low, clear deliberate voice. "Think what it would mean to you if you gave the alarm—the wrecking of your own life, and the arrest of your friend Mullet! But I give you perfect liberty to choose your future course of action. I have no wish to coerce you."

"You could not, even if you wished!" she declared, yet through her brain surged thoughts of what the loss of Frank would mean to her.

The man before her was a blackguard. He had shown himself as such. With perfect coolness he could besmirch her fair name in such a manner that it could never again be cleared.

At that moment the girl was fighting for her own honour as well as her father's secret which this man had gained. It was a secret no longer—it could never be. Their enemies had triumphed!

She set her teeth hard, and tried to think.

Jim Jannaway was quick to notice her change of manner.

"Remember," he remarked, "one word to your father regarding this visit of mine, and your lover and your father shall know the truth!"

"They will know whatever lies you invent regarding me!" she said in a voice of intense bitterness.

He only shrugged his shoulders and smiled. She, a mere innocent girl, had no chance against his quick intellect, sharpened as it had been by years of crafty cunning and double dealing. To the "crooks" and silk-hatted adventurers of London the very name of Jim Jannaway was synonymous of all that was perfection in kid-gloved blackguardism.

"Well," he said a moment later, "I haven't time for further argument, Miss Griffin. I'm sorry I can't stay longer. Perhaps the front door would be a less conspicuous exit for me."

And so saying he stepped out upon the balcony, untied the silken rope from the railing, rolled it up swiftly, and placed it in his pocket.

A moment later he was again standing before her.

She stood glaring at him with a look of bitter hatred, while he recognised that her lips were already effectually sealed.

She dare not risk the suspicions which he could with a word place upon her. Hence he, alas! held her in his power!

"Remember!" he said, "I shall say nothing until you dare to give me away. It is a compact between us. Silence for silence!"

Then, without further word, he moved across to the door, unlocked it, and next second had disappeared noiselessly down the stairs.

And with him had gone the great secret of the hiding-place of the treasure of Israel which her father believed to be his—and his alone!

The girl cast herself into a chair, and gave way to a paroxysm of tears.

Jim Jannaway and his friends had again triumphed.

Chapter Thirty Five
Shows Further Complications

At nine o'clock next morning the hunch-backed Doctor, pale and eager, was closeted with the Professor, to whom he related what he had witnessed while watching outside the house in Berkeley Square on the previous night.

In consequence of this, the good-looking Laura was summoned to the study, closely questioned, and returning impudent answers, was summarily dismissed and left the house.

"So it is Sir Felix Challas who is desirous of ascertaining our secret," remarked Aminger Griffin, greatly surprised, "He is such a great churchman, and such a high-minded philanthropist, that I can hardly believe that he should employ such methods. Why, only this very week I saw in the papers that he has made a fourth donation to Guy's Hospital of two thousand pounds."

"He is a swindler, hiding himself beneath the cloak of religion," declared Diamond emphatically. "I have seen Mullet this morning, and he has promised to call and have a chat with you. He will come to-day, I expect."

"Well," exclaimed the Professor with some hesitation, and with a smile of triumph upon his lips, "we need have no further fear of our enemies, Doctor, for we have forestalled them. Yesterday I succeeded in deciphering the whole record in Ezekiel, and convincing myself of the existence of a similar cipher in Deuteronomy. I have here the complete translation in English." And he placed the document in the Doctor's trembling hands.

The ugly little man read it through eagerly, and then sat staring straight into the Professor's face.

"Then the secret of the treasure of Israel is revealed!" he gasped in a low voice, as though fearing to be overheard. "But is it not probable that your servant listened, and heard you tell Miss Gwen the manner in which the cipher could be read?"

"No doubt. But fearing that, in a matter of this magnitude I might be the victim of treachery, I deviated slightly from the correct key, in such a manner as to throw out the whole reading!" laughed the Professor. "I told my daughter so afterwards."

"Mullet has told me a good deal. I stayed with him in his rooms last night," the Doctor said. "It appears that Sir Felix Challas's methods are, on occasions, so unscrupulous as to be criminal. In his employ he has a dangerous scoundrel named Jim Jannaway—a thief and gaol-bird, though his exterior is that of a gentleman. He has served several terms of imprisonment for burglary. To this man the philanthropist of Berkeley Square, who received a Baronetcy for his good deeds, leaves his dirty work. From what Mullet told me I should not be surprised that it was he who arranged that your servant should spy upon you."

"Mullet is also an outsider, is he not?" remarked the Professor with some suspicion.

"Of course, but of necessity. Though he may rob the rich, he prides himself on never having done a mean action to a poor person, or a woman."

"Ah! Doctor," laughed Griffin. "I see you believe in degrees of crime— eh?"

"In this case, yes. 'Red Mullet' has greatly assisted us. It was he who telegraphed to me from his retreat in Kent to watch the house in Berkeley Square. And now he has explained to me many points which were hitherto mysteries."

"We need have no fear of our enemies now," remarked the Professor, as at that moment Gwen, looking fresh in her white blouse and navy serge skirt, entered the room brightly and greeted the ugly little hunchback. "It only remains for us to call Farquhar into conference, and decide how we shall act. Somebody should proceed at once to Jerusalem, decide the exact spot, and purchase the land. We can have time for further operations when once the land on both sides of the hill is ours. Farquhar has promised that Sir George will find the necessary funds for that, if we so desire."

Gwen, holding her breath, walked to the window and looked out upon the gloomy London street.

Her position was hideous. Her father believed that the great secret was his—and his alone. Frank would believe it—and by remaining silent she would be misleading her lover into a false sense of security.

She knew, alas! that their enemies would hesitate at nothing—that the Treasure of Israel was already lost to them—lost to the Jews for ever!

With her back turned to her father and his visitor she stood listening, her clenched hands trembling. What could she do? How could she act?

Suppose she told the truth, and bore the inevitable blow?

"It's certainly fortunate that you did not explain to Miss Gwen the actual mode of deciphering the record," the Doctor was remarking, "for Sir Felix and Haupt, at any rate, cannot gain the knowledge we have gained."

"Sir Felix—who—dad?" inquired the girl, turning quickly.

"Sir Felix Challas, my dear," was the Professor's reply. "The Doctor has discovered that it is he who is our enemy. He poses as a great philanthropist as you well know. His portrait is in this week's *Tatler*—over yonder."

The girl crossed quickly, took up the paper, and searched the pages eagerly. Then when her gaze fell upon the picture, the journal nearly fell from her nerveless fingers.

She recognised the brutal, red-faced man who had been her inquisitor, and who would have struck her had not Mullet interfered, and stood her champion.

Beneath the portrait was a laudatory notice of the hypocrite's noble contribution to the funds of charities of London.

"You see, Doctor," her father went on, not noticing the girl's blanched face and horror-struck eyes, "Erich Haupt will only be entirely misled by the statement I made to Gwen. By using the cipher in that manner, he will obtain a jumble of Hebrew letters which represent nothing. No. We need not fear Sir Felix and his anti-Semitic views in the least. We alone know the place of concealment of the sacred treasure of Israel."

"I have already telegraphed to Farquhar at Horsford. He should be here before twelve."

"And when he comes, we shall decide what to do," remarked the Professor. "I think he should go out at once to Palestine. Only one of us must go to purchase the land, otherwise suspicion might be excited. And if so, then good-bye to all our chances."

"Sir Felix, if he cannot obtain the secret, may endeavour to upset our plans out there," remarked Gwen. "He is a man of wealth and power, dad."

"But he does not possess the information which we possess. Professor Holmboe's secret is now ours—and ours alone!" he declared triumphantly.

"Could we not get Mr Mullet to assist us, dad?" suggested the girl puzzled to distraction as to how she should act. She was divided between her love and her duty.

"No. He will only help us in his own way," responded Doctor Diamond.

The girl walked back to the long window which led out upon the balcony—the window which Jim Jannaway had been prepared to use as an emergency exit—and stood with her hands clasped behind her back, while the two men further discussed what they believed to be a most satisfactory situation.

The land on both sides of the mount must be purchased in secret, they agreed, and not a word must leak out regarding the discovery until actual operations had commenced. Then the Professor was to launch his startling statement upon the world in the form of an article in the *Contemporary*. After the purchase of the land, the Professor, the Doctor, and an engineer were to go out to Jerusalem and make secret investigation. The surveyor, whom Griffin proposed to send out with Farquhar to make secret survey upon the measurements contained in the cipher, was a young man in business at Richmond, a friend of his, to whom he proposed to give a small interest in the syndicate.

"We are agreed, I suppose, Doctor, that at all hazards the most sacred relics and the archives of the Kingdom of Israel which are no doubt preserved there, shall be restored to the Jews?" Griffin said.

"Most certainly," was Diamond's reply. "This man Challas intends, it seems, to revenge himself upon the Jews by desecrating the treasure."

"But, dad!" cried the girl, "surely he would never be allowed to desecrate sacred relics!"

"If he discovered them upon land he had purchased he might very easily destroy them before he could be prevented," her father pointed out. "There lies the great danger. Fortunately, however, he will be unable to do that. Farquhar must go out to Jerusalem at the earliest possible moment. And I'll get young Pettit, the surveyor, up from Richmond this afternoon."

Gwen's face was blanched, she stood rooted there, still staring down into the street, inexpressibly gloomy that winter's morning. Lights were in the rooms of some of the houses opposite, while outside Notting Hill Gate Station, at the end of the road, the big electric globes were shedding their brilliance, as they did each night.

How should she act? She was calmly contemplating what might occur. Her head reeled, for she had not closed her eyes since she had last stood in that room face to face with her enemy—the man who had filched the secret from them and departed.

His threats rang in her ears. If she revealed the truth, then Mullet would be arrested, and in addition a foul lie, which alas! she could not refute, would be told both her lover and her father! She shuddered and held her breath. Had she not already promised secrecy to Mullet! Could she, after his self-sacrifice, deliberately bring ruin upon him?

No. She was hemmed in on every side by the impossible. And even if she told the truth, it was now too late, alas! Sir Felix Challas, great financier that he was, had agents in all the capitals, and possessed secret channels of information against which their little combination would be utterly powerless. Alas! they were now only tilting at the wind.

That red-faced blatant parvenu, that Jew-hating hypocrite who did his evil doings behind his moneybags, had triumphed!

Whatever she said, whatever allegation she made against the Baronet or Jim Jannaway—for she now for the first time had learnt his name—would make no difference. The bitterness of it all must fall upon her, and her alone.

Her young heart was crushed, stifled, broken.

If she spoke, or if she were silent, it was the same—she must play her lover false.

Chapter Thirty Six
The Victim of Shame

The tall red-moustached man stood in the dining-room with Gwen Griffin.

She had seen his approach from the window, and dashing downstairs, had admitted him. Taking him at once into the room she had closed the door, and in a few brief hasty words had admitted him to her confidence.

"What!" he cried, staring at her in amazement. "Jim Jannaway has dared to come here, to read the documents, and then to threaten you with this! Look here, Miss Griffin, the matter is much more serious for you than I had imagined. Those fellows, Felix and Jim, will stick at nothing, but they shall not ruin your reputation. Leave that to 'Red Mullet'."

"But, Mr Mullet," she cried, "he threatens your arrest if I tell my father the truth. Besides, have I not promised secrecy to you?"

"My dear child," he said, "go at once and tell your father the truth. Then leave the rest to me."

"But what will he think of me?" she asked, her face blanched to the lips.

"Let your father—indeed, let the world—think what it will of you, Miss Griffin. You are an innocent victim of the avarice of these men, just as I am. I stood your friend that day when I released you from bondage—and I will stand your friend still!"

"They possess our secret."

"That is a most unfortunate fact," he admitted. "Still we must try and defy them. I will do my best. But if I fail," he added in a low earnest voice, "it will not be for want of endeavour, I promise you. I tried to save you and your father once—and I will try again. We must win even if we make some sacrifice."

"But do not imperil yourself," she urged. "Do not, I beg of you, Mr Mullet."

"I shall act with both firmness and discretion, and if we but unmask these blackguards who have tried again to entrap you, we shall have done a service to society at large. Unfortunately," he added with a sigh, "my own hands are none too clean."

"You will see my father. The Doctor is upstairs with him," she urged.

"No—later!" he exclaimed hastily. "At the present moment not a second is to be lost. I must go to them, and see what we can do by firmness. Tell your father of Jim's visit here, but do not say you have seen me, and say nothing regarding the past—remember, nothing. Promptness of action is now our only safeguard."

And leaving the girl standing there bewildered, he passed out of the room, and next second she heard the front door closed behind her.

Of his power to avert the natural flow of events she had but little confidence. He was beneath the thumb of Sir Felix Challas, therefore, how could he hope to wrest back the secret which Jim Jannaway had learned?

In any case, the good-looking scoundrel to whom a woman's honour was of no account, would carry out his threat, and Frank must, ere long, turn his back upon her, as he had done before.

Her heart beat fast, and she placed her hand upon her breast, as if to stay its anxious throbbing.

Mullet, though an adventurer himself, was right. It was her duty to tell her father the truth, and not allow him to continue further in that sense of false security.

Yet at what cost must her statement be made! At cost, alas! of her own honour.

Ere long she would not be able to look Frank in the face, for Jim Jannaway would lie so circumstantially that both her father and he would believe it to be the shameful truth. Mullet would not admit the past. "Say nothing regarding the past," he had urged! He had some strong motive in this—a motive that must, of itself, prevent him revealing the truth, and clearing her of the blemish placed upon her good name.

Besides, would Frank ever accept the excuses made for her by a man of "Red Mullet's" stamp? The actual truth was an ugly one. She had been absent from home, and on returning, had refused to give an account of where she had been. And now it was to be revealed that she had lived in "Red Mullet's" chambers!

She burst into a flood of tears on recognising her own utter helplessness.

Circumstances were entirely against her. She could never hope to defend her own honour in the face of such dark facts.

Suddenly she dried her eyes with a great effort, and looked at herself in the big mirror at the back of the high, old-fashioned carved sideboard. She started to notice how pale she was, and how dark beneath the eyes.

Then slowly she went out of the room, and up the stairs, in obedience to her protector, "Red Mullet."

Hardly knowing what she did, or what words escaped her, she re-entered the study where her father, her lover and the Doctor were in consultation, and standing before them, described the scene that had occurred in that room during the night-hours.

The three men, when they heard the astounding truth, started to their feet with one accord.

"You!—Gwen—my daughter!" gasped the old Professor in a voice of bitter reproach. "And you have allowed this—you allowed that man to gain our secret without alarming me! I am ashamed of your conduct—heartily ashamed!"

"I could not, father," answered the girl, panting and pale-faced, "I—I was afraid—I feared him!"

She raised her eyes to Frank's, and saw in them a look of blank disappointment. She now fully realised that if she had raised the alarm, the communication of the secret to Challas might perhaps have been prevented. She pointed to the broken bell-push, and explained how before her entry there, the resourceful scoundrel had disarranged it as a precaution.

Diamond paced the room in a frenzy of despair. The little man raised his clenched fists above his head and uttered curses upon his enemies, for he saw that through his fingers at the very moment of success, there had slipped a colossal fortune.

"Frank!" exclaimed the girl, in a low piteous voice, standing before him with bent head, "forgive me. I—I was helpless last night. I am helpless now!"

"Forgive!" echoed her father in furious anger. "How can he ever forgive you—how can I forgive you? You might have been in fear of him at that moment, but upon your own showing, you knew him, is not that so?"

"Yes, father," she faltered. "I—I did know him."

"Then you have had dealings with our enemies before!" Frank cried, all his dark suspicions now suddenly aroused by her fears and apprehensions.

"I told them nothing, though they tried to force me to."

"You knew this man, Jim Jannaway, while I was in Copenhagen," said Frank, his eyes fixed upon her very seriously. "Come, tell the truth, Gwen."

She nodded in the affirmative, and unable to utter another word, burst again into tears.

And the three men standing there saw that her tears were tears of shame.

Two hours later, Frank Farquhar, dark-faced and determined, stood in one of the smaller rooms in Sir Felix Challas's house in Berkeley Square, while before him, seated easily on the edge of the table, was Jim Jannaway.

"Well, Mr Farquhar," he said, "what you've just stated is to a certain extent correct. I have no reason whatever to hide the truth, now that you have come to me and demanded it. The investigation of Holmboe's story has simply been a matter of business in which the keenest wits win. We have won."

"By trickery—and by a burglary, for which Professor Griffin intends to have you arrested."

Jannaway laughed impudently in his face.

"My dear sir, pray don't be foolish," he answered, "why it was Miss Griffin herself who let me in, and who showed me her father's decipher of the message in Ezekiel. And if you don't believe me," he added, "here's the telegram which the sent me."

Frank took the telegram he handed him, and read the following words: "Shall place candle at my window at two to-morrow morning. Come. Have something very important to communicate. Love, Gwen."

Love! The word danced before Frank's eyes.

"Why should she be acting in your interests, Mr Jannaway, and not in her father's? That seems to me a very curious point," he said, for want of something else to say.

"There was a reason—a very strong reason," replied the fellow, with a mysterious grin, pretending, of course, to be unaware that Farquhar was the girl's lover; "the little girl is a particular friend of mine."

"What do you mean?" gasped Frank, his face paler.

"Well—what I say. Need I be more explicit? It is not usual for a man to imperil a girl's reputation, is it?"

"Come," said Frank; "tell me the truth. Is your acquaintance an intimate one?"

The fellow nodded and laughed. He plainly saw the result of his cruel aspersions upon the girl's character.

"I don't believe it," declared Frank.

"Oh! perhaps you are her friend also!" exclaimed Jannaway with a smile. "If so, you'd better ask her if she did not remain with me during a recent absence from home. I wanted her to go back, but she seemed afraid, and preferred life in a bachelor's chambers."

"You lie!" cried Frank, crimson with anger.

"No, not so quick, Mr Farquhar," exclaimed the scoundrel coolly. "Just inquire of her, that's all. Ask her if she did not meet me in secret late one night, and whether she didn't remain with me in my chambers off Oxford Street. She will certainly not have forgotten the incident," he added with meaning sarcasm.

"I don't believe you!" declared Frank, "but even if she had, you're a cursed blackguard for giving her away!"

"You asked me for the truth, and you've got it!" was Jim Jannaway's response. "Anything more you wish to know? If so, I am entirely at your service."

It was one of Jannaway's characteristics that the more angry he became, the more cool was his exterior.

"I want to know nothing from one who is a liar, a thief, and a slanderer of women," Frank responded, in a hard, bitter voice.

"I understand that the object of your visit was to inquire the reason why I called so early this morning at Pembridge Gardens. I have simply replied that I called at the Professor's in response to this invitation," and he indicated the telegram which he still held in his hand, and which, if the truth were told, he had taken the precaution to send to himself, as additional evidence against the innocent girl whom he had all along intended should be his victim.

"And you repeat your allegation that Miss Gwen has been your guest at your chambers for several days—eh? Remember, if untrue, such a statement is actionable."

"I repeat it. And I ask you to satisfy yourself as to its truth by asking her. But," he added, "I may as well tell you that the little girl is annoyed with me just now for betraying her father's secret to my friends. Yet, after all, as I've already said, it was only a matter of business, and with business women ought never to meddle. They always burn their fingers."

"And your friends—that is Sir Felix Challas and his associates—intend, of course, to profit by this secret which you've stolen—eh?" asked Frank, his face darkening.

"That's their affair—not mine."

"I hear that you bribed the parlour-maid at Pembridge Gardens—the crafty scoundrel that you are!"

"That's it!" Jim laughed, "and I squeezed the cook, and kissed the kitchenmaid! Anything else? No, I really haven't any more time to waste, Mr Farquhar. All I need add is, that if you doubt my statement, please ask Miss Griffin herself."

Chapter Thirty Seven
Reveals a Woman's Face

A cold bleak afternoon in Kensington Gardens. The frozen gravelled path was lightly powdered with snow, and against the bare black branches showed the pale yellow light of the wintry afternoon. Bent to the biting wind, men and women, wrapped to the ears, passed up the Broad Walk, and among them was Gwen Griffin, a lonely, solitary, sweet-faced little figure, neat with her black bow in her hair, her blue doth skirt, fur bolero, and fur toque and muff to match.

She walked very slowly, her sad eyes cast upon the ground. She always went into the gardens when she wanted to think. Near Hyde Park Gate, she turned into one of the narrow and little-frequented paths, for she wanted to be alone.

That afternoon the great blow which she dreaded had fallen, and her young heart so light and happy, was crushed and broken.

Frank Farquhar had sent her, by messenger from Half Moon Street, a cruel, brief letter, in which he told her plainly of the allegation which Jim Jannaway had made, and explaining that, in consequence, he must ask her to consider their engagement at a complete end.

Its rigid formality showed that he believed every word of that vile calumny. Ah! if only Mullet would speak! If only he would consent to the truth being told.

But alas! though a fortnight had passed since his hurried departure from Pembridge Gardens after hearing of the betrayal of the secret, he had sent her no single word. He was a will-o'-the wisp, gone abroad, in all probability, in order to escape arrest.

For a fortnight, too, she had not seen Frank. After her admission of Jim Jannaway's visit, he had left the house in evident disgust and anger, and had not returned. He had not even written to her, for she understood that he had gone abroad. That afternoon, however, he had sent her the note which for fifteen long anxious days she had been dreading.

She sank upon one of the seats quite alone, yet within sound of the dull roar of the traffic in Kensington Gore, and taking his letter from her muff, re-read it, her vision half obscured by hot bitter tears.

"The scoundrel told such a circumstantial tale," she murmured to herself, "that Frank has believed it without question. Yet—yet if he had come to me, and asked me, what could I have said? It was true that I stayed in that hateful place, even though against my will. Ah! I wonder what foul lies he has told against me—what—"

And hiding her face in her muff, she burst again into a flood of tears.

Her sweet, bright countenance had, alas, greatly changed in those past few weeks. Instead of bearing the stamp of inward happiness, she was now wan and pale, with thin cheeks and dark, deep-sunken eyes—the face of a woman whose heart was troubled, and who existed in terror of the future.

Both the Professor and Diamond—who was still a frequent visitor and had long conferences with her father—had noticed the change. But neither had made any remark. They attributed it to her heartfelt regret at not having raised the alarm on finding Jannaway prying into their secret.

The girl's mind, racked by the tortures of conscience and frenzied by the cruel calumnies uttered against her, was now strained to its greatest tension. She was utterly friendless, for even her father now avoided her, and at meals treated her with a cool and studied aversion. Instead of being petted and indulged as she had been all her life, she was now shunned. He asked of her no advice, nor did he invite her to his study each evening to chat, as had been his habit ever since she had left school.

One friend she possessed in the world—"Red Mullet," the adventurer who posed as a mining engineer! Where was he? Ay, who could tell?

"That man threatened his arrest if I did not remain silent," she said, speaking aloud to herself, her eyes fixed upon the bare, cheerless prospect before her. "I have told the truth, and already he has carried out one of his threats. Perhaps he will carry out the other. Probably he will, and then—and then I shall lose my only friend! He may allege, too, that because 'Red Mullet' is my friend, he is my lover! Ah! I wonder what shameful scandal he has told Frank! I wonder! Oh! Why has Frank not come to me for an explanation for proof of those abominable lies uttered by a man whom he knows as a blackguard and a thief. It is cruel!" she sobbed, "cruel—too cruel! Ah! Frank, my own Frank, I love you with all my heart—with all my soul! You are mine, mine!" she cried, raising her clenched hands to heaven in her frenzy of despair, "and yet I have lost you—lost my father's great secret—lost everything—*everything*!"

Her white lips moved, but no sound came from them. Her eyes were closed, her hands clenched tightly as there, with none to witness her agony of soul, she implored the protection of her Maker and the clemency of Providence in that, the greatest trial of all her life.

She prayed in deep earnestness for assistance and strength to withstand the evil machinations of her enemies.

With Frank's departure, the sun of her existence had set. The future was only grey and darkening, like the dismal, dispiriting scene that spread before her.

Love and life were, alas, lost to her for ever.

Away over those leafless trees, eastward beyond Hyde Park and Grosvenor Square, a curious scene was, at that moment, being enacted in the house of her enemies.

Challas, stout and pompous, was standing with his back to the library fireplace, while in an armchair near, sat the white-bearded old German Professor.

"You see from this 'wire' from Jim, that all goes along beautifully Erich," the Baronet was saying. "He has engaged a Turk to purchase the land on both sides of the Mount, the price asked being a little bit stiff— eight thousand pounds for the lot. I 'wired' him this morning to close at the lowest price possible, and at the same time I've placed him a credit of ten thousand at the Ottoman Bank in Jerusalem."

"Then by this time the deal is closed," remarked the old German, rubbing his thin hands in satisfaction. "Ah! I wonder how our friend Griffin now feels?"

"Yes," laughed Sir Felix, "thanks to Jim we obtained the whole secret without the trouble of deciphering it. That was a smart move of his to capture the little girl as he did."

"Yes," laughed the old man, "it seems that we're on the straight road to success."

"The road!" echoed the great financier. "Why, by this time, I expect the land is ours, and if so, I shall start myself on Saturday. I mean to keep my intentions 'dark,' of course. The papers will say that I've gone to Vienna, for if it were known that I'd gone to Jerusalem there are men in the City who would be keeping a wary eye on me. They know that when Felix Challas goes abroad, it's generally to see some good thing or other. That's the worst of this cursed popularity. The public eye is upon one the whole time."

As he spoke, the old butler tapped at the door, and handed him another telegram, which he broke open eagerly.

"Ah!" he exclaimed after consulting a little note book which he took from a drawer—the code which Jim always used. "Another from Jim! He's closing at seven thousand eight hundred, the deeds to be signed to-morrow. The story he has told is that the land is to be used for building purposes."

"I suppose the surveyor you sent out with him has fixed the exact spot?"

"Of course. They did that four days ago. It was a difficult task to accomplish without attracting attention, but Jim succeeded. He always does!" added the Baronet with a grin.

"I understood that the Mount was nearly covered by the Jews' cemetery," remarked the German.

"So it is. But the plots we want are fortunately rocky places, where burial is impossible. I think it a big stroke of luck—don't you?" he added with a self-satisfied laugh.

"Certainly," was the German's response in his deep, guttural voice, "but what of Mullet? Have you heard anything of him lately?"

"Nothing. He's abroad somewhere. I believe Jim and he have quarrelled. I only hope they won't get to serious disagreement—if they do it will be very unpleasant for us all. 'Red Mullet' hasn't acted straight in this affair at all. He fell in love with Griffin's girl, I think—and became heroic—like the chicken-hearted fool he is."

"You haven't any fear of him turning upon you, I suppose?"

"Fear of him!" laughed Sir Felix heartily.

"Why, my dear Erich, I could put him away for ten years, to-morrow, if I wished, and fortunately he knows it. No. He'll keep a very still tongue, never fear. He still draws his money from Paris, which shows that he doesn't intend mischief."

"Ah! that's all right," declared the Hebrew scholar, greatly satisfied. "I—well, I've always had suspicions that he meant to play into Griffin's hands."

"So he did, undoubtedly, but Jim and I were rather too clever for him."

At that moment the elderly butler re-entered with a card upon the salver.

Sir Felix took it and his face changed in an instant. His mouth was open, and for a second he seemed speechless.

"Not at home—not at home," he snapped to the man. "Never at home to that person—you understand?"

"Yes, Sir Felix," replied the grave-faced servant, who bowed and withdrew.

Erich Haupt noticed that the visitor, whoever it was, seemed a most unwelcome one.

From the Baronet's subsequent movements the old German realised that he wished to get rid of him.

Therefore, he rose and departed, promising to call next day, and hear the latest report of Jim Jannaway's progress in Jerusalem.

Then, the instant Erich had left the house, Sir Felix rang for his valet, a young Italian, giving him a note to take in a taxi-cab to his office in the City and await a reply.

The man was gone an hour, during which time his master ascended to the great drawing-room, and advancing cautiously to the window, peered out into the grey twilight of the square. He stood behind the curtains so that any one watching the house from the outside could not observe him. From his nervous anxiety and restless movements it was apparent that he feared his unwelcome visitor might still be watching outside.

As he peered through the crack between the heavy curtains of blue silk brocade and the window sash, his eyes caught sight of a figure, and he sprang back breathless, his face white and drawn, as though he had seen a ghost.

It was a ghost—a ghost of the past that had arises against him in that hour of his greatest triumph.

The young Italian returned, and handed him a bulky letter which he placed in his pocket without opening. Then, having sent him forth with a note to the Ritz Hotel, a mere excuse, he ran up to his dressing-room, quickly exchanged his frock-coat and fancy vest for a suit of rough tweed, and putting on a bowler hat, returned to the library. Upon his face was a haunted look of terror. The unexpected had happened.

From his safe he took a small sealed packet of folded papers which he opened and cast quickly into the fire, waiting in eager impatience until all had been consumed. Then, unobserved, he slipped out by the back in the evening gloom, hurrying down the mews, and through into Hill Street, where he hailed a hansom and drove quickly away.

For the ghost of the past was still watching, silent and hideous, against the railings of Berkeley Square.

Chapter Thirty Eight
Contains a Surprise

That short February day was indeed an eventful one, both for the rival investigators, and for the whole Hebrew race.

Almost at that same hour when Sir Felix Challas left his London mansion so hurriedly, and in such fear, "Red Mullet" was being conducted up a long, wood-built, unpainted corridor where the uncarpeted floor was full of holes and the broken windows were patched, to a small shabby little reception-room—the waiting-room of the Sublime Porte, or Government Offices at Constantinople.

A Turkish servant in a dingy red fez, handed him the usual formal cup of blade coffee and cigarette, and he was left alone to await his audience with the Grand Vizier of his Imperial Majesty, the Sultan.

It was not the first time in the course of his adventurous career that he had had audience at the Sublime Porte. He knew the shabbiness and the decay of that great shed-like building, its lack of order, its seedy-looking officials, and its altogether incongruous appearance as the centre of the administration of a great empire.

Smoking the cigarette, he stood gazing thoughtfully out upon the rubbish heap in the courtyard below. Beyond, lay Pera, and the blue Bosphorus. The room, with its bare walls, faded Oriental carpet, rickety writing-table and few shabby chairs, was the apartment where the Ambassadors of the Powers awaited audience of the Grand Vizier, or of his Excellency, Tewfik Pasha, his Majesty's Minister for Foreign Affairs. A contrast indeed to the fairylike glories of the palace of Yildiz.

Five minutes later, the tall, red-moustached Englishman was conducted to a private room, shabby as was all at the Sublime Porte, where, at a table, sat a benevolent white-bearded old gentleman in frock-coat and fez, the Grand Vizier of the Sultan.

The high official greeted him in French, and having motioned him to a chair on the opposite side of the table, said:

"I am greatly obliged to you, M'sieur Mullet. I have read with intense interest the document you gave me yesterday, and last evening I placed the matter before his Majesty, my sovereign, at the Palace. As you are aware, his Majesty is always tolerant of other religions that are not our Faith, and has ever been most lenient towards the Hebrew race. This discovery, and your statement that certain persons hostile to the Jewish religion are in search of the supposed sacred relics, have both interested him, and he has commanded me to tell you that inquiries have been made by telegraph in Jerusalem. It appears that a certain Englishman named James Jannaway is staying at the Park Hotel, and is in treaty with the owners of two plots of land at the base of the Mount of Offence, one belonging to Poulios, a Greek, and the other to a certain Hadj Ben Hassan, an Arab. The Governor of Jerusalem reports that the price is fixed, and only the contracts remain to be drawn."

"The man Jannaway, your Excellency, is the agent of Sir Felix Challas," declared Mullet.

"As you yourself have been when you have visited Constantinople to obtain concessions from us on previous occasions, M'sieur!" remarked the wily Turkish official. "Why have you betrayed your employer?"

"For reasons which I have already explained in the document I handed to you. Your Excellency has always been extremely good to me personally, and I deemed it but my duty to inform you of the secret excavations about to take place in Jerusalem."

"You have no ulterior motive—eh?" asked the old man, fixing his eyes keenly upon him.

"None whatever, your Excellency. On the contrary, I shall be the loser."

The Grand Vizier stroked his beard for a few moments in thoughtful silence. Then he said:

"His Majesty never fails to repay generously any service rendered him. I may as well tell you he considers the rendering of this information a very valuable service. It might easily have happened that the most sacred relics of the Hebrews could have been taken from our country in secret by enemies of the Jews, a circumstance which would have caused his Majesty the utmost annoyance and anger."

"Your Excellency has already satisfied yourself that I have told the truth, I hope?"

"Certainly; during the night I have had several long telegrams from the Governor of Jerusalem, all of which bear out your allegation of a secret attempt about to be made to excavate in the Mount of Offence."

"And what action will the Ottoman Government take?" asked "Red Mullet," eagerly.

"His Majesty has already taken action," was the Grand Vizier's reply. "This morning he signed an irade which I placed before him, prohibiting the sale of any of the land of the Mount of Offence to any foreigner, and forbidding any excavations or any investigation whatsoever being made there."

"Red Mullet" was silent. The situation was an unexpected one. Such an irade would prevent Griffin and Diamond—the rightful holders of the secret—from taking any action, or making any investigation! By successfully opposing Challas, he had unfortunately also opposed Professor Griffin!

"Is not that—well—well, just a little in opposition to his Majesty's well-known policy of progress? The Imperial irade forbids any investigation whatever, I take it?"

"It forbids every investigation, of whatever nature," slowly replied the white-bearded mouthpiece of the Sultan. "Besides, there is a Jewish cemetery in close proximity; we will not have that desecrated, by either archaeologists or treasure-hunters."

"Then the secret cipher elucidated by Professor Griffin is to remain an unsolved problem?" Mullet said in a tone of great disappointment.

"For the present, yes," was the old gentleman's response. "There are many difficulties. Suppose the sacred relics were really discovered, to whom would they belong?"

"To the Hebrew race—and permit me to express the opinion, your Excellency, that they should be searched for, and given over to the Jews."

"I am not yet in a position to advise his Majesty upon that point. For the present, investigation and excavation are absolutely prohibited. But, rest assured, that no one is more alive to the importance of Professor Griffin's discovery than his Majesty himself. Indeed, he wishes for an exact transcript of this extraordinary record in your Bible."

"That investigation by the anti-Semitic group should be prohibited, I am, of course, much gratified, your Excellency. But I do hope sincerely that one day his Majesty will allow the right of research to the rightful holders of the secret—who, as I have stated, are the discoverer, Professor Griffin, and his friends."

"Including yourself, M'sieur Mullet—eh?"

"Yes, including myself, your Excellency," laughed the red-moustached man. "I would most humbly petition his Majesty, through you, to grant to me the concession to search after the truth, if his Majesty ever grants one."

"For the present, rest assured, Mr Mullet, that no permission will be given to any one. There are many eventualities to be considered, as well as international complications. But if any concession be granted in the future, his Majesty will certainly accord it to you, in consideration of the important and timely information which you have so generously furnished to us."

"Then we need not fear the success of our enemies," laughed the tall Englishman, with much gratification.

"Certainly not," answered the venerable old gentleman with a smile. "See here," and he pointed to an open telegram before him, "this is the last despatch from the Governor of Jerusalem, an hour ago. By my orders the Mount of the Offence is surrounded by a cordon of military, who have instructions to allow no one to pass. I have taken this precaution in case the affair gets into the press, and the spot is visited by great crowds, as it well may be. So," laughed the Grand Vizier, "you have to-day given your friend, M'sieur Jannaway, a rather unpleasant surprise, I should fancy."

Chapter Thirty Nine
Is the Conclusion

The anxiety of Erich Haupt may easily be imagined when, next day at the Waldorf Hotel, he received a telegram from Challas, despatched from an obscure place in Holland, saying that he had been called away unexpectedly, and telling him to go to Berkeley Square and open any telegrams that might be there.

He drove westward in a "taxi" — and found one message. It was in code from Jim Jannaway. The old German had noticed where the financier kept the code-book, and had but little difficulty in finding it.

"We have been given away," it ran. "The spot is now guarded by military. Sale of land, and all investigation forbidden, and we have received an intimation to leave Palestine at once. Coming home."

Haupt's dismay and chagrin was complete. He drove to the nearest telegraph-office and "wired" to Jannaway that Sir Felix had been called away.

This telegram, however, did not reach Jerusalem before Jim had left. Therefore, when he alighted from a cab in Berkeley Square some days later and knocked eagerly at the door of Sir Felix's house, he was surprised to find it opened by a strange man.

When the hall door had closed behind him again, another man advanced, and asked:

"I believe you are Mr Jannaway?"

"That's my name," replied Jim. "Where's the gov'nor? Who the dickens are you?"

"I'm Inspector Attwell, Criminal Investigation Department," replied the other, "and I arrest you, on a warrant granted in France, for the wilful murder of Henri Laroche, banker of Rue de Rouen, Bordeaux, on December 6, 1907."

Jannaway stood as though turned to stone. His face was bloodless, his mouth wide-open.

Frank and Gwen have just returned from their sunny honeymoon in Italy and Tunis to their pretty, semi-rural home at Chislehurst, whence every day Farquhar comes to London to direct the fortunes of the Gavin group of newspapers.

Only now, in these pages, is the truth revealed; a strange, astounding truth which one day, ere long—for diplomatic representations are at present being made by the Powers—must cause his Majesty the Sultan, and his reformed Government, to reverse the former prohibition regarding it. And for that Professor Griffin and his friends are patiently waiting.

Then will the words of the prophet be fulfilled the secret place of concealment in the Mount of Offence be opened, and, after nearly two thousand five hundred years, to its just ownership, that of the Hebrew race, will be given back the most sacred relics of that colossal and wonderful hoard, the Treasure of Israel.

"You—you've made a mistake—a very big mistake!" he managed to exclaim with a sorry attempt to laugh. "Where's the gov'nor—I mean Sir Felix Challas? I must see him at once."

"I'm afraid, Mr Jannaway, you'll never see him again," replied the officer. "Yesterday he was arrested in Breslau on a charge of complicity with you in the crime at Bordeaux, but an hour later he poisoned himself in the police-cell. It'll all be in the papers this afternoon, I expect."

"Suicide!" gasped the adventurer, utterly staggered.

"Yes, it seems that the dead man's daughter, Louise Laroche, whom you believed you had also killed, though ruined and destitute, has searched and found you both out, and made a startling statement to the Préfet de Police of Paris. Hence this warrant. But, come along. I must warn you that any statement you make may be used against you upon your trial."

"Louise!" he gasped, staring straight before him. He recollected that woman's pale, pinched face at the corner of Berkeley Street that night—that face which he had tried to forget and believe to be a mere fancy. "Louise alive—a living witness!" he cried, plainly terrified. "And Felix always told me that he—he'd killed her with his own hand to prevent her giving the alarm! She came into the room and discovered me at the safe, and she paid for it, I always thought, with her life. Then the young woman found dead must have been the servant!"

"Come, you'd better say no more," urged the officer, who, turning to the man who had opened the door, said: "Just whistle a cab, Hall."

"No!" cried Jim Jannaway, hoarsely; "You—you shan't take me alive. I—I'll—I'll die game, too!" and before the inspector could prevent him he had whipped out his revolver, placed the muzzle in his mouth and fired, falling lifeless next second at the officer's feet.

God's wrath had fallen upon the evil-doers.

Next day—the very day when the great sensation of Sir Felix Challas's tragic end, which every one recollects, appeared in the papers—"Red Mullet" ascended the stairs at Pembridge Gardens, and grasped the hand which the Professor stretched forth.

At his side stood Frank Farquhar, to whom he was introduced by the Professor.

"I'm most delighted, Mr Mullet, to have the opportunity of at last knowing you," Frank exclaimed. "The Professor has to-day shown me your letters and telegrams. In the circumstances, the situation is as satisfactory as it possibly can be. We can only hope that the Sultan will, after all the eventualities have been fully considered, grant to you the concession to search. It is fortunate, indeed, that you enjoy the friendship of the Grand Vizier."

"Yes," laughed the tall fellow, "his Excellency has been good enough to give me quite a lucrative appointment in the Department of Mines. I'm entering the Turkish service on the first of next month, when—well—I hope I'll be able to lead an honest life in the future."

"Let's hope so," exclaimed the Professor. "These revelations concerning Sir Felix Challas and your friend Jannaway, in the papers to-day, are most astounding."

"Not so astounding, Professor, as the story which I could tell. But both men are dead; therefore, for me to speak is now unnecessary. They were as crafty a pair of scoundrels as there were in the whole of Europe: and from them, your daughter Miss Gwen, had, indeed, a very narrow escape."

"Ah!" cried Frank. "Tell us the whole truth—do!"

"Not without Miss Gwen's consent," he laughed. "My daughter is out," Griffin said, "I expect her to return every moment. She has been expecting you daily."

"Red Mullet" smiled.

"Well, you know," he said, "your daughter, Professor, is my particular little friend."

"And you have been her good friend and protector, if what she tells me is correct," remarked her father. "But I want to hear the story from your lips. She refuses to say anything."

"Because I bound her to secrecy. It was imperative," he assured the grey-haired man. "And to you, Mr Farquhar," he said, "I must apologise. Some of my actions must have appeared mysterious—even suspicious."

"Well," replied Frank, with some hesitation. "I saw Jim Jannaway and—and he told me a very strange story."

"He lied to you," said Mullet quickly. "Ah! I know! He told you that he was her lover—eh? It was a lie—an infernal and cowardly lie! Look here, Mr Farquhar, I'm older than you, a good deal, and I'm a man who respects a woman's honour—I've a daughter of my own in Diamond's care. You know my little Aggie, to whom I'm devoted. Well, I tell you upon my oath—if you will accept the oath of an outsider like myself—that Miss Gwen is innocent, and that she loves only you—has thought of only you—and is as devoted to you as I am to my own dear child."

Frank hesitated, his eyes fixed upon the speaker. He saw that the man before him spoke the truth: that the evil-tongued coward who, cornered, dare not face the music, had uttered foul lies.

At that moment the door suddenly opened, and Gwen in her warm furs stood upon the threshold, her face full of surprise at seeing their visitor.

"Why!" she cried, "Mr Mullet!" and rushing forward, she grasped his hand eagerly.

"I have told them, Miss Gwen, I have just told them the truth," he said simply.

"Yes!" cried Frank Farquhar, stepping forward quickly, and taking the girl's hand he kissed her upon the lips there, before both her father and Mullet. "I have misjudged you, my darling!" he said. "Forgive me. That man lied to me, and, alas, I believed him. But to-day I know the truth. The death of that scoundrel Challas and his 'cat's-paw' has released Mr Mullet from his bondage. He has now no further fear of their reprisals, and has spoken—spoken the truth, and cleared you of that shameful scandal which Jannaway placed upon you."

"Did I not tell you, Frank, that Mr Mullet had been my very best friend?" said the girl simply, as, at that moment, the little Doctor entered, fussy and excited as usual.

"I did not believe it once," he replied, "but now I know it to be the truth." And turning to the man who had staked his own liberty to protect Gwen's honour, he grasped him warmly by the hand, uttering words of heartfelt thanks.

And so again, and for ever, two hearts became united, and the dark clouds of suspicion opened to give way to the sunshine of life and love.

All these stirring events happened not quite a year ago.

Though the Ark and the sacred vessels still remain hidden beneath the Mount of Offence till such time as his Majesty the Sultan thinks fit to rescind his prohibition, one interesting circumstance has occurred, namely the joyous marriage at St. Margaret's, Westminster, of Frank Farquhar and Gwen Griffin, which was celebrated a couple of months ago.

The tragic and sensational end of Sir Felix Challas, followed by that of friend Jim Jannaway, was a mere one day's wonder, as are all the sensa of our daily press nowadays. The whole facts were never revealed a inquest, and the public quickly forgot the mystery connected with the

They are in ignorance of that colossal and startling secret which the final *dénouement*, or of the remarkable discovery by Arminger G

"You—you've made a mistake—a very big mistake!" he managed to exclaim with a sorry attempt to laugh. "Where's the gov'nor—I mean Sir Felix Challas? I must see him at once."

"I'm afraid, Mr Jannaway, you'll never see him again," replied the officer. "Yesterday he was arrested in Breslau on a charge of complicity with you in the crime at Bordeaux, but an hour later he poisoned himself in the police-cell. It'll all be in the papers this afternoon, I expect."

"Suicide!" gasped the adventurer, utterly staggered.

"Yes, it seems that the dead man's daughter, Louise Laroche, whom you believed you had also killed, though ruined and destitute, has searched and found you both out, and made a startling statement to the Préfet de Police of Paris. Hence this warrant. But, come along. I must warn you that any statement you make may be used against you upon your trial."

"Louise!" he gasped, staring straight before him. He recollected that woman's pale, pinched face at the corner of Berkeley Street that night—that face which he had tried to forget and believe to be a mere fancy. "Louise alive—a living witness!" he cried, plainly terrified. "And Felix always told me that he—he'd killed her with his own hand to prevent her giving the alarm! She came into the room and discovered me at the safe, and she paid for it, I always thought, with her life. Then the young woman found dead must have been the servant!"

"Come, you'd better say no more," urged the officer, who, turning to the man who had opened the door, said: "Just whistle a cab, Hall."

"No!" cried Jim Jannaway, hoarsely; "You—you shan't take me alive. I—I'll—I'll die game, too!" and before the inspector could prevent him he had whipped out his revolver, placed the muzzle in his mouth and fired, falling lifeless next second at the officer's feet.

God's wrath had fallen upon the evil-doers.

Next day—the very day when the great sensation of Sir Felix Challas's tragic end, which every one recollects, appeared in the papers—"Red Mullet" ascended the stairs at Pembridge Gardens, and grasped the hand which the Professor stretched forth.

At his side stood Frank Farquhar, to whom he was introduced by the Professor.

"I'm most delighted, Mr Mullet, to have the opportunity of at last knowing you," Frank exclaimed. "The Professor has to-day shown me your letters and telegrams. In the circumstances, the situation is as satisfactory as it possibly can be. We can only hope that the Sultan will, after all the eventualities have been fully considered, grant to you the concession to search. It is fortunate, indeed, that you enjoy the friendship of the Grand Vizier."

"Yes," laughed the tall fellow, "his Excellency has been good enough to give me quite a lucrative appointment in the Department of Mines. I'm entering the Turkish service on the first of next month, when—well—I hope I'll be able to lead an honest life in the future."

"Let's hope so," exclaimed the Professor. "These revelations concerning Sir Felix Challas and your friend Jannaway, in the papers to-day, are most astounding."

"Not so astounding, Professor, as the story which I could tell. But both men are dead; therefore, for me to speak is now unnecessary. They were as crafty a pair of scoundrels as there were in the whole of Europe: and from them, your daughter Miss Gwen, had, indeed, a very narrow escape."

"Ah!" cried Frank. "Tell us the whole truth—do!"

"Not without Miss Gwen's consent," he laughed. "My daughter is out," Griffin said, "I expect her to return every moment. She has been expecting you daily."

"Red Mullet" smiled.

"Well, you know," he said, "your daughter, Professor, is my particular little friend."

"And you have been her good friend and protector, if what she tells me is correct," remarked her father. "But I want to hear the story from your lips. She refuses to say anything."

"Because I bound her to secrecy. It was imperative," he assured the grey-haired man. "And to you, Mr Farquhar," he said, "I must apologise. Some of my actions must have appeared mysterious—even suspicious."

"Well," replied Frank, with some hesitation. "I saw Jim Jannaway and—and he told me a very strange story."

"He lied to you," said Mullet quickly. "Ah! I know! He told you that he was her lover—eh? It was a lie—an infernal and cowardly lie! Look here, Mr Farquhar, I'm older than you, a good deal, and I'm a man who respects a woman's honour—I've a daughter of my own in Diamond's care. You know my little Aggie, to whom I'm devoted. Well, I tell you upon my oath—if you will accept the oath of an outsider like myself—that Miss Gwen is innocent, and that she loves only you—has thought of only you—and is as devoted to you as I am to my own dear child."

Frank hesitated, his eyes fixed upon the speaker. He saw that the man before him spoke the truth: that the evil-tongued coward who, cornered, dare not face the music, had uttered foul lies.

At that moment the door suddenly opened, and Gwen in her warm furs stood upon the threshold, her face full of surprise at seeing their visitor.

"Why!" she cried, "Mr Mullet!" and rushing forward, she grasped his hand eagerly.

"I have told them, Miss Gwen, I have just told them the truth," he said simply.

"Yes!" cried Frank Farquhar, stepping forward quickly, and taking the girl's hand he kissed her upon the lips there, before both her father and Mullet. "I have misjudged you, my darling!" he said. "Forgive me. That man lied to me, and, alas, I believed him. But to-day I know the truth. The death of that scoundrel Challas and his 'cat's-paw' has released Mr Mullet from his bondage. He has now no further fear of their reprisals, and has spoken—spoken the truth, and cleared you of that shameful scandal which Jannaway placed upon you."

"Did I not tell you, Frank, that Mr Mullet had been my very best friend?" said the girl simply, as, at that moment, the little Doctor entered, fussy and excited as usual.

"I did not believe it once," he replied, "but now I know it to be the truth." And turning to the man who had staked his own liberty to protect Gwen's honour, he grasped him warmly by the hand, uttering words of heartfelt thanks.

And so again, and for ever, two hearts became united, and the dark clouds of suspicion opened to give way to the sunshine of life and love.

All these stirring events happened not quite a year ago.

Though the Ark and the sacred vessels still remain hidden beneath the Mount of Offence till such time as his Majesty the Sultan thinks fit to rescind his prohibition, one interesting circumstance has occurred, namely, the joyous marriage at St. Margaret's, Westminster, of Frank Farquhar and Gwen Griffin, which was celebrated a couple of months ago.

The tragic and sensational end of Sir Felix Challas, followed by that of his friend Jim Jannaway, was a mere one day's wonder, as are all the sensations of our daily press nowadays. The whole facts were never revealed at the inquest, and the public quickly forgot the mystery connected with the affair.

They are in ignorance of that colossal and startling secret which led to the final *dénouement*, or of the remarkable discovery by Arminger Griffin.

Frank and Gwen have just returned from their sunny honeymoon in Italy and Tunis to their pretty, semi-rural home at Chislehurst, whence every day Farquhar comes to London to direct the fortunes of the Gavin group of newspapers.

Only now, in these pages, is the truth revealed; a strange, astounding truth which one day, ere long—for diplomatic representations are at present being made by the Powers—must cause his Majesty the Sultan, and his reformed Government, to reverse the former prohibition regarding it. And for that Professor Griffin and his friends are patiently waiting.

Then will the words of the prophet be fulfilled the secret place of concealment in the Mount of Offence be opened, and, after nearly two thousand five hundred years, to its just ownership, that of the Hebrew race, will be given back the most sacred relics of that colossal and wonderful hoard, the Treasure of Israel.